Secrets Well Kept

By
Lynn Ames

SECRETS WELL KEPT
© 2019 BY LYNN AMES

ISBN: 978-1-936429-18-9

OTHER AVAILABLE FORMATS

eBOOK EDITION
ISBN: 978-1-936429-19-6

PUBLISHED BY
PHOENIX RISING PRESS
PHOENIX, ARIZONA
www.phoenixrisingpress.com

CREDITS
EXECUTIVE EDITOR: ANN ROBERTS
AUTHOR PHOTO: JUDY FRANCESCONI
COVER DESIGN: TREEHOUSE STUDIO

Dedication

To James Edward "Ed" Westcott, without whom the world would never have seen the full story of the Secret City—Oak Ridge, Tennessee—and its extraordinary role in ending World War II. Your dedication and skill behind the camera provided a lens through which history will always remember the men and women who created the fuel for the atomic bomb. Your photographs and generosity in making them available in the public domain brought this chapter in our history to life for me and countless others.

Ed Westcott
January 20, 1922 – March 29, 2019

Acknowledgments

Secrets Well Kept is a work of historical fiction. I have done my best, in every instance, to hew to the truth of what happened in the secret city of Oak Ridge, Tennessee during World War II. I have painstakingly re-created the atmosphere, the living environment, the social life, the timing of events, and the work done by 75,000 individuals who came to a place in East Tennessee to help the war effort. In fact, the only products purely of my imagination are the characters I created, and in all instances, the ways in which they interact with real historical figures.

In order to succeed in uncovering and laying bare the truth about a place that's very existence was meant to be a secret, I needed a lot of help. My deepest gratitude to official Oak Ridge historian, D. Ray Smith, who gave freely of his time, knowledge, and expertise to give me guidance, to check my facts, and to provide me with historical/historically accurate documents and information. To Ruth Huddleston, one of the original cubicle operators at Oak Ridge, my thanks for sitting down for an interview and answering all of my questions so that I could get the technical details and mindset right. To Ed Westcott, to whom this book is dedicated, a posthumous thank you for your remarkable photographs that so richly captured life at Oak Ridge.

Beyond the primary resources, there were many other resources that proved helpful. Chief among these were: *The Girls of Atomic City*, Denise Kiernan, *Now It Can Be Told*, General Leslie M. Groves, *City Behind a Fence*, Charles W. Johnson and Charles O. Jackson, *Ignored Heroes of World War II: The Manhattan Project Workers of Oak Ridge, Tennessee*, Richard Cook, *The New York Times Complete World War II*, The Atomic Heritage Foundation, The American Museum of Science and Energy, and Edward R. Murrow "Orchestrated Hell" broadcast—CBS Radio, December 3, 1943.

To my team... To my wife, Cheryl, who traveled to Oak Ridge with me multiple times and was invaluable in helping me with research and imagining the perfect ending to this book, I couldn't have gotten this right without you. To my first readers, you always make my work better and I am deeply grateful for your time and helpful feedback. To my editor, Ann Roberts, my thanks for adding spit-shine and polish and for your steady hand. To my cover designer, Ann McMan, there aren't enough superlatives in the world to describe your beautiful work; I love you, little sister. To my e-book and web store guru, Toni Whitaker, thank you, thank you.

And to all of you readers, I am most grateful to you. Without you, I couldn't do what I do. Thanks for the love.

Other Books by Lynn Ames

Stand-Alone Romances
Chain Reactions
Bright Lights of Summer
All That Lies Within
Eyes on the Stars
Heartsong
One ~ Love

Romantic Comedies
Great Bones

The Kate and Jay Series
The Price of Fame
The Cost of Commitment
The Value of Valor
Final Cut

The Mission: Classified Series
Beyond Instinct
Above Reproach

Anthology Collections
Outsiders

Specialty Books - Humor
Digging for Home

Lynn Ames books are available in multiple formats through www.lynnames.com, from your favorite local bookstore, or through other online venues.

MARCH – MAY, 1943

CHAPTER ONE

Hey, Lindstrom."

Nora didn't turn around. She grew weary of the taunting, the inappropriate cat calls, and the constant buzz of emotionally stunted sophomoric boys that populated the physics lab at Pupin Hall. No matter, she would be graduating with a doctorate in physics from Columbia soon, and they could just call her Dr. Lindstrom after that.

"Lindstrom. Are you deaf or something?"

"Is there something in particular you want, Dennis?"

"No. But there's something you're going to want."

This time Nora wheeled around to face her classmate, determined to give him a piece of her mind.

Before she could utter a word, he waved an official-looking letter in front of her. "This came for you. But if you don't want it…"

"Give it here. Right now." Nora snatched the envelope from his hand. The return address read: E.O. Lawrence, The Radiation Laboratory, University of California, Berkeley.

Nora's hands began to shake. Ernest Lawrence was the Nobel Prize-winning father of the cyclotron. He was a legend. What could he possibly want with her?

"Aren't you going to open it?"

Nora frowned. She'd forgotten Dennis was standing there. "When I'm ready." She adjusted the settings for the mass spectrometer for what seemed like the thousandth time. If she could find the sweet spot, she could produce the results her male counterparts had failed to achieve the entire semester and prove what she'd known all along—she was every bit as smart and capable as they were. Naturally, as a woman in a man's field, she had to work ten times as hard simply to be taken seriously.

"Women." He shook his head and walked away.

When Nora was sure she was alone, she carefully slit open the envelope and teased out the single sheet of paper.

March 23, 1943

Dear Dr. Lindstrom (please excuse the presumption of title, as I know you will not officially receive your doctorate until May):

My colleague and friend, Robert Oppenheimer, says he met you recently at Columbia and he has apprised me of your work in Pupin Hall. He tells me you have some interesting theories and a keen understanding with regard to uranium-isotope separation using electromagnetic fields. Dr. Oppenheimer also tells me you are a scientist of the highest integrity.

As it happens, I have need of someone meeting your description, especially a female. While I cannot relate more details, I wonder if, upon your graduation, I might entice you to embark upon an important scientific assignment that will be of utmost importance in the war effort.

I assure you that the pay will be more than you can imagine and that the work will be tremendously satisfying. The assignment will require your relocation to a new, secret environment. All of that will be disclosed at a later date should you choose to accept this offer of employment.

Time is of the essence, so if you could please respond to this letter as soon as practicable, I would be most appreciative.

Thank you for your consideration, and congratulations on your upcoming graduation.

Sincerely,

Ernest O. Lawrence

Nora blinked. The inventor of the cyclotron wanted to hire her. She wasn't due to graduate for another two months, and already she was a sought-after scientist. She re-read the letter twice more, returned it to the envelope, and tucked it away in her locker. Was she interested? You bet she was!

ໄ໑໐

"Mary Elizabeth Trask, you'd better have finished your homework!" Mabel Trask hollered from the yard where she was hanging the laundry to dry.

"I've got to go. Mother is on a rampage," Mary whispered into the telephone.

"Can I see you tonight? We could go for a drive."

She rolled her eyes. "Sam, I told you, I need to study for my English test. I've simply got to do well. Graduation depends on it." Mary gazed furtively out the window. "She's coming. 'Bye." She hung up the phone without waiting for a reply.

Her mother poked her head in the doorway. "Well? Have you finished all your assignments? I thought I heard you on the phone. Was that Samuel? He's such a nice boy. He'll make a good husband."

"That's it, Mother." Mary's nostrils flared. "If I've told you once, I've told you a thousand times, I'm too young to get married. For gosh sakes, I'm only eighteen. I'm not even out of high school yet and you've already got me married off."

Mabel pursed her lips and put her hands on her hips. "I married your father the day after graduation; God bless him and bring him home safely from the war. That's worked out just fine. When a good man shows interest and wants to marry you, thank your lucky stars and say yes."

"I'm not having this conversation with you, Mother. I have a test to study for." She stomped out of the kitchen and up the stairs to her room, where she slammed the door and flopped down on the bed.

For the past eighteen months, ever since her father had enlisted in the Army and gone off to fight, Mary's mother had been pressuring her to hitch her star to Sam. Yes, he was a nice boy, but she wasn't ready to settle down. There was a great big world out there she hadn't explored yet. If she married Sam, she'd never get farther than the Philadelphia city limits. She was sure of it.

She imagined herself nursing an infant and pregnant with another. The image turned her stomach. Motherhood and domesticity weren't for her. Then again, schooling wasn't for her, either.

"Mary, Mary quite contrary, what in the world are you going to do?" She sighed dramatically and sat up. "Crack open that school book and try to make sense of it, that's what."

She grabbed the book out of her satchel and turned to the bookmarked page. Despite her twenty-twenty vision, she squinted at the words to help her focus. She blinked, and then blinked again, but the letters still jumbled together. That familiar feeling of helplessness washed over her. How was she going to bluff her way out of this one?

∽⌖∾

Nora virtually floated on air as she let herself into her parents' well-appointed Greenwich, Connecticut, home. "Mor? Far? The prodigal daughter has returned." She could hear voices in the living room, so she headed in that direction.

"Dr. Tompkins. I didn't know you made house calls." Nora glanced from the family doctor to her parents on the sofa and her brother, Bill, sitting in the Queen Anne chair. Which one of them was ill?

"In this case, I was happy to stop by, young lady." The doctor winked. "Oskar, Elsa, William," he said, ruffling Bill's hair. "I know you're going to do great things. I'll be seeing you." On his way out, he patted Nora on the shoulder. "Nice to see you, Nora."

Nora frowned. "What was that about? She addressed her parents. Are you sick? Mor? Far?" Neither of her parents appeared ill.

"We're fine." It was her mother who answered. "Dr. Tompkins stopped by as a favor to your father."

"He wrote me a 'Get out of service' letter," Bill said.

Nora bristled at his smug expression. "What are you talking about?"

"Far had Doc write a letter saying I have a chronic condition that prevents me from serving in the military."

"You're perfectly able-bodied. You had him concoct something false just so that you don't have to go fight for our country?" Nora glared at Bill and then at her father. "You encouraged that?"

"You watch your tone, young lady," Elsa Lindstrom warned.

"I'm proud of it. Now I'll never have to go to those God-forsaken places and get my head shot off."

Nora barely restrained herself from cold-cocking her brother. "No. You'll leave that for the courageous boys and men who aren't busy frittering their lives away."

"That's enough, Nora." Oskar Lindstrom finally spoke.

"Far, you can't be serious about this. You're perpetrating a fraud." Nora pointed at her brother. "He's nineteen and fully capable of going to war. Boys much younger than him are willingly lining up outside recruiting stations all over the country for the honor of representing our country."

"Your brother is destined for big things, Nora. You should be grateful that he'll be spared."

"Oh, for Heaven's sake, Mor. That boy," she said the word derisively, "isn't anything more than a sniveling coward, and you're enabling him. I should think you'd want him to serve his nation with pride and dignity. Maybe he would come back a real man."

Bill stepped threateningly in her direction, but his father positioned himself between them. "Both of you, stop it. Bill will come to work for me in the shop, and one day he'll take my place. There will be no further discussion of this, not now, not ever. It is done. Do you understand me?"

Nora's hands balled into fists. Her chest heaved with unspent anger. Bill's eyes flared dangerously. Finally, he blinked first and backed away to stand by the large bay window.

"Why are you here?" her mother asked.

"Nice to see you too, Mor." Nora unclenched her fists. "Actually, I came to share some really exciting news with all of you. Given what I just witnessed, though, I imagine you'll be less enthusiastic than I hoped."

"Nonsense. What is it? What's the news?"

"Sit," Her father's tone softened. "Tell us."

Bill continued to stare sullenly out the window, and Nora debated whether she should simply leave without further comment. Her parents looked at her expectantly. *Tell them. Don't let that yellow-bellied sapling ruin your moment.*

"All right." Nora squared her shoulders. "I've got a job offer and I'm going to take it."

"What? That's fabulous!"

"I didn't realize you were applying anywhere."

"I wasn't. I received a letter from Dr. Ernest Lawrence from the University of California, Berkeley."

"California is so far away."

"I don't think I'll be going to California, Mor. I don't really know where I'll be going. I only know that whatever it is, it's important, and it's for the war effort. Unlike Bill," she practically spat out his name, "I can't wait to do my part and make a difference."

"What do you mean you don't know where you'll be going? How can you accept an offer if you don't know where it is?"

"What will you be doing for this Dr. Lawrence?" her father asked.

"I'm not really sure."

"That's rich," Bill interrupted. "You're taking a job someplace, to do something, and you have no idea what, or where it is. That's my brainy sis. Head in the clouds and no idea how to navigate the real world. Do yourself a favor. Keep your head in the books you love so much and leave the living to those of us who know how to do it."

"You mean cowards like you? No thanks. I'm happy to do my part, whatever, wherever that takes me." Nora strode out of the living room, through the foyer, and out the front door without so much as a backward glance.

Why she'd ever thought they'd understand or want to celebrate with her was a mystery. It wasn't as though they'd encouraged her to seek higher education. That had been her high school science teacher, and later her college and graduate school physics professor, Enrico Fermi. Well, she'd show them. By golly, she'd show all of them.

"How is your father? Any word from the Front?"

Mary skipped over the sidewalk crack as she cradled her books against her chest. Phyllis's dad also was in the Army, and that bond had brought them closer together. They lived around the corner from each other and often walked home from school together.

"Mother and I listen to the news every night for a mention of the 36th Infantry Division. Nothing so far. We did get a letter from him last week. He didn't say where they were, just that the bugs were horrible, the ground was so muddy his boots sunk in all the way to his calves, and the food was awful."

They reached Mary's street—Larchwood Avenue—and came to a halt. "How about your father? How's he doing?"

"Hard to say. Mom and I haven't gotten a letter from him in three weeks." Phyllis bit her lip and Mary feared she might cry.

"Don't worry about it. There are dozens of reasons you might not have heard from him. He could be in some remote outpost, or maybe his company is on the move. I'm sure you'll hear something soon."

"I hope so."

"I'm certain of it." Mary nodded, as if the matter was settled. "I've got to get going. Mother is expecting me at home."

"Okay. See you tomorrow?"

"You bet." Mary waved as she headed down the sidewalk and through the gate into her front yard. She bounded up the steps and into the house. As she placed her books down on the foyer table, Sam's unmistakable voice wafted from the sitting room. The sound made her irrationally angry.

"Thank you for the refreshments, Mrs. Trask. This was mighty nice of you."

"You're welcome, Samuel. Feel free to stop by anytime. I'm always happy for your company, and I expect to see a lot more of you going forward. I'm sorry Mary's not here yet. I can't imagine where she could be. She should've been home by now."

"She is home." Mary strode into the room. There was Sam, sitting comfortable-as-could-be on the sofa, drinking a soda. Her mother was in her customary rocking chair. Following First Lady Eleanor Roosevelt's lead, she was knitting a sweater for the boys at the Front with yarn procured from the Red Cross.

"There you are. Samuel dropped by a little while ago and he and I were having a wonderful chat."

"I can see that. He looks right at home."

"Hi, Mary." Sam stood. "You look very nice today."

"What are you doing here? Why aren't you at work?"

"Mary, where are your manners? Samuel came all the way over here to see you."

Mary continued to stare at Sam. Of course, her mother was right; she was being unreasonably curt. Still…

His gaze flitted back and forth between Mary and her mother. "I missed you. I thought maybe we could go for a walk or something."

"I have homework to do."

"That can wait until after dinner. You two run along."

Mary opened her mouth to protest. Her mother, the one who constantly nagged her to get her homework done from the moment she walked through the door after school, wanted her to fritter away an hour or more with Sam.

There was nothing for it. If she continued to resist, she'd catch heck from her mother later. "Give me a minute to freshen up. I'll be right down."

She fixed her makeup, checked her breath, combed her hair, and was back downstairs within five minutes. "I'm ready."

Sam beamed at her. "You look fetching."

"Thank you. I'll be back in time for dinner," she called over her shoulder to her mother.

"Don't rush. Samuel is welcome to join us."

"Sam has better things to do." She fairly shoved him out the door in front of her. When they turned the corner and Mary was sure her mother could no longer spy on them from the living room window, she stopped short and rounded on him.

"What do you think you're doing?"

"What are you talking about? Can't a guy miss his girl?"

Mary sighed. "You know I'm working my tail feathers off to pass this English test. I can't be gallivanting around with you when I should be studying." She resumed walking, adjusting her pace to match his uneven gait, a remnant of his bout with polio as a child.

"Come on. You know deep down you're happy to see me."

"I know deep down that if I don't pass this test, I don't graduate." She kicked a stone on the path. "So, why aren't you at work?"

"I got off early. Old man Bailey said some sprockets we needed to fix Mrs. Hadley's watch hadn't come in yet, so I didn't have anything to do."

They walked along in silence for a time, and when Sam interlaced his fingers with hers, she allowed it.

"Your mom says you're going to start a full-time job at Meyer's after graduation. Do you know what your hours are going to be?"

Mary groaned. "I don't want to talk about it. That whole thing depresses me."

"Working a steady job right out of high school depresses you? Do you have any idea how lucky you are? Meyer's Drug Store is a staple in town. You could have a job for life."

Mary disentangled their fingers. "I don't want to spend the rest of my life working behind the counter at a drug store. Working there part-time on weekends is bad enough."

"What do you want, Mary? Because I don't understand you. You're super smart, but you're not good enough at school to go to college, and even if you were, how would you pay for it?"

"I want to go places and see things. I want to shake off the dust and live a little." She twirled in a circle with her arms outstretched.

"Now be realistic. Work at Meyer's for a year, and then we'll get married. I'll take care of you for the rest of your life."

"On a watchmaker's salary? No, thanks. I don't want or need you to take care of me. I want to take care of myself."

"You're crazy, you know that? Stop daydreaming. There are plenty of girls who would jump at the chance I'm giving you."

"Then go date them!"

"I don't want to date them. I love you!"

They'd stopped walking and were face to face, both of them breathing heavily. Sam pulled Mary to him and kissed her sloppily on the mouth. She planted both hands on his chest, shoved him away, and wiped her mouth with the back of her hand.

"Are you nuts? People will see."

"What if they do? You're my girl. Folks expect me to kiss you."

"Not in broad daylight out on the sidewalk, and not as though you want to swallow my tonsils. You're embarrassing me." She checked her watch. "I'm going home now. I'll be late for supper."

"Go to the diner with me Friday night?"

"We'll see. I have to work early on Saturday."

"Can I call you?"

Mary waved without answering and hustled down the sidewalk. She couldn't explain it, but every time Sam kissed her, she wanted to wash her mouth out with Listerine. Her mother was right. Sam was a nice boy, he didn't mind her working, and, because of his disability, she was never going to lose him to war. She should be counting her lucky stars. So, why wasn't she?

CHAPTER TWO

Nora paced impatiently in front of the restaurant where she and her closest childhood friend, Anna, had agreed to meet. She checked her watch. As usual, Anna was ten minutes late. She would blame it on the traffic, her roommate, or... The list went on and on. Truthfully, Nora didn't care about the excuses, but she was in the middle of an experiment she needed to finish before morning. At present, her lab partner was monitoring the reactions of the ions to a variety of stimuli, but she didn't completely trust him to keep a close enough eye on things and to accurately reflect the data in their reports.

"Hi, hi," Anna said breathlessly. She waved as she approached, her smile incandescent as always. "I'm so sorry I'm late. You wouldn't believe..."

Nora tuned out the rest of the explanation and instead focused on the dimple in Anna's chin. She could've told Nora she'd incinerated her favorite pair of shoes and Nora would've forgiven her. All throughout their childhood years, it had been like this. *Stop this madness. She's a woman, you're a woman. End of story. She doesn't feel the way you do. You know that. It's time to let it go.*

"Hello? Where are you?" Anna snapped her fingers in front of her face.

"What did you say?"

"I said, let's go inside. The wind is messing up my perm."

"Right." Nora opened the door and followed her in. It took a minute for her eyes to adjust to the low lighting. The restaurant was crowded for a Wednesday, but they managed to get a booth in the back.

Once they'd ordered, Anna asked, "So, what's this big news you wanted to share? Have you found a fella?"

"Huh?" Nora barely managed to right the glass of water before it spilled in her lap. Her face turned beet red. "N-no!"

Anna threw her head back and laughed, and Nora wanted to crawl under the table. Instead, she stared at the tablecloth. She nearly jumped out of her chair when a soft hand covered hers.

"I'm sorry. I didn't mean to embarrass you or make you uncomfortable. I was hopeful, is all. I want you to be happy. You spend too much of your time alone in the lab or with your head in a book."

Nora wanted to stay miserable, but warmth radiated from where their hands touched through the rest of her body, making her uncomfortable in an entirely different and foreign way. She withdrew her hand and put it in her lap. It was time to get back on safe ground.

"I've got a job offer."

"Wow! Already? That's fabulous! Tell me all about it."

Nora scanned the room to make sure no one was paying them undue attention. "I wish I could…tell you all about it, I mean."

"Why can't you?"

"It's classified."

"Oh, the plot thickens. I love a good mystery. Spill."

"No can do."

"C'mon. I can keep a secret."

Nora made a motion as if to zip her lips.

"Why would you invite me here just to tease me?" Anna pouted.

"I'm not trying to be difficult. Even if I wanted to, I couldn't tell you much."

"You've got to give me something."

Nora had to give Anna credit, she had a flair for the dramatic. "Okay. The letter I received came from Ernest Lawrence, himself."

"Who's Ernest Lawrence?"

"Who is…" Nora took a deep breath and willed herself to be patient. It wasn't as though Anna kept up on the latest scientific discoveries. Her interests shaded to the arts and she wanted to be an actress.

"Ernest Lawrence invented a machine that won him the Nobel Prize in 1939."

"That's good, right?"

"That's very, very good. He's tops in the field."

"What did he want? In the letter, I mean."

"He asked me to come to work on something crucial to the war effort."

"I always knew you'd do great things." She winked at Nora. "Where are you going?"

Nora shrugged.

"C'mon. Surely you can at least tell me where you're off to on this super-secret assignment."

Nora shook her head. "They haven't told me."

"Wait a minute. So, you don't know where you're going and what you'll do when you get there?" Anna's eyes grew large and round.

"You make it sound—"

"Like you've lost your mind? Yeah. Because I'm pretty sure you have."

"Shh." Nora glanced around. "Keep your voice down."

"You're my best friend. It's my job to tell you when you've gone cuckoo. And boy, have you. They could send you to...to...Minnesota or some other Godforsaken place."

"Maybe."

"How are you going to pack, if you don't know what the weather will be?"

Leave it to Anna to be ever-practical. "I guess I'll have to pack a little of everything and hope for the best."

Anna stared at her a long time, long enough to make her squirm. "You're really serious about this?"

"I'm more than serious. I'm going to do it. I've already sent a return letter accepting the offer of employment."

"Does this fancy-schmancy job at least pay well?"

"Top dollar." Nora breathed a sigh of relief. Maybe Anna was coming around.

"What does your family think? Wait." Anna held up a hand. "I don't care what that no-account brother of yours thinks. What did your parents say? You've told them, right?"

"I did."

"And?"

"They had much the same reaction as you. I think they would've had me committed if they could've worked it out and not had it bring shame on the family."

"I hate to agree with them, but they've got a point. Not the having you committed part, but I'm worried for you. I'm sure your folks are too. You're brilliant. There's no question about that. But you don't know anything about the world out there. You don't even like people. How are you going to get along?"

"I'm going to miss you."

"You'd better miss me. Who else would put up with your bookwormy ways?"

"That's not even a word."

"It is if I say it is." Anna frowned. "Will you promise to write? Even if you can't say much, it will be good to hear from you."

"I promise to write if they'll let me."

"America is a free country. They'd better let you write your best friend!"

"I expect to see you on the newsreels every time I go to the theater." Nora tried not to choke up.

"Forget the newsreels. I'm going to be in the main feature."

"Of course you are."

"Are there going to be lots of boys where you're going, you think?"

"I don't know. Probably far more guys than gals."

"Well, good odds for you, then. Just don't lock yourself away in some science lab, okay? Live a little. Find a fella. It wouldn't hurt you to go on a date, you know."

Nora blushed again. "I'm not you. Boys don't flock to me the way they do you."

"Nora Lindstrom. You're a real looker. Boys don't ask you out because you don't give them the time of day. Let 'em see that beautiful smile. Flash those pretty hazel eyes. Style that luxurious blond hair in curls. You'll be beating them off with a stick."

For reasons Nora didn't want to examine, the idea nauseated her.

❖❖

The movie theater was hopping, as it always was on a Friday night. It mattered not that the feature film, *The Pride of the Yankees*, had been out for two months, nor, for that matter, that Mary already had seen it three times. Thanks to her dad, Henry, Mary had been raised with a baseball in her hand, and Lou Gehrig's tragic story tugged at her heartstrings.

Henry Trask was a huge Philadelphia Phillies fan. He and his only daughter were regular fixtures at the ballpark, and Henry, a conductor on the Pennsylvania Railroad's *Broadway Limited*, often liked to boast about how the team preferred to take *his* train when they traveled for road trips.

Seeing this movie over and over again helped Mary feel closer to her dad.

Sam's hand brushed her breast and Mary shrugged him off. "I'm trying to watch the movie! Cut it out!" she whispered harshly. She shifted in her seat and distanced herself from Sam.

"C'mon! It isn't like you don't know the scene by heart. Gary Cooper gives Gehrig's emotional farewell speech and chokes up, etcetera, etcetera, etcetera."

"It's the best scene in the movie. I tear up every time I see it."

"I'm the one crying here. I haven't seen you in days! I missed my girl." Sam put his arm around Mary and drew her closer but stopped short of trying to touch her breast this time.

Mary studiously ignored him until the end credits rolled. "Could you have been any ruder? I came to the theater to watch the movie, not to be groped by a hormonal teenaged boy. You're nearly twenty. You'd think you would've outgrown such boorish behavior."

"For God's sake! There wasn't another couple here actually paying attention to what was on the screen. It's a darkened movie theater! No red-blooded guy brings his girl to the pictures on a Friday night and really expects to see the movie!"

She faced him. "Let me see if I understand this. You spent sixty-four cents on the movies so that you could try to put the moves on me?"

Sam frowned. "When you say it that way, I sound stupid."

Mary nodded. "You said it, not me." She slung her purse over her shoulder and stood. "At least one of us got your money's worth."

He jumped up and followed her. "Can I still take you out for a burger and a malt?"

She turned and smiled sweetly at him. "Of course. I'm hungry and I'm not stupid." He mumbled something under his breath that she didn't quite catch. She didn't bother asking him to repeat it.

They were silent on the short drive to the diner, and she was impressed when he came around and opened the door for her and helped her out of the car. He really was a nice boy, and when she and her best girlfriends compared notes, he wasn't any different than their boyfriends. They all had one thing on their minds. She shouldn't be so hard on him.

To make it up to him, she ordered a less expensive Coke instead of a malt.

"Have you heard anything more from your dad? Is he at the front lines yet? Has he killed any Nazis?" Sam licked ketchup from his fingers.

"Sam Abel, what a question to ask."

"What? That's why he's over there. We have to win the war, and the only way to do that is to take care of those damn Nazis and the Japs. I mean, darn. Sorry."

Mary rested her chin on her hands. "I wish nobody had to die. This whole war business makes me sick to my stomach. People are dying, and for what?"

"I'd go in a heartbeat if they'd let me. Instead, I'm 4-F'ed and sitting on the sidelines, watching the other guys get all the glory."

"Stop feeling sorry for yourself. I doubt there's a lot of glory in getting sick from slogging through cold mud day after day. That's mostly all Daddy talks about."

"That's probably because he doesn't want to worry you and your mother. I bet he's seen things that would curl your toes." Sam talked around a mouthful of burger. "He isn't telling you, is all."

Mary shuddered. "I hope you're wrong. I hope he hasn't had to hurt anyone, or watch anyone else be harmed."

"Don't you want us to win the war?"

"Of course I do! That doesn't mean I have to like that the world is at war or that my father is part of it. I worry for him. Every night I pray that he comes home safe. Is it wrong that I wish he didn't have to be over there and that nobody had to be killed?" Mary blinked back tears.

If Sam noticed, it wasn't obvious. He bit into his last French fry. "Nah. But I bet if your father was here, he'd tell you he's happy to be hunting Nazis. Besides, they started it. They're shooting at him. Don't you want him to shoot back?"

"Of course, if someone's trying to hurt you, you should defend yourself. But what about innocent people minding their own business who get caught in the crossfire? What about them?"

"What about them?"

She crossed her arms. "Let's talk about something else."

Sam threw some bills on the table. "How about if we go for a drive?"

"At this hour?"

"It's a clear night. We could go up to the lookout and see the stars. What do you say?"

It was a beautiful night—the moon was full and the stars shone brightly. Some of her fondest childhood memories were of picking out the constellations with her dad. Maybe this would be another way to feel closer to him. Who knew? He might be looking at the very same stars at the same time. "Okay."

Mary's hair whipped around her face as they wound their way up to the lookout, a popular hangout for couples. Conversation was impossible with the convertible top down. Between the wind and the radio blaring, she could barely hear herself think.

Sam found a place to park near the end of the strip and cut the engine. "You warm enough?" He pulled Mary to him on the bench seat and wrapped an arm around her.

"I'm fine." She pulled her sweater tighter around her and looked up at the sky. "It's so pretty up there."

"I suppose."

"Do you think there's anything out there?"

"You mean, like aliens?"

"I mean, people, or life, or… I don't know what."

"I don't think there are little green men running."

"The sky seems so big. I can't believe there's nothing out there."

They were silent for a time as they stared into space. Sam repositioned himself and leaned in to kiss her. His upper lip scratched her face and his breath tasted of onions. She stilled his roaming hand after he undid the top button of her blouse. When his kiss became more insistent, she pulled back.

"Argh. What is it with you? You want to be my girl, don't you?"

Did she? "It isn't that. I've told you before—I want to wait until I'm married. I'm not some floozy. If that's what you want, you'll have to go elsewhere."

"For God's sake." Sam pulled back. "I was going to wait to do this, but…" He reached into his jacket pocket and pulled out a small velvet box.

Mary swallowed hard. Could he be…?

"Mary Elizabeth Trask, will you marry me?" He opened the box to reveal a sparkling diamond solitaire.

Mary's heart pounded so hard she was certain he would feel it.

"Well, say something."

"I…"

"I already asked your mother for your hand. That's why I was at your house that day when you came home from school. She said she'd be proud to have me as her son-in-law."

Whatever trepidation she'd been feeling morphed into red-hot anger. "You went to my mother behind my back?"

"It wasn't like that. I-I wanted to do this the right way. Your father isn't around, so I had to ask your mother."

"What about me?"

"What about you?"

Mary ground her teeth. "Why is it more important to you what my mother thinks than it is what I want?"

"What are you talking about?"

"Is it my mother you want to marry?"

"What? Of course not! I want to marry you."

"Then what does asking my mother have to do with anything?"

"It may seem old fashioned to you, but I was trying to be chivalrous. It's customary to ask the father for his daughter's hand in marriage. I can't very well ask your father, now can I? So I did the next best thing."

"Unbelievable."

"What did I do wrong?"

"What did you do wrong?" Mary tried to buy herself more time. What had he done wrong? She tried to make sense of her rage. Sam still held the box open between them. She resisted the urge to run. "Take me home."

"What?"

28

Mary faced forward and slid as far away from him as she could. "I said, take me home, Sam. Now. I want to go home." She worked to keep the edge of panic out of her voice.

He looked crestfallen. "You're not going to give me an answer?"

Mary remained mum.

Finally, Sam closed the box and tucked it back in his pocket. He started the car. "Just... Just promise me you'll think about it. Please? Don't say no. Maybe I should've asked you differently. I don't know. This is the first time I've ever proposed to a girl."

Mary thought he might cry. She stopped short of putting a hand on his arm to comfort him. She couldn't. Her own emotions were too much of a jumble.

"Please take me home," she said quietly.

Sam put the car in gear and drove her home. She opened her door before he came to a full stop.

"Mary?"

"Not now, Sam." She ran up the sidewalk, through the gate, up the front steps, and into the house without a backward glance. She didn't stop running until she was in her room. She clicked the door shut as quietly as she could and leaned heavily against it.

Sam had asked her to marry him. It should've been the happiest moment of her life. Instead, she felt like she'd been sentenced to prison.

CHAPTER THREE

Nora lifted the goggles from her face and rubbed her eyes. *If you'd slept last night, you might be able to concentrate better today.* She sighed. No matter which way she'd turned, she hadn't been able to get comfortable. The full portent of her decision to accept Dr. Lawrence's offer weighed heavily on her mind.

Were Anna and her parents right? Had she lost her senses? "No. No, you did exactly the right thing. Stop second-guessing this."

"Talking to yourself, Lindstrom? You know that's a sign of madness, don't you?"

Nora startled and swiveled around on her stool. "Is your only purpose in life to annoy me, Dennis?"

"No. That's a bonus."

"What do you want?"

"You've got some very official-looking visitors. They're waiting for you in Dr. Fermi's old office."

Nora threw down the goggles, shrugged off her lab coat, and rearranged her dress. She didn't have time to go to the restroom and fix her hair, which she was sure must look a fright.

When she reached Dr. Fermi's office, she could hear raised voices behind the closed door. She hesitated.

"...and I'm telling you..."

She closed her eyes, took a deep breath to steady herself, and rapped her knuckles on the door.

"Come!" The voice was gruff, and the invitation was more a growl than a greeting.

Slowly, Nora opened the door and peeked around it. There were three men in the room, two standing and one sitting. She'd met Dr.

Oppenheimer before, of course. He'd examined some of her hypotheses and experiments. The other man standing she knew right away from pictures and newsreels—Dr. Ernest Lawrence. These were two of the greatest scientists of the day, and they were here to see her. She thought she might faint.

"Come in, Dr. Lindstrom."

Nora stepped forward. "D-Dr. Lawrence, Dr. Oppenheimer." She shook their proffered hands.

The man behind the desk was a hulking figure in a military uniform. "I'm General Leslie Groves, Dr. Lindstrom."

"General." Nora nodded to him. She wasn't sure if she was supposed to salute or shake his hand, so she remained frozen to the spot.

"Dr. Lawrence here thinks very highly of you. Dr. Oppenheimer, as well."

Nora wanted to interject that neither of them knew her very well. Instead, she said nothing.

"I was just telling the general that you've accepted my offer—our offer—to undertake this crucially important job on behalf of the war effort. You're the perfect choice. No one will do it better." As he said the last, Lawrence glanced pointedly at General Groves.

"She's a girl. The ink isn't even dry on her diploma. You want to entrust her with perhaps the most important function in the place."

Nora stared at a spot on the wall.

"I'm telling you, she's got the perfect temperament for the job at hand, and she knows the science behind it far better than any of her classmates. She's absolutely the right one. We need her." Oppenheimer slapped the desk with his open palm for emphasis.

"No." The general crossed his arms, brooking no argument.

"You're wrong about this," Dr. Lawrence broke in. "Hear us out. She's a she."

"That much is obvious."

"It will be invaluable to have a woman scientist in charge of a gaggle of younger, inexperienced girls. Who better to do the job? She'll understand them and their moods. She'll be better at motivating them to do the work without asking questions, and they'll relate better to her than to a man in a similar position."

"No," General Groves said.

Nora wondered if she really needed to be here for this argument. It seemed they were doing fine without any of her input.

"Dr. Lindstrom?" Lawrence wheeled around and faced her.

"Yes, sir?"

Before Lawrence could ask his question, Oppenheimer broke in. "What is your opinion on the advisability of hiring a cadre of female high school graduates and training them to sit at cubicles all day and operate machines very much like the ones you've been working on, using some of the principles you've been exploring in your research? Do you think it can be done? They wouldn't have to understand the science behind it. In fact, we don't want them to. You'd instruct them to twist the knobs and pull the levers in such a way that would achieve the correct results."

Nora knew she must look like a deer caught in the glare of automobile headlights. "I—"

"More specifically, do *you* think you could train them to do it?" Lawrence asked. "So far, only my male Ph.D. students have been able to operate the machines. You'd have to teach unskilled girls to produce results similar to those of Ph.D. students."

Nora straightened to her full height. These…men…were just like the boys in the lab. They all believed they were superior in every way to girls and women. That was what this was about? She'd take that challenge and prove them all wrong.

"I know I could, and we'd get better results." She hadn't meant to say it so forcefully, but there it was.

"Is that right?" General Groves's eyebrows rose nearly to his hairline.

"Yes, sir."

"And if you're wrong? You realize the war effort might hinge on your ability to deliver on that boast?"

"I'm certain…sir."

Groves rocked back in his chair. "I like her pluck." He turned to Lawrence and Oppenheimer. "If you're wrong and she fails…"

"If we're wrong—"

"Which we're not—"

"We'll chalk it up to her being a girl and replace her with a man," Lawrence finished.

Groves steepled his fingers as he regarded her. Nora refused to wilt under the scrutiny. "Very well. We'll do it your way." He pointed at her. "You are sworn to secrecy. If you're as smart as these geniuses seem to believe you are, I'm sure you've figured out the basic outline of what we're attempting to accomplish. There are precious few people who know or understand the scope of this project. One wrong word uttered in the wrong company could spell doom for the Allies. Do you get my drift?"

"I do, sir. I promise you, I will not speak of it to anyone."

"You couldn't even tell your boyfriend."

Nora blinked. "I don't have one of those, sir."

Groves smiled. "Good. You're dismissed. You'll be hearing from me when we're ready to move on this."

"Yes, sir. Thank you, sir. You won't be sorry."

"I'd better not be."

She clicked the door shut behind her and made it to the bathroom on shaky legs. When she'd scoured every stall to be sure she was alone, she collapsed against the brick wall. Her hands shook. Three things were clear to her. Lawrence and Oppenheimer hand-picked her for this assignment. The assignment entailed separating uranium isotopes. The outcome of the war very well could depend on how well she did her job.

She would not fail.

༺ঌ৵༻

"Samuel called for you, dear. Again."

"Okay, Mother." Mary took the stairs to her room two at a time.

"We haven't seen much of him lately," her mother called after her. "Why is that?"

"I've been busy studying. I've got that big English essay test coming up, remember?"

"I do." Mrs. Trask stood in the doorway. "But you can't study all the time. You should go out with Samuel and get some fresh air."

"I can go out with him after this test is over. Honestly, Mother, I should think you'd want me to put all my energy into doing well on this exam. This could make the difference between graduating or not. I don't understand why my seeing Sam is so important to you."

"We've had this discussion before. That young man wants to marry you. He's got a good head on his shoulders, he's never going to die in war..." Her voice caught. "He has steady, reliable employment. What more do you want?"

I want to be in love. "I want to study. Please, close the door on your way out."

"Don't be rude, young lady."

"I'm not being rude. I barely have time to breathe between studying and working at the drugstore. I'll deal with Sam later, after the test."

"What am I supposed to tell him when he comes calling?"

"Tell him the truth. I'm focused on schooling."

"You are impossible, you know that?"

"So you keep telling me. Please let me study in peace."

"Dinner will be on the table at six thirty. Don't be late."

"'Bye, Mother."

When her mother left, Mary closed her eyes in relief. She knew she couldn't avoid him forever, but at least for a little while, she could put him off.

Nora breathed deeply. Spring was in the air; she smelled it in the blossoms on the dogwood trees, in the grass that covered the fields of Central Park, and in the scent of the lilac bushes as she strolled past.

It felt good to be outside after being cooped up in the lab for so many hours. She almost felt human...almost. A good soak in the tub once she got back to her place would do the rest of the job.

"Nora. Hey, Nora!"

She wanted to keep walking, but she knew from experience that her nosy neighbor wouldn't quit until she acknowledged her. "Hi, Bunny."

"Something really official-looking came for you a little while ago. It's from the War Department in Washington."

Nora furrowed her brow. The idea of Bunny snooping through her mail was an ongoing source of irritation, but Bunny was waving the envelope in front of her like a matador waving a red cape in front of a bull.

"Thank you, Bunny." Nora struggled not to snatch the envelope out of her hand. Instead, she waited patiently for Bunny to deliver it to her. Then she hustled up the stairs and into the building, ignoring the string of questions that followed her.

When she was safely alone, she used a letter opener to slit open the envelope from General Leslie Groves, The War Department, Office of the Chief of Engineers, Washington, D.C. Inside was a single, typewritten sheet of paper signed by Groves himself.

May 1, 1943
Dear Dr. Lindstrom:
As we discussed previously, you have agreed to employment at my discretion.

Please present yourself at Pennsylvania Station in New York City on May 7, 1943, at one o'clock in the afternoon. You will be met at the station, provided with a ticket, and escorted to the train by my representative. A hired private car will meet you at your designated stop and transport you the rest of the way to your final destination.

This assignment carries with it the burden of absolute secrecy. You must tell no one of these instructions, nor convey any information whatsoever to anyone, including your parents and family members, for the duration. Your country is counting on you.
Sincerely,
General Leslie R. Groves

Nora read the letter twice. May seventh? That was less than a week away. Graduation was scheduled for May sixteenth. How would she explain to her parents that she was going to miss graduation? Not only that, but she couldn't tell them anything, including where or when she was going, how she was getting there, how long she'd be gone, or what she would be doing.

What am *I going to be doing?* Although she knew the rough outlines from her meeting at Pupin Hall, she didn't know her job title, what the work environment would be, her salary, hours, or living situation. In fact, she knew absolutely nothing, not a single thing more than what Dr. Lawrence, Dr. Oppenheimer, and General Groves had told her, which amounted to pretty much nothing.

For the briefest of moments, all she could hear was her parents' derision and Anna's incredulity. Doubt crept in, followed by its close cousin, insecurity. Nora set the letter aside. "You know exactly what you're doing. You're using your education to help win the war. The details aren't important. What matters is that you're going to make a difference—and not by sitting around knitting scarves, either."

Nora clenched and unclenched her fists. The strength of conviction surged through her. Not only could she do this, she absolutely would do this. And when it was all over, her parents would be proud and Anna would be in awe of her and what she had accomplished.

She threw open the closet doors, pulled down her suitcase, and hoisted it onto the bed. Tonight she would begin to pack. Tomorrow she would tell her parents she was going away, and she'd be in touch when she could.

Mary wiped her sweaty palms on her pretty red-and-white-checkered gingham dress as Mrs. Platt passed by her with the stack of graded exams for the second time.

"Nice job, Penelope. You showed an excellent grasp of the subject."

"Thank you, Mrs. Platt."

Mrs. Platt returned to the front of the room and faced the class. "I have to say, I was impressed with your test results. It appears as though you learned something this quarter, after all."

Mary stared at the wooden desk. Her heart sank. She was the only student without a graded paper in front of her.

"Mary Trask?"

"Yes, ma'am?"

"I'd like to see you after class."

"Yes, ma'am."

"Class dismissed."

Slowly and with trepidation, Mary gathered her books and trudged to the teacher's desk. "Mrs. Platt—"

She held up a hand. "I'll do the talking, young lady."

"Yes, ma'am," Mary mumbled.

"I have to say, I'm very disappointed in you. I know you read *Great Expectations*. I saw your mother at bridge club and she told me how diligently you'd been studying. I don't understand it. This paper," she waved it in the air between them, "would lead me to believe you'd barely opened the book."

Mary caught a glimpse of the big red "F" at the top of the paper and gasped. "Mrs. Platt, I did read the book, I swear. It took me forever, but I finished it. Heck, I could tell you everything that happened in that book. I studied and worked hard. I…"

She lowered her head and wrung her hands. "I don't do well on tests. I don't know why. The words don't look right on the page. I have trouble reading the questions. Then, when I think I do understand what you're asking, I know all the answers in my head, but when I try to write them down, it seems like everything comes out wrong."

To her mortification, tears formed on her lashes. Without a high school diploma, she'd never amount to anything. She'd have to marry Sam or someone like him.

"What are we going to do about this, Mary? I know you often struggle. But this exam? This one is completely beyond salvaging."

Mary shook her head. The lump in her throat was so big, she didn't think she could speak around it. "Please, don't tell my mother," she choked out. "I couldn't bear it."

"Put your books down and look at me."

Reluctantly, Mary did as she was told.

"I'm going to ask you the same question that was on this test. I want you to stand right there, without opening the book, and tell me the answer."

She straightened up. "Yes, ma'am."

"Who is Pip in love with, and is it a case of requited, or unrequited, love?"

Mary smiled. "Pip's in love with Miss Havisham's adopted daughter, Estella, who, as it turns out, is really the escaped convict Magwitch's daughter, but we don't find that out until much later." She warmed to the topic. "For most of the book, Estella treats Pip badly. She looks down on him. Then she marries Bentley Drummle, even though Pip doesn't want her to, but he dies and she becomes a widow. Pip meets her again after Bentley dies." Mary began to pace in front of the teacher's desk.

"This is where it gets confusing. In the version we read, Dickens gives the impression that Pip is going to get the girl. But when he first wrote *Great Expectations*, he made it clear that Estella remarries someone else, leaving Pip in the lurch. Dickens rewrote the ending and changed it to a 'hopefully ever after' kind of thing after he got guff for writing such a miserably unhappy conclusion. Personally, I think the first ending was more appropriate, considering how unhappy the first two-thirds of the book are. I mean, the change in tone in the newer ending kind of doesn't fit with the rest of the book and waters down the moral of the story."

When Mary came to a stop, the room was so quiet that the only sound was the second hand marking time on the wall clock. Mrs. Platt stared at her, open-mouthed. "D-did I say something wrong?"

Mrs. Platt blinked. "No. No, Mary, you said everything exactly right. In fact, you answered the question in a more detailed and nuanced fashion than most college students."

"Oh."

For several moments, Mrs. Platt stared out the classroom window. More than once, she shook her head and tutted. Finally, she placed Mary's exam paper on the desk and took out her red pen. With a single slash mark, she put a diagonal line through the "F." Then she wrote in big, bold strokes at the top of the page.

I have given this student a follow-up oral exam. From this exam, it is clear that Mary has a full and above-average understanding of the themes and concepts in this novel. As a result, I have re-evaluated and re-graded this exam. This student deserves an "A."
She signed the note and beamed at Mary.

"Gosh. Thank you, Mrs. Platt. Thank you. Thank you." Mary ran behind the desk and hugged her around the neck.

"Now, now. That's enough of that." She pushed her glasses farther up onto the bridge of her nose. "I'm still going to need the principal's approval to make such a drastic change to a grade."

"Oh." Mary felt the air rush out of her lungs.

"Don't worry. Principal Wegman has always trusted my judgment before. I doubt this time will be any different."

"Thank you, ma'am. Thank you so much."

"You're welcome, Mary. I knew something had to be terribly wrong. You're too smart to turn in an exam like this."

"Yes, ma'am."

"Stay here. I'll be right back."

Mary watched out the window as the school bell rang and the students piled out of the building, spilled onto the sidewalk, and dispersed in pairs and small groups. She saw Mrs. Platt approach Principal Wegman, who was standing on the top landing, presiding over the end of the school day. The discussion was brief but animated.

Please say yes. Please say yes. Please say yes.

Mary lost sight of Mrs. Platt as she walked back through the heavy front doors, and she skedaddled away from the window to stand at attention once again in front of the desk. The classroom door opened seconds later.

"Principal Wegman wasn't very happy with the situation, but he agreed to the grade change."

Mary let out a breath and whooped with joy, which garnered her a raised eyebrow. "I'm sorry, ma'am. It's just... My graduation depended on that grade. I don't know what I would've done if I hadn't passed."

"I don't know if your plans include college or higher education of any kind, but I strongly recommend you find yourself a reading tutor over the summer."

"Yes, ma'am. May I go now?"

"Yes, Mary. You're dismissed."

She let herself out of the classroom, scurried out of the building, and continued down the sidewalk until she was off school property. Then she dropped her books, spun in a circle, and did a victory dance. She was going to graduate on time, after all.

"Hey. Everything okay?"

Mary's hand flew to her chest. "Lord have mercy. You nearly scared me to death."

"I'm sorry," Phyllis said. "I waited for you by the big tree. When you didn't come out for so long, I got worried."

"That's all right." Mary picked up her books and the two girls fell into step together.

"What's got you in such a good mood?"

Mary explained about the exam and the grading change.

"Wow. Lucky you. I wish some of my teachers would do something like that for me..." Phyllis stopped walking.

"What is it?" Mary followed her line of sight down the street, where Phyllis's mother was crumpled on the sidewalk in front of their house. Her wailing was loud enough that Mary could hear her, even from this distance.

"No. No, no, no." Phyllis broke into a run, and Mary followed close on her heels.

In this time of war, everyone knew what a tableau like this meant. They reached Phyllis's mother as several neighbors knelt on the ground next to her, trying in vain to console her. She held a telegram loosely in her hand, and Phyllis liberated it from her grasp. She covered her mouth with a hand as a sob burst forth.

Mary didn't have to ask what the telegram said. She knew. "Phyllis? What can I do to help?"

Phyllis shook her head. She fell to her knees on the sidewalk and took her mother in her arms. Together, they rocked and cried. The sound pierced the peacefulness of the tree-lined street.

Mary tried to decide whether she should stay or go. Phyllis seemed to have forgotten that she was here. The front door was wide open. After a moment, she came to a decision. Gently, she rubbed Phyllis's shoulder and spoke into her ear. "I'm going to make you both some hot tea. Bring your mother and come inside."

Mary's mother wouldn't be happy that she would be late getting home, but when she explained why, she was certain her mother would understand.

CHAPTER FOUR

A re you going to come inside, or are you going to continue to wear out the sidewalk?" Bill stood with his arms folded in the front doorway of their parents' house. Nora's face reddened. She should've known he'd be there and that he'd be only too happy to make her look like a fool if he thought he could get away with it. She stalked up the steps and brushed past him without a word.

"Nice to see you too," he muttered, as she passed him.

Her parents were seated in the living room. They were listening so intently to the news on the radio, she doubted they'd even heard her come in.

"Mor, Far."

"Shh." Her mother waved her away.

"They sunk six German U-boats today, and it looks as though we're about to win surrender in North Africa," her father said. "Finally, things are starting to go our way."

"It's about time," Bill said.

Nora helped herself to a glass of water from the kitchen. When she returned to the living room, Edward R. Murrow was signing off in his characteristic fashion.

"To what do we owe the pleasure?" Nora's father turned off the radio.

"I came to say goodbye."

"You going somewhere?" Bill asked.

She ignored him and instead addressed her parents. "I expect I'll be gone for a long stretch, but I'll write or call when I can."

"Your brother asked you a question. Where are you going?"

"Away."

"Don't be vague, dear. Coy doesn't suit you."

Nora frowned at her mother. "This is the opportunity I told you about—the job I accepted. It's not a question of being evasive, Mor. I'm simply following orders."

"Orders?" Bill scoffed. "What, you're in the military now?"

"No. But I'm not going to sit around like a coward and hide from doing my duty."

He took a menacing step in her direction, and their father stepped between them.

"We've been through this before. Your brother is coming to work for me. I need him. End of discussion. That's enough from you."

Nora's nostrils flared. "You're right, Far. It is enough. I didn't come here to fight. I came because I thought you'd like to know I was leaving and I wanted to tell you in person. Also, it won't be necessary for you to come to graduation, since I can't be in two places at once."

"You won't be able to come back to accept your diploma?"

"No, Mor."

"But you've worked so hard to earn it."

"I have. I expect they'll find a way to send it to me."

"How can they send it to you if you can't tell them where you are?" Bill had retreated to the other side of the room, where he stood with his arms crossed, glaring at her like a petulant teenager, which, of course, he was.

Again, Nora ignored him. "Anyway, I'd best be going. I have to finish packing."

"You're leaving so soon? But you just got here."

"I'm sorry, Mor. There's so much to do."

"You'll write if you can?"

"She said she would, dear."

"I will." Nora hugged her mother and father. She breathed deeply to memorize the scent of her perfume and his aftershave. It likely would be a very long time before she'd see them again. "Bill." She nodded at him as she took her leave.

When she arrived home, Anna was sitting on her doorstep. "Hi."

"Hi. What are you doing here?"

"I've been thinking. The truth is, I felt badly for the way I reacted to your news last time I saw you. If you're going away to God-only-knows-where and you're happy about that... You're still happy about it?"

"I am."

"Then I'm happy for you."

Anna looked up at her from under long lashes, and Nora's heart stood still.

"When do you leave? Do you know yet?"

It took several seconds before Nora's brain registered Anna's question. "Tomorrow."

"Tomorrow? So soon?"

"Mm-hmm."

"Did they tell you where you're going? I mean, I know you can't tell me, but at least you know, right?"

"No."

"No, you can't tell me, or no, you don't know?"

"Both."

"Gee whiz. That's crazy." Anna stood. "In that case, it's a good thing I stopped by when I did. Otherwise, I might've missed you." She handed Nora a package wrapped in a brown paper bag.

"What's this?"

"I know my friend. She's been keeping a diary since we were old enough to read and write. I thought she might need this."

Nora smiled. "Ever-thoughtful Anna."

"Open it."

Nora tore open the paper. The smell of fine leather assaulted her senses. "Oh, my." She ran her fingers over the soft cover and the embossed gold initials in the bottom left corner, N.L. She swallowed hard and regarded her friend. "This is too much. It must've cost you a week's salary."

"Pshaw. It's the least I can do. Consider it my contribution to the war effort."

Nora laughed. "Well, it's very thoughtful of you." She pulled the leather strap free of the buckle and fanned the blank parchment pages. "There are enough sheets in here to last me the rest of my life."

"I'm planning for your future. I expect those pages to be filled with fascinating adventures. And I want to hear about each and every one when you can tell me." Anna leaned forward and kissed her on the cheek.

Nora blushed to the roots of her hair.

"Be safe for me. Do great things. Always remember me."

As if I could ever forget you. "I will."

Anna sashayed down the street, looked back, and waved. Nora watched after her until she disappeared from sight. She held the journal up to her face and inhaled deeply. Then she held the journal to her chest and hugged it tight. Instantly, it had become her most favorite and treasured possession. She wasn't positive she was allowed to chronicle the things she'd be doing, but surely she could record her own personal story in these pages. After all, Anna was counting on her.

⤝⤞

"Mary, I wanted you to know that they've changed the color of the label on the penicillin package. It's the one with the red outline."

"Thanks, Doc." She was grateful that Doc never made her feel stupid for having trouble reading the labels on the medicine bottles. They'd worked out a system. He would tell her what color label or what bottle shape held which medicine, and she would stock the shelves accordingly. "By the way, Doc, we got that cough serum in that you've been waiting for."

"Good. Mrs. Meriweather will be glad to hear. She's been waiting on that prescription going on two weeks now."

Mary finished stocking the antibiotics shelf and stowed her lab coat in her locker. She grabbed the duster, unlatched the half door and exited the pharmacy station.

Unlike Mildred, who worked up front, Mary didn't mind dusting the shelves. In truth, she enjoyed the mindless work. It gave her time to daydream.

Most often, she imagined being one of those big movie stars she saw in the pictures—Ingrid Bergman, or Ava Gardner, Katharine Hepburn, or Gene Tierney. Of course, it was only a dream. After all, she'd never be able to read scripts well enough to play a part.

What are you going to do if you don't marry Sam? As much as she loved and respected Doc, she wouldn't...couldn't...spend the rest of her life working behind a drugstore counter. Somewhere out there were jobs for girls like her—jobs that weren't dependent on her ability to read and write.

Already, she'd crossed the usual suspects off the list. She couldn't be a secretary or a teacher, and if she were going to take a retail job at a department store, then she might as well stay here at Meyer's, where she was comfortable and Doc helped her compensate for her shortcomings.

Something will come up. You'll see. Keep your eyes open. Graduation was next week. She could work here until she had a better option.

In the meantime, she needed to figure out what to do about ever-persistent Sam. She'd been avoiding him for weeks. Finally, to get him off her back, she'd agreed to let him take her out to dinner after graduation. She wasn't looking forward to it.

She caught the deodorant can as it teetered on the shelf. *Pay attention, Mary Elizabeth. You almost made a mess. You can deal with what to do about Sam later.*

Pennsylvania Station bustled with boisterous reunions, soldiers and civilians hustling to and from designated tracks, heartfelt goodbyes, and the sound of train whistles. Nora turned in a circle. General Groves's letter said only that a representative would meet her at the station. She wondered if the general had been to Penn Station. It was enormous. Without knowing her destination, it was impossible to know where to wait.

She readjusted her grip on the suitcase and pushed the purse strap higher on her shoulder. Her feet hurt from being stuffed into high heels she was unaccustomed to wearing, and her hose were slipping.

"Ugh. This is ridiculous." She'd half a mind to turn around and go home. Instead, she decided to make one last pass through the terminal. She turned left at the flower vendor, and that's when she saw him. He was a stern-looking gentleman in a business suit and hat, and he held a sign that had her name on it. She broke into a run.

"I'm Nora Lindstrom." She skidded to a halt in front of him, nearly decking him with the suitcase. She put it down and fumbled in her purse for identification.

He glanced at the ID, nodded, picked up her suitcase, and pivoted on his heel. "Come with me. We don't have much time."

47

Just like that, he was on the move. He hadn't even told her his name. She jogged to keep up. She couldn't even get close enough to ask him a question. When he stopped short, she nearly ran into the back of him.

"This is your train." He reached into his suit-jacket pocket, pulled out a train ticket, and handed it to her. "I'll come with you and get you settled."

They crossed through three cars until they arrived at an empty berth in a sleeping compartment. He stepped inside and placed her suitcase next to the wardrobe.

Nora read the ticket. "There's no destination listed."

"Don't worry about it. Someone will fetch you when you've reached your stop and a car will be waiting for you when you get off. The driver has your name." He turned to go.

"Wait!"

He paused.

"This is a sleeper car."

"Yes."

"Am I to understand that the trip will last through the night?"

"So it would appear. Get comfortable, Dr. Lindstrom; you'll be riding for a while."

When he was gone, Nora folded herself into one of two small chairs that would convert into the bottom bunk for sleeping.

"Here you are, miss."

Nora jumped up. A luggage-carrying Pullman porter escorted a young woman into the car.

"There must be some mistake. This is way too posh for my blood." The woman's dress was neat and well-pressed, but somewhat worn around the edges.

"No mistake, miss. We're full up everywhere else. This is where I was told to put you."

The woman shrugged. "I guess it's okay, then." She turned and seemed to notice Nora for the first time. "Hi there, I'm Josephine."

"Nora. Nice to meet you."

The two women shook hands as the porter stood by waiting. "Miss? Shall I put your suitcase over there?" He indicated the space next to Nora's suitcase.

"Oh, my. Where are my manners? Yes, please." Josephine waited until he had retreated from the compartment. "Isn't this exciting?"

"You've never traveled by train before?"

"No."

"You're in for a treat. I love trains."

Josephine cocked her head to the side as if sizing her up. "You look as though you might do this a lot."

Nora wasn't sure how to take the comment, so she remained mum.

"Where are you headed?"

She'd been dreading this question. How could she explain it? *Keep it honest and simple.* "I don't know my destination yet."

Josephine's eyes opened wide. "You too? I thought maybe I was the only one."

"What do you mean?"

"My brother-in-law works for the War Department. He heard they were hiring a lot of clerical staff for some big project and he got me an interview here in New York. They hired me on the spot and told me to show up at the train station today. They wouldn't tell me where I was going, only that it was for the war effort, and that I should pack as if I was moving. So here I am." Josephine sat down opposite her.

Nora processed this information. In addition to scientists, they were hiring secretaries. Who else might they be hiring? What did secretaries have to do with uranium-isotope separation?

"Are you a secretary too? You don't look the type."

Nora tuned back in to the conversation. "I don't?"

"Nah. You look too smart for that." Josephine stared so long that Nora squirmed in her seat. "Definitely too smart to be taking dictation."

"T-thank you. I think."

"You're welcome."

Nora braced herself as the train lurched forward.

"What was that?" Josephine gripped the armrest so hard her knuckles turned white.

"Relax. We're pulling out of the station."

"Oh." She followed Nora's lead and leaned back in her chair. The train whistle blew and her hand flew to her chest. "My heavens that's loud."

"It will stop in a minute. Don't worry, that's perfectly normal." Josephine pointed at the window. "It's pitch black."

"We're in a tunnel. Once we're clear of the station, you'll see the scenery pass by."

"I'm sure glad you're here with me. I'd probably have died of fright already if I'd been by myself."

They fell silent as the train picked up speed. Nora felt sorry for her. Her skin was pallid and her pupils were big as saucers.

"There's a toilet and sink behind that door." Nora pointed. There, that was helpful advice.

"Thanks."

She detested small talk, and what more was there to say, anyway? Nora collected the journal and a pen from her suitcase. She opened to the first page. For a long time, she sat with the pen poised over that blank sheet of paper. What could she say and stay within the rules? *It isn't as though anyone but you is going to see this.*

"Writer's block?"

Nora's head snapped up. "I'm sorry?"

"Writer's block. It's what my brother calls it when he can't figure out what to say. He's a playwright. Well, he was a playwright. Now he's a Naval intelligence officer, serving God knows where. He's a sensitive guy, you know? I hope this darned war doesn't change him."

"Mmm." Nora didn't know what else to say. If she didn't write something soon, Josephine likely would keep talking.

May 7, 1943
Dearest Diary,

We are underway. I still do not know our destination, but I can tell you that we're headed south. There is at least one other woman on the train who appears to be bound for the same destination. She is similarly ignorant of any details. Truly, I imagine she has even less information than I do about what lies ahead.

I have to admit to a bit of trepidation. My parting with my parents and brother was less cordial than I would have preferred. I don't worry about Bill—he's a horse's behind. But Mor and Far...

I shall miss them. Far isn't as young as he used to be, and the stress and strain of keeping the shop running is taking a toll on him.

I know he says he helped Bill avoid service because he needs him at work, but I also know my brother. He's a coward through and through. He led Far to believe he'll ease the burden at work. The truth is, he's afraid to serve and too selfish ever to put himself in harm's way. Put country before self? Not Bill! He'll be of no use to Far, and he'll bolt as soon as he sees a better opportunity. Poor Far. Poor Mor. They've poured everything into Bill and their return on investment, I fear, will be pitifully low.

Still, I regret the harshness of my words in front of our parents. I would have preferred to say a private goodbye without Bill's noxious presence, but that was not to be. Perhaps once I'm settled, I'll be able to write a letter to Mor and Far and mend any damage I might have done.

Enough of that. It's time to focus my gaze forward. What kind of environment awaits? Am I to settle in a big city? A small town? Is the setting rural or cosmopolitan? Have I brought the right clothes? Enough books to read? Will I be living by myself or with other young women? Will we be sorted by education? By job? By age?

I have so many questions and not a single answer, save for the knowledge that wherever we are going, we are, I expect, all of us anxious to make a difference. Our objective is singular—to win the war. Whatever our roles, I trust the words of Groves, Oppenheimer, and Lawrence.

I suspect the mystery of why they chose me will eventually be answered by the surroundings and the circumstances. For now, how about a game of solve this puzzle? I know we are headed south. I know I'm in a sleeper car, and the voyage will last at least one night. That rules out Philadelphia, Baltimore, and Washington, D.C., as none of those destinations would require an overnight.

I suppose it's pointless to guess beyond that. Who knows? We might veer west instead of south, or hug the coast all the way to Florida. Florida? Dear God, I hope not. It's so buggy and humid down there.

The train slowed and Nora peered out the window.

"What's happening?"

"Looks like we're making our first stop."

"Are we supposed to get off here? What are we supposed to do?" Josephine stood, then sat, and then stood again.

"First, I suggest you sit down. If you're standing when we stop you'll become unbalanced."

"Oh. Thank you." Josephine sat down. "Should we prepare to get off?"

"No. If this was our stop, someone would've told us by now." Nora squinted at the sign as they chugged into the station. *Philadelphia.* Well, she'd been right so far. They were headed south.

More later, dear diary. For now I must sign off with a promise to write as often as I can.

All my best, dearest diary.

Nora

CHAPTER FIVE

Mary finished packing the basket she and her mother had prepared. She still hadn't seen Phyllis since that awful day. When she'd called to check, Phyllis told her that she wouldn't be walking to school with her for the remainder of the school year; she couldn't leave her mother alone. They weren't going to hold a funeral until her father's body was shipped home, and no one seemed able to tell them when that would happen.

Mary found her mother out back hanging the laundry on the line. "I'm going to take the basket over to Phyllis's house now."

"Let me see what you've got in there." Mrs. Trask peeked underneath the gingham cloth.

"I've got the casseroles and pies we baked, plus I went out and picked some vegetables and fruit from the victory garden."

"That's nice. I'm sure they'll appreciate it. One of the gals at bridge club lost her son at Pearl Harbor. She said the hardest part was a few weeks after she got the news. At first, lots of people came over and they had plenty of support. But after a while, everyone moved on with their lives. She said rattling around the house by herself when there weren't any distractions was the worst."

"I can understand that."

"What I'm trying to say is that I think your timing is good. It's been a couple of weeks. What you're doing is very thoughtful. I'm certain Phyllis and her mother will really appreciate it."

"I'd better get going. I'll be back for dinner."

"Be careful."

"I will."

Mary cut through the side yard and let herself out through the front gate. She made it to Phyllis's house in no time flat and knocked on the screen door. A minute later, Phyllis's mother answered the door.

"Hi, Mrs. Campbell. I came by to see how you and Phyllis were doing." Mary noted that her eyes were red-rimmed and puffy, and several strands of her normally perfectly coiffed hair were out of place.

"Well, isn't that nice. Thank you, Mary. Come in. I'll let Phyllis know you're here."

Mrs. Campbell held open the screen door, and Mary stepped into the foyer. "I brought you both some goodies. Mother and I made the casseroles and the pies, and the veggies are from our garden."

"That's mighty neighborly of you, Mary. Make sure to thank your mother for me."

"I will."

Mrs. Campbell disappeared down the hall. When she returned, Phyllis was with her.

"Hi."

"Hi, yourself." Mary wasn't sure what else to say.

"Want to come to my room? We can talk there."

"Sure."

"I'll take the basket and put it in the kitchen," Mrs. Campbell said.

Mary followed Phyllis down the hall. Her wall was plastered with magazine pictures of movie stars, including Jimmy Stewart, Cary Grant, Humphrey Bogart, and Gary Cooper. As always, Mary wondered why she didn't have any pictures of some of her female idols. If Mary's mother would've allowed her to hang magazine pictures in her room, she would've put up pictures of Gene Tierney, Vivian Leigh, Ingrid Bergman, and Katharine Hepburn. They were exquisite.

They settled on the bed—Phyllis with her back against the wall, Mary sitting near the foot of the bed.

"How are you?" Mary shook her head. "Never mind, that's a stupid question."

"No. It's okay. It's hard, you know? I worried from the second we said goodbye to him that he wouldn't come back. I always anticipated the worst, and then it happened. Now I feel so…hollow,

I guess. Like there's never been a before and there won't be any after." She paused. "That probably doesn't make a lick of sense."

"No. It does. It's like being suspended in time."

"Yeah. It's hard to know what's real and what's in my mind. Mom cries herself to sleep every night. She hardly touches her food and I can barely get her to get out of bed in the morning."

"I'm sorry."

"I can't go to school. I can't leave her. I don't know what she'll do."

"You don't think she'd try to hurt herself, do you?"

Phyllis shrugged. "Honestly? I don't know what to think. Dad was her entire world. Without him…" She stared out the window.

"What are you going to do? You can't watch her every second for the rest of your life. And what about school? You have to finish."

"I know. I haven't figured it out yet. I have to earn some money. Otherwise, how will we live? Mom could be a seamstress; she's good enough. But I'm not sure she'll recover from this enough to work."

"That's tough."

"Truman is determined to marry me, but I wonder how he'd feel if I told him my mother would have to come live with us?"

Mary's ears perked up. "Did he propose?"

Phyllis nodded. "I was about to tell you when…"

"How did he do it?"

"You mean, how did he propose? Oh, it was dreamy. We went for a long walk, and then he took me out for dinner. At first, I was confused, because the sign on the door said the restaurant was closed. He knocked on the glass, and the chef let us in. There wasn't another soul in the place. Turns out the chef was Truman's uncle. We had a private dinner for two and he proposed over dessert."

Mary hung on every word. "Did you say yes?"

"Uh-huh. We were going to get married right after graduation, before Truman gets called up, but then this all happened."

"What are you going to do now?"

"I don't know. Truman still wants to go ahead with it, but I'm worried about Mom. Besides, how would it look, us getting hitched right after Dad passed away?"

"A lot of girls are marrying their fellas before they ship out. I think it would be fine. If you wanted to, I mean." Mary bit her lip.

This probably wasn't the best time to ask, but she might never get a better opening. "Can I ask you something?"

"Sure. Anything."

"How did you feel?"

"How did I feel about what?"

"When Truman popped the question."

"Are you kidding? I was in Heaven. My heart nearly pounded out of my chest. I would've married him right there if we'd had a minister."

Mary frowned.

"Why are you asking me this? Is Sam going to propose?"

"That's the trouble. He already has."

"Oh, Mary! You're kidding me? Why are you only now telling me this?"

She shrugged.

"You said yes, of course."

Slowly, Mary shook her head. Quietly she said, "I haven't answered him."

"How long ago did he ask you?"

"I don't know, a few weeks?" She couldn't make eye contact.

"Have you lost your mind? Sam is about the most handsome guy in town and he's never going to have to go to war. What are you waiting for?"

What was she waiting for? *I'm waiting to fall in love with him.* "I don't know. I guess... I'm not sure I feel for him what I should feel for the man I'm going to marry."

"How do you want to feel?"

"How do you feel when you're with Truman?"

"That's easy. Like nobody else in the world exists. Like if the two of us were stranded all alone on a deserted island, I'd be perfectly happy. Like if I never saw him again I'd just die." Phyllis sighed dreamily.

"Have you...? You know."

"Not yet," Phyllis whispered, "but we've come really close a couple of times."

Mary's mood continued to plummet. "Did you want to? I mean, was it hard for you to hold back?"

"Heck yes!" Phyllis threw her head back and laughed. "I thought I would combust on the spot. And Truman? Oh, boy. Let's just say he had a hard time coming back from the edge."

"And all that felt good to you? The kissing and…stuff?"

"Better than good." Phyllis narrowed her eyes. "Why all the questions? Isn't Sam a good…kisser?"

"No… I mean, yes. I mean… I suppose."

"Maybe he needs more practice. None of the guys our age are any good at this stuff. They need to do it more to figure it out. At least that's what I've heard."

Mary doubted the veracity of that. It sounded like something a guy would say to get a girl to give in. "Yeah," she answered dubiously. Idly, she wondered what it would feel like to kiss Phyllis. Her lips looked soft, like rose petals. *I bet that would feel a lot better than kissing Sam. Oh, my gosh! Where in the world did that come from, Mary Elizabeth?* She shook her head to clear it.

"You've got to give him an answer. You can't leave him hanging like that. It's not fair."

"I know." Mary swallowed hard.

"Guys like Sam don't grow on trees. If the quality of…hanky-panky…is your only problem with him, I say marry him and train him." She winked.

"Right. Train him." Mary thought she might throw up. She stood. "I've got to go. I told Mother I'd be home for dinner."

"Thanks for stopping by. I'm glad you did."

"Me too." Mary hugged her friend. "Take care of yourself and your mom. I'll come by again soon."

"I'd like that."

"Me too." Mary opened the bedroom door. "I can see myself out." She took her leave.

Her stomach churned all the way home. Her experience with Sam didn't sound anything like what Phyllis described. What was she going to do?

Nora followed the porter as he carried her suitcase down the train steps and onto firm ground. She rubbed her eyes and smoothed her dress. It seemed like everyone on the train was disembarking at the same moment. People of every size and shape swarmed over the platform, many of them talking excitedly.

The station sign read, "Knoxville." Nora knew that Knoxville was in Tennessee. Beyond that, she knew virtually nothing of the place.

"Oh, my goodness. That's a lot of folks," Josephine exclaimed, coming up alongside her. "Do you think we're all going to the same place?"

"I don't know."

"I guess we'll find out soon enough."

"I imagine so." In the near distance, Nora spotted a man in a suit holding a sign with her name on it. "I must go."

"Go? Go where?" Josephine stretched. "Will I see you again?"

"I don't know."

"I hope so. But just in case, it was nice to meet you, Nora."

"You too."

"See you."

Nora and the porter made their way over to where the sign-wielding man stood. "I'm Nora Lindstrom." As she did at Penn Station, she showed her ID.

"Excellent. Welcome. If you'll come with me." He relieved the porter of Nora's suitcase.

She barely had a chance to thank the porter before the driver and her suitcase were almost out of sight. She hurried to catch up. "Am I permitted to ask where we're going yet?"

The driver loaded her bag in the trunk of a limousine. "You'll know soon enough." He opened the back door and helped her inside.

They left the station, and with the positioning of the sunrise in the rear window, it became clear to Nora that they were heading due west. She breathed deeply. The air was warm—warmer than at home—and more humid. The smell of pine trees from her hometown were replaced by the aroma of cows. Pastures and rolling green hillsides dotted the land, punctuated by farms and homesteads, barns and hayfields.

She watched the scenery fly by as they traveled in silence. The pinks and oranges of the sunrise gave way to blue skies, and the rocking motion of the car nearly lulled her to sleep.

She hadn't gotten much in the way of shuteye last night, between the jostling of the train on the tracks, Josephine's snoring, and the periodic shrill sound of the train whistle blowing in the stillness of the night. The loud pre-dawn pounding on the door and the man announcing that they'd be arriving at the station within the hour added to the disorientation. Now, all Nora wanted was some rest in a comfortable bed.

The limo glided to a halt, nudging her back to the present. She ducked to peer out the windshield and was shocked to see a military checkpoint up ahead, and a line of cars in front of them. "Where are we?"

The driver either didn't hear her or chose not to answer. A large sign on top of the guard post read: *MILITARY AREA, Weapons, Ammunition, Explosives, Cameras, Field glasses, Liquors, Telescopes, Radio Transmitters PROHIBITED. All vehicles and passengers subject to search.* Guards with armbands that marked them as Military Police manned the booth.

Wherever they were, it was like no place Nora ever had been before. She swallowed hard when it was their turn and the guards approached the car. The driver opened his window and a stern soldier asked for his papers, the purpose of his request for entry, and whether or not he had anything in the trunk.

If the driver was rattled by the inquisition, he didn't show it. He explained who his passenger was and that they were headed for someplace called The Castle on the Hill. A second soldier searched the trunk and the undercarriage. The first soldier knocked on her window. She lowered it.

"Do you have some ID, miss?"

Nora fished out her ID with a shaky hand and gave it to him. He examined it, looked her over one more time, and handed it back.

"You're cleared."

She rolled up her window to keep the bugs from coming inside. She wanted to ask where and what The Castle on the Hill was. Instead, she remained mum and tried to stay calm. *He'll only say you'll find out soon enough.*

The scene outside the window was organized chaos. Construction workers and equipment covered every available square inch of acreage. Muddy roads snaked throughout the fenced-in complex, bulldozers leveled the land, and cranes hoisted heavy steel and wood. Partially finished barracks, apartment complexes, and houses dotted the landscape, along with the beginnings of massive buildings that seemingly rose out of nowhere.

Nora knew her mouth must be hanging open. The sheer scope of this undertaking was mind-boggling. A large billboard caught her attention: *Your PEN and TONGUE can be Enemy WEAPONS. Watch what you Write and Say.* The accompanying image was of a fountain pen pierced through an Army helmet. Nora's heart lurched as she thought about the gorgeous leather journal in her suitcase. There was no way she could forego her daily diary entries. She'd lose her mind.

What you see here, what you do here, what you hear here, when you leave here, let it stay here. The drawing of the three monkeys, one covering its eyes, the next its ears, and the last its lips, illustrated the point. Nora reminded herself that she had nothing to fear. The signs reflected the same message General Groves imparted to her in person. Everything about this project was top-secret. As long as she followed the rules, kept her mouth shut, and did her job, all would be well. Again, her mind strayed to her journal, buried underneath some dresses in her suitcase. One thing was certain—if she chose to keep it, that journal was never to leave her home, nor to be visible or mentioned to anyone else.

"This is our stop," the driver said. He pulled into a parking lot in front of a sprawling complex.

The Castle on the Hill. Except that the sign in front of the massive structure read, Administration Building, Clinton Engineer Works, Manhattan Engineer District, U.S. Army Corps of Engineers. Nora cocked her head to the side. She could see why folks would think it resembled a castle. The building was comprised of one long center section and a series of wings on either side.

The driver came around and opened the door for her. Nora stretched to get her circulation moving. Could it really have been less than twenty-four hours since she started this journey? This place was so foreign that it might as well have been a lifetime ago. She took her suitcase, thanked the driver, and walked through the front door.

"Hello," she said, as she approached the front desk. "My name is Dr. Nora Lindstrom. My driver just dropped me off here. I'm not sure if I have an appointment to see someone, or…"

The receptionist held up a hand as the index finger of her free hand trailed down a list.

There must be a hundred names on that list.

"Here you are. Okay, hang on a second." She picked up the phone, spoke a few words, and hung up. "If you'll wait over there," she indicated some chairs in the vestibule, "someone will be right with you."

Right with you turned out to be the better part of an hour, during which time Nora fidgeted with her watch, ran through ten science experiments in her head, and did her best not to rue the day she said yes to this mysterious job.

"Dr. Lindstrom? Sorry to keep you waiting. My name is Barbara, I'm Colonel James C. Marshall's assistant."

She said it as though Nora was supposed to know who this Marshall fellow was.

Barbara walked away and turned back only to beckon Nora to follow her.

They arrived at an office bustling with clerks and administrative personnel. "We'll get you an ID badge and a Townsite Resident's Pass. You can't go anywhere on the Reservation without them."

"The Reservation?"

"Clinton Engineer Works. CEW. This place." The woman waved her arms as if to encompass the entirety of this nameless town.

"Is this place a city? A military base? What is it?"

"It's the Clinton Engineer Works," she said pointedly, with a look that told Nora she'd better not ask any more questions.

Nora nodded as if those three words elucidated everything.

"Sit here. They'll take your picture for your ID badge. As I said, you'll need to wear that everywhere, and carry your resident's pass, also. You were pre-cleared, so that will make things go more quickly for you."

Nora had no idea what that meant, but whatever it was, if it cut red tape, she was all for it. Her escort whispered something to the clerk taking fingerprints and pictures, and then she was gone.

Another half hour later, Nora was equipped with an ID badge and resident's pass, and then she was shuffled off to another administrative cubbyhole for housing processing.

This clerk examined her badge, ran a finger down a list, and tapped an entry. "Hang on a second." She got up and conferred with a colleague. Their whispers were loud enough for Nora to hear.

"...I know, but her badge indicates that she should be eligible for a Cemesto. They've got her in a dorm room. That ain't right."

"It's on the list. We have to follow the list. It's not ours to ask questions."

Nora had no idea what a Cemesto was, but she already knew she wanted one. A dorm room? She shuddered.

"Okay, Dr. Lindstrom. This is where you're going to be bunking." The woman showed her a map and indicated a building designated W-1. "Go get settled and unpacked. You're due to report for orientation at 0800 hours tomorrow."

"0800?"

"Eight o'clock tomorrow morning."

"Ah. Where should I report?"

"Come back to the reception desk. Someone will direct you."

"Thanks." Nora turned to go. "Um… How do I get out of here?"

"Turn right, go down the corridor until you can't go anymore, then turn left, go down the stairs, and follow the exit sign."

"Okay. Thanks." Nora picked up her suitcase and accepted the proffered map. Whatever she'd been expecting when she said yes to Dr. Lawrence's invitation, what she'd seen and been through so far left her questioning her judgment.

CHAPTER SIX

The cap tilted at an angle and Mary feared that if she turned her head too quickly, it would fly off and poke somebody's eye out. The graduation gown was several inches too long and a size too big for her petite frame. She pulled up the sleeves so that they didn't swallow her hands.

"Stop fidgeting."

"I can't help it."

"Try," Phyllis whispered.

Mary was glad the school had decided to let Phyllis graduate, despite missing the last few weeks of classes. "Your dad would be so proud of you right now. I bet he's up there looking down on us."

Tears sprang to Phyllis's eyes. "I hope you're right. I bet your father is really proud of you too."

Mary fingered the letter she carried in the pocket of her gown. Her mother had handed it to her right before she'd gotten out of the car. She hadn't read it yet, beyond seeing that it was from her father and that it was addressed to her. She didn't want to read it now in front of Phyllis—that would be insensitive. Besides, she didn't want to invite scrutiny over her reading abilities.

The principal stood in front of the students. "Class? It's time to line up. As we discussed, you'll be seated alphabetically by last name. Since you're about to graduate, I sincerely hope you can figure out where you belong. Just in case, I'll make it easy for you. Line up behind the big sign displaying the first letter of your last name, and the teacher assigned to your group will call your names in order."

Mary found the "Ts" and took her proper spot, between Sylvia Topsail and Lucius Turner. She fingered the letter again, determined to open it.

"Aren't you nervous? I'm terrified," Sylvia said.

"No. I can't wait for it to be done with."

"Rumor has it Sam proposed to you. Is that true?"

Mary's eyes flashed angrily. Apart from Phyllis, who hadn't been back to school, she hadn't told a soul about the proposal. So Sam must have shared it with his buddies. How dare he...

"Is it?" Sylvia stared at her expectantly.

What should she say? "I don't respond to idle gossip."

"You don't have to be snippy about it. I was only asking whether or not it was true. It's not gossip if you ask the source."

"Okay, everyone," the principal intoned. "The band is about to play 'Pomp & Circumstance.' When you hear the first notes, that's your cue to start marching in. As we practiced, fill in the seats until there are no empty chairs in the row, then start the next row."

The sound of the trombones playing saved Mary from having to respond to Sylvia, though she continued to seethe about Sam's obvious indiscretion. She marched in with the rest of her classmates and took a seat toward the end of the second-to-last row. She twisted in her chair, craning to see where her mother and Sam were sitting. The auditorium was packed with graduates and spectators, and she couldn't pick them out, although she knew they were somewhere in the throng. Maybe it was just as well that she couldn't see Sam at the moment.

As the first speaker droned on, Mary nearly dropped off to sleep. She willed herself to pay attention. When that didn't work, she removed her father's letter from her pocket and unfolded it. Slowly, painstakingly, after reading each word and sentence multiple times, she managed her way through it.

My dearest Pumpkin,

I'm sorrier than you know that I can't be with you on your big day. I'm sure you'll be the prettiest girl on that stage, and I am the proudest father of any of the graduates.

Your mother tells me that you've been at logger heads with her over Sam, and that he's asked you to marry him. She says you haven't yet given him an answer. I wish I was there in person to advise you.

Please know that no boy is going to be good enough in my eyes for my only daughter, but what I've seen of him over the time you've been dating leads me to believe he'd be a good husband to you and a good father.

Having said that, I know how strong-willed you are and that you have a mind of your own. Your mother and I want what's best for you, but only you know what that is. Search inside your heart, Pumpkin. The truth lies in there. Whatever you decide, whatever path you choose, I will support you and your right to make that choice. Yes, even if your mother wants to kill me for it. I might be more afraid of her than I am of any of the Krauts we've faced over here, but I'll always stick up for my little girl.

Above all, know that I love you more than anything. I kiss your picture and your mom's every night before I go to bed, praying for God to keep me safe so that I can come home to you both.

I love you.
Dad

Mary sniffled and blinked away a tear. "I love you too, Daddy."

"Class, please rise."

Mary stuffed the letter back in her pocket and stood.

"As your name is called, please approach the stage."

By the time they got to the Ts, Mary thought she might die of boredom. But when she arrived at the edge of the steps and gazed out at the sea of faces, her heart nearly pounded out of her chest. She really was going to do this—she was about to start a whole new chapter in her life. As she climbed the stairs and started across the stage, she heard a holler and a whistle. She turned in the direction of the sound. There was Sam, standing and waving. Her mother sat next to him, looking proud, if a little embarrassed.

Mary wanted to crawl underneath the stage. She hurried to the president of the school board, who shook her hand and placed the diploma in her other palm.

"Congratulations."

"Thank you." Mary finished the walk, exited the other side of the stage, and returned to her row. The sound of Sam's cheers echoed in her ears, and she squirmed in her seat.

Half an hour later, when the ceremony ended, Mary tried to locate Phyllis. She stood on her tiptoes and scanned the crowd. Finally, she saw her standing off to the side, quietly hugging her mother as Truman stood nearby. She headed in their direction.

"There's my girl." Sam intercepted her, swept her up into his arms, and twirled her around. "I'm so proud of you I could bust."

"Put me down." Mary squirmed and twisted out of his grasp.

"Well done." Her mother joined them. "Your father would be so happy. I wish he could've been here."

"Me too." She removed the mortar board and handed it to her mother. Then she removed the letter from her pocket, yanked the gown over her head, balled it up, and gave that to her mother too. She smoothed the wrinkles in her dress. "Do you have my purse?"

"Here." Mrs. Trask separated the strap from her own purse and Mary's and handed Mary the bag.

"Thanks." She placed her father's letter in the purse. "I'll be back in a minute." Without waiting for a reply, she ran in Phyllis's direction.

"Phyllis! Hey, Phyllis!" She caught up to her as she headed for the exit.

"Hello, Mary."

"Hi, Mrs. Campbell. Hi, Truman." Mary took Phyllis's hand. "In case I don't see you later, I wanted to say congratulations and good luck."

"Thanks." Phyllis hugged her. "You too. I'm sure I'll see you around."

"Sure. Take care." She knew Phyllis was right. It wasn't like she was going anywhere; she'd be working down at Meyer's. The thought depressed her beyond measure. She made her way back to Sam and her mother.

"Samuel tells me you two have plans for the evening," Mrs. Trask said when she returned. "Don't stay out too late and be careful."

"We will. I promise to have Mary home before midnight."

"Before eleven, you mean, right, Samuel?"

"Yes, ma'am. Before eleven."

"Goodnight, Mother. Don't wait up." Mary kissed her on the cheek.

Sam put his arm around Mary. "I thought I'd take you to dinner at The Victor Café. What do you say?"

Mary's stomach rumbled, a stark reminder that she hadn't eaten all day. "Sure. That sounds nice."

The restaurant was busy, but they were able to get a table in the front window. When they'd ordered and the waiter had retreated, Sam took Mary's hands across the table.

"Now isn't this nice?"

"It is."

"When you marry me, I'll treat you to dinners like this once a month, at least."

Mary tried to liberate her hands, but Sam held fast.

"What's the matter? You want to go out more often than that? Okay. I just thought we'd be saving to buy a house."

Mary's queasiness was back. "You've got it all planned out, don't you?"

"Well, yeah. Isn't that what the man is supposed to do? Take care of his wife and plan for the future? I thought that would make you happy—show you how responsible and reliable I am."

Suddenly, Mary felt as though she couldn't breathe, as though she was trapped with no way out. "Excuse me." She threw her napkin on the table and hastened to the restroom. For long seconds, she stood at the sink, trying to take air into her lungs. She splashed cold water on her face and dried herself off. *This is natural. You're panicking over nothing. He's saying the kinds of things anyone in his position would say. And what's so bad about a guy who's crazy about you wanting to take care of everything? Relax. Enjoy a nice dinner. You don't have to answer him right now.*

"Are you okay?"

Mary hadn't noticed the woman standing at the next sink, re-applying her makeup. "I'm fine, thanks. Just a little light-headed from lack of food."

"Well then, a restaurant is the right place to be."

Mary smiled weakly. "You're right. I'm sure I'll be fine as soon as I have something to eat."

"Have a nice night."

"You too." She exited the bathroom and returned to the table. Sam jumped up as she approached. He held her chair for her.

"Are you all right? I was worried about you. You were pale as a ghost."

"I'm fine. I-I just didn't have time to eat anything today."

"Dig in." Sam indicated the steaming plate of spaghetti with marinara sauce that had arrived while she was in the lavatory.

She was hungry and ate without pause. Afterward, she wiped her mouth and sat back.

"I think you liked it." Sam grinned.

"Delicious. Thank you."

"You're welcome. The sky is clear. Want to take a stroll and walk off all that pasta and garlic bread?"

"Sure."

Sam settled the bill and held the door for her. He looped his arm through hers and they wandered the streets of South Philly.

"This is nice." Mary meant it. For once, he wasn't pressuring her or pushing her to decide.

"It is nice," Sam agreed. "We could do this all the time when we're married. You'd like that, right?"

There it was again. Mary's heart stuttered.

"Right?"

Sam pulled them up short, spun her toward him, and kissed her hard on the mouth. Mary struggled against him. Finally, she stomped on his foot.

"Ouch!" He released his hold.

"Sam Abel, don't you ever, *ever* do that to me again like that without my permission."

"I have to *ask* you if it's okay to kiss you? What the hell? I mean, what the heck? What is wrong with you?" He was breathing heavily.

Mary crossed her arms. "I don't enjoy being pawed. I don't know any girls that do."

"And I don't like being treated like I'm some sort of pervert just because I want to get close to my girl... You know, the one I've asked to marry me?"

They stood facing each other, less than a foot separating them. In truth, Mary noted ironically to herself, they were worlds apart.

"Are you ever going to give me an answer?"

"If you keep pestering me, you won't like the answer, I can promise you that much."

"Will I like the answer anyway, Mary? Will I? Are you just leading me on? Stringing me along?"

"N-no." Was she? "I need more time. For Heaven's sake, I just graduated tonight. My father is off fighting this horrible war and could die any minute... I can't breathe. I need to breathe."

"I'll let you breathe, all right. You can find your own way home." Sam stalked off.

"But..." How would she get home? *Walk, that's how.*

It took her an hour and a half to make it to her house. Her feet were sore and blistered, her whole body ached, and she was chilled, not to mention that she was twenty minutes late for curfew.

"Mary? Is that you? I didn't hear Samuel's car pull up."

"Yes, it's me, Mother. Go to bed. I'll lock up down here."

"Did you have a good time?"

"Splendid." She hoped the sarcasm wasn't evident. She dragged herself upstairs and ran a bath. A good soak in the tub. That would make everything better.

You've got to be kidding me. Nora lost her grip on the suitcase and it clattered noisily to the floor. The lobby of the only completed women's dormitory was overrun with young women scrambling around, looking for a room to call their own.

A woman who introduced herself as the housemother approached. "Welcome to bedlam."

"Thanks, I think. I was told to report here to get settled."

"You and everyone else." The housemother squinted to get a better look at Nora's badge. "Oh, my." Her eyebrows rose into her hairline. "Give me a second."

Nora wasn't sure what it was about the badge that seemed to get people's attention, but she wasn't about to question it.

"All right. It took some wrangling, but I was able to get you a spot to yourself. It's on the second floor. Rosalie here lives next door. She'll show you the way. Curfew is at ten o'clock sharp, unless you have shift work. Otherwise, you'll need my permission to be out past ten. Bathrooms are shared, so don't tarry in there. You'll have your own mail slot here in the lobby. Oh, and no men."

Nora wondered if maybe she shouldn't write it all down. There certainly seemed to be a lot of rules. "Yes, ma'am."

"C'mon. I'll show you the way."

Rosalie, Nora noted, spoke with a very southern drawl. She would need to listen carefully to catch every word. "So, where're you from?"

"Connecticut." Was she allowed to say that?

Rosalie nodded, as if that made all the sense in the world. "I figured you for a Yankee."

"Really? Why?" Despite her exhaustion, Nora was intrigued.

"The clothes. The accent. Heck, you sure aren't from around these parts."

That surprised a laugh out of her. "I guess I'll need to work on blending in."

"Nah. Different is good, I think. Connecticut is near New York, right? I always wanted to see New York. Never got there."

Nora sized her up. "You've got your whole life ahead of you. I'm sure you'll get there."

"Honey, I'm from a podunk town in middle-of-nowhere Tennessee, about ninety miles from here. Knoxville is the biggest city I'll ever see."

"You don't know that. Don't give up on your dreams."

"I like you." Rosalie opened the second door on the left side of the hallway. "You're nice—not like I've heard Yankees are."

Nora wasn't sure what to say to that, so she followed Rosalie into the room.

"Here you go, sugar."

Nora put the suitcase down and turned in a circle. The space was small. It held a night table, a small dresser, a closet barely big enough for half her clothes, and a twin bed. The closet had no door, only a curtain separating it from the rest of the room.

"It's probably not what you're used to back up north, but you'll adapt. Honestly, I'm surprised they sent you to bunk here."

Nora walked over to the bed and tested the mattress with her hands. It seemed to be hard enough, but not too hard. She sat down and invited Rosalie to do the same. "Why does everybody keep saying that?"

"Saying what?"

"That I'm not in the right place. You must be the third person who's made that observation."

Rosalie shrugged, and Nora surmised that she was buying time until she could figure out how much was safe to say. Everyone in this place measured their words as if the walls had ears.

"You don't have to answer that. I don't want to violate any rules. I don't even know what all the rules are yet, but I know I don't want to put you in an awkward position."

Rosalie leaned over and tapped Nora's ID badge. "That's why."

"My name?"

"No. The "A" on your badge. That letter designates where you're allowed to go in this place, who you're allowed to talk to, and what you can hear. That "A" on your badge means you've got a really high-level clearance. I've only ever seen men with a clearance that high."

"I see."

"I work as a housing clerk at The Castle. I can tell you that none of the men with that level of clearance live in a dorm room."

"They don't?"

"No. They live in Cemestos, or at least Flat Tops."

There was that word again. "What's a Cemesto?"

"It's a prefabricated house made of asbestos and cement. They come in several models, depending on the size of the family. They're mostly for married folk, but high-level muckity-mucks live in those too, even if they're single." Rosalie covered her mouth. "Sorry, I didn't mean to imply that you were a snob or anything. Obviously, you're not."

"That's okay. No offense taken."

"Anyway, I'll leave you to get settled in. The bathroom is two doors down to your left at the top of the stairs. I'm next door to your right if you need anything."

When Rosalie was gone, Nora flopped back on the bed. ID badges, Cemestos, Flat Tops... She felt like Alice falling through the looking glass.

Outside the door, she heard girls chattering away. From the snippets of conversation, it sounded like they were going dancing on a tennis court after dinner. Dancing on a tennis court?

Nora's stomach rumbled, reminding her that it had been too long since she last ate. There was no icebox, stove, or anything resembling a kitchen. Where was she supposed to eat?

"Hey, Nora? It's Rosalie," her neighbor called through the closed door. "I forgot to tell you, there's a cafeteria not far from here. That's where we mostly eat. If you want, you can join me and some of the girls for dinner."

Nora opened the door. "I'd like that."

"Okay. Let's go. You can unpack later."

As if on cue, doors opened along the hallway and girls piled out and down the stairs. As much as Nora wanted to disappear into her own space and write in her journal, she knew she needed sustenance. Besides, the more she could learn about this place by listening, the better. She checked her hair in the little mirror over the dresser, grabbed her purse, and followed the crowd.

MAY – OCTOBER, 1943

CHAPTER SEVEN

M eyer's Drugstore was hopping. Every stool at the ice cream counter was taken, and the line at the pharmacist's station snaked around aisle three. Mary wiped the perspiration from her forehead with a handkerchief. She wished she could stick her head in the ice cream freezer. The air in the store was stagnant. *Just like my life.*

She surveyed the crowd. Of the ten people waiting for prescriptions, she knew eight of them. That was the thing about a neighborhood drugstore—everyone knew everyone. *And everyone knows everyone else's business.*

She recognized that she was in a foul mood. The truth was, she'd been in the same lousy frame of mind ever since graduation night.

"Can we get some service around here?"

"This line is moving slower than molasses."

"By the time I get my prescription filled, I could be dead."

Mary let the comments roll past her. It wouldn't do to answer these folks, although she would've loved to give them all a piece of her mind. She worked through the line, despite the fact that she should've been on lunch break.

Twenty minutes later, she'd waited on the last customer. "I'm going on lunch break, Doc."

"Okay. When you get back, we've got some more orders to place. We're running out of bicarbonate and phosphorus."

Mary stowed her lab coat and grabbed the lunch bag out of her locker. The old oak tree in the park across the street beckoned to her, as it did every day.

"Oh, I'm sor—"

"Hello, Mary."

"Phyllis! I'm sorry. I didn't mean to run into you."

"That's okay. You were very…focused."

"I've got half an hour for lunch and I am determined to spend it in the shade. How are you doing? How's your mother?" She hadn't seen either of them since graduation.

"She's still spending her days sitting in the living room chair, staring out the window. I think she believes that if she sits there long enough, my dad will somehow mysteriously appear, walking up the street."

"I'm sorry. That must be so hard for you."

"Honestly, I'm at my wit's end. The only thing that makes it bearable is planning for our wedding."

"Have you and Truman set a date? Do you want to come sit with me? You can tell me all about it. I'm starving."

Phyllis checked her watch. "Sure. I've got a few minutes."

They settled on a picnic blanket under the tree and Mary pulled out a tomato sandwich and an apple. "Do you want some?"

"No thanks. I had lunch a little while ago."

Mary bit into the sandwich. "So, tell me about the wedding and what you're going to do about your mother."

"The wedding will be in October. Truman thinks we should sell the house and buy one of our own with an in-law suite for my mother. He thinks the change of scenery will be good for her so that she's not constantly surrounded by reminders."

"Truman's a smart man. He's willing to have her live with you?"

"Oh, yes. He's fine with it. He and my mother get along famously."

Mary thought about her mother and Sam. They were thick as thieves. Not a day went by that her mother didn't ask why she hadn't seen him in a while.

"What did you decide to do about Sam?"

Had she read her mind? Mary sighed heavily. "We had a terrible fight the night of graduation. We've been sort of in limbo ever since."

"I'm sorry to hear—"

"Mary? Can I speak to you for a minute? I know it's the middle of your workday, but…"

Sam stood above them. He held a half-dozen red roses in one hand.

"I've got to get back to Mom," Phyllis said. She rose and brushed off her skirt. "It was good to see you, Mary."

"Tell your mother I said hello."

"I will." Phyllis waved.

"I'm sorry. I didn't mean to run Phyllis off, only… I feel horrible and I can't get what happened out of my mind." Sam handed the flowers to Mary. "These are for you. A peace offering." He sat down opposite her. "Aren't you at least glad to see me?"

She set the flowers on the blanket. "You should be glad to see me. I could've been dead on the side of the road the way you left me stranded in the middle of the night."

"I know. I said I'm sorry. I lost my head. I didn't know what to do. All I know is, I want to spend the rest of my life with you. I can't eat, I can't sleep. All I think about is you."

"You have a funny way of showing it." The queasiness had returned; Mary stuffed the remains of the sandwich in the bag.

"You said you needed time. So I've hung back and waited. But the wait is killing me, Mare. I know what I want. I want you and me to be together forever. I've given you room to breathe. What do you say? Please. I'm begging you here, and that's not easy for me."

Mary plucked a buttercup from the ground and twirled it in her fingers. To her mortification, tears sprang to her eyes.

"What is it? What is it, Mare?" Awkwardly, Sam reached out to comfort her.

"I don't know." She shook her head and shrugged off his touch. "I have to get back. Doc will be missing me." Hurriedly, she wiped her eyes and rose.

Sam stood, as well. "Say you'll at least meet me at the park tonight after dinner. We can just sit and talk. I promise, I won't lay a finger on you."

He looked so lost. "Okay." She grabbed the lunch bag and ran across the street.

"Wait! You forgot the flowers and your blanket."

She ignored him and kept running until she reached her locker. Her hands shook and her breathing was shallow. She rested her forehead against the cool metal of the locker. She couldn't keep doing this. She simply…couldn't.

❧❧

Nora hid a yawn behind her hand. The air in the auditorium was stale and hot. Several of the women among the fifty or so new hires fanned themselves with paper fans. The speaker, an ominous-looking fellow, droned on about the enemy having eyes and ears everywhere.

"You must never say what it is we are doing here. If someone asks you, tell them you're making donuts."

At first, Nora thought he was kidding.

The woman sitting next to her whispered, "I heard one girl asked what the big magnet was for. The next day, she was gone. Poof. No one ever saw her again."

Nora wanted to say she was sure no harm came to that girl, but the way the speaker was talking, she wasn't so sure.

"The person sitting right next to you might be a spy. Ask no questions, offer no information, do your jobs, and we'll win the war."

He finished speaking and an older woman stepped to the podium. "Girls, come with me. Men, stay put. Mr. Chaucer will continue your orientation."

Nora followed the throng of young women as they headed down the corridor to a classroom. As she entered, someone handed her a pamphlet. *Between Us Girls and the Gatepost.* She sat at the front of the classroom and opened to the first page.

She needn't have bothered, as the woman from the auditorium read them the entire pamphlet out loud, word for word.

"Women must be well-groomed at all times. No midriffs, no shorts, no short skirts. Be industrious on the job and do not take advantage of those times of the month. Above all else, conduct yourselves with proper decorum and do not flirt with the men and distract them from their very important jobs."

Nora arched an eyebrow at the last. What about the men distracting the women from doing their jobs? She glanced around her. All of the girls seemed to be taking everything very seriously. Well, almost all of the girls.

One young girl—Nora gauged her to be barely out of high school—raised her hand.

"Yes?"

"Is it okay to flirt with the boys when we're not working and they're not working?"

The room erupted in titters.

"You all are dismissed."

As they were filing out, Nora noticed that young girl being led in the opposite direction. She wasn't laughing anymore.

"Dr. Lindstrom?"

"Yes?" Nora was startled by the appearance out of nowhere of an impeccably dressed woman carrying an official-looking folder. The woman seemed familiar, but she'd met so many since her arrival, she couldn't quite place her.

"Colonel Marshall would like to see you." The woman must've registered Nora's blank stare, because she added, "I'm Barbara. You met me yesterday when you checked in at the Castle. I'm Colonel Marshall's assistant."

"Oh, yes. Of course." Recognition dawned.

"Come with me, please."

When they arrived, Barbara knocked on a partially opened door. "Come."

"Dr. Lindstrom is here as requested, sir."

She stepped aside to allow Nora to pass.

"Come in and have a seat." He indicated one of the guest chairs across from the desk.

The office wasn't anything fancy. In fact, it seemed almost like a converted supply room.

"I'm glad I happened to be here when you arrived. Are you settling in okay?"

Although she realized it was most likely a rhetorical question, Nora was eager to take advantage of the opening. Who better to talk to than the man in charge? "Actually, sir, I think there might have been a mix-up with my accommodations."

"Is that so?"

"I was placed in the women's dormitory, but I understand that I qualify for something called a Cemesto."

"Really?" The colonel rocked back in his chair.

"Yes, sir."

"Are you married with children, Dr. Lindstrom?"

"N-no, sir."

"Are you married at all?"

"No, sir."

"Cemestos are reserved for married couples with families."

"But I was led to believe that Cemestos were also for those with a higher clearance."

"You were led to believe wrong. Listen, Dr. Lindstrom, I realize you're new around here, and maybe where you're from you're used to pulling rank. Let me make this perfectly clear. If I had my druthers, you wouldn't even be here. But I'm given to understand that Dr. Lawrence has a fondness for you, so here you are. I can easily change that."

As much as she knew his words were meant to intimidate her, Nora had no intention of being bullied. "I understand that, Colonel. I'm simply asking for what is fair."

He rocked forward suddenly so that he was as close as he could get to her without going over the desk. "Winning this war is all I care about. Surely you and I can agree on that. Winning the war is not dependent on you sleeping cozily at night. You are not getting a Cemesto. I'll have my assistant put you on a waiting list for a Flat Top. That's the best I'm going to do. And let me make it perfectly clear that we are never going to have this conversation again. Understood?"

"Yes, sir. Thank you for your consideration."

He straightened his uniform tie and sat back. "Now can we get on with the business of why you're here?"

"Yes, sir."

"Good." He shook his head. "Women," he muttered under his breath. "It will be your job to oversee a bunch of unqualified, green-behind-the-ears female high school graduates and to train them to perform one of the most vitally important jobs in this war. I thought perhaps you'd like a tour of the plant and a primer on how the machine works."

"Yes, sir." She was happy to be back on safe ground.

"Dr. Ludlow, who works under Dr. Lawrence's tutelage at Berkeley, will take you to the Pilot Facility, familiarize you with the calutron machine, and give you a tour."

"That would be great, sir."

"Lindstrom?"

"Yes, sir?"

"There's a lot riding on the success of this operation. Up until now, nobody except specially trained Ph.D.'s have worked on these machines. It's dubious at best to think you'll be able to make this work. The odds are against you. I want you to succeed. Keep your girls quiet and make sure they don't ask any questions about what they're doing or why. It's best if all they know is that what they're doing will help us win the war."

"Yes, sir. Mum's the word."

"Barbara!"

"Yes, Colonel?"

"Is Ludlow here yet?"

"Yes, sir."

"All right. Get out of here," he said to Nora.

"Yes, sir." When she reached the door, she turned back. "I'm sorry if we got off on the wrong foot, sir. I do appreciate the help with housing. Thank you."

"Not another word, Lindstrom. Don't make me regret it."

"No, sir." Nora left and closed the door behind her. Clearly, she'd done all she could about her living situation. Now it was time to see what this mysterious assignment was really all about.

"Is something wrong? You've barely touched your dinner."

Mary roused herself from her thoughts. "No, Mother. Everything's fine." She pushed the green beans around the plate. "Can I ask you a question?"

"Of course."

"When you agreed to marry Daddy, were you in love with him? I mean crazy, head-over-heels in love?"

Mrs. Trask set down her fork and wiped her mouth with a napkin. "What a question!"

"I know you got married the day after graduation, but what about before that?"

"Your father was the kindest, most considerate boy I knew. He wasn't a blowhard like some of those boys. He wasn't pushy or overbearing. He was gentle and understanding."

"That's not what I asked. Were you nuts about him? Were you so in love that you couldn't imagine life without him?"

"Is this about Samuel?"

"Please, Mother. I've asked you a question."

Mrs. Trask gazed out the kitchen window. "I can hardly remember back that far. I was enamored of him, I can tell you that much. Your grandparents thought him an excellent catch. He already knew everything there was to know about trains. Right from the start he wanted to be a conductor, and by golly, he did everything to make that happen. He had drive."

Mary closed her eyes. "That's not about love. That's about whether or not he could provide for you. I'm asking specifically about love."

"Love is fleeting, Mary Elizabeth. Kindness, consideration, and respect—these are the things that sustain a marriage."

There's your answer. "I'll do the dishes, Mother. Then I'm going out for a little while. I won't be late."

"You worked all day. I'll take care of the kitchen. You go on ahead."

"Thank you." Mary kissed her mother on the temple, a rare display of affection. Then again, her mother had, however indirectly and unwittingly, helped her reach a momentous decision.

When she arrived at the park, Sam was sitting on their favorite bench, waiting for her.

"Hi." He stood. "I brought these back for you." He handed her the roses, looking a tad more wilted than they had several hours ago. "And the blanket, I brought that for you too."

"Thank you. That was very thoughtful." She sat down and he followed suit.

"How's your mother?"

"She's fine, thank you."

"Any more word from your dad?"

"No."

"I'm sure he's fine."

"How's business?"

"Booming. We had to hire someone to work second shift."

"That's great." She was fresh out of small talk. "I... I know this has been hard on you. You asked me a question, offered me a ring, and you deserve an answer."

He shifted so that he was facing her. He reached for her hands and then apparently thought better of it and pulled back. "Before you say anything, this has been hard on you too. As you said, you had a lot on your mind, what with graduation, and your dad, and taking on a full-time job. I understand why you weren't ready to answer me right away."

Mary bit her lip. She didn't really want to make this a discussion. She wanted to say her piece and get it off her chest. "Sam—"

"I wasn't finished. I'm sorry if you thought I was too pushy. I guess I panicked because I'm so sure how I feel, and I wanted to lock you down before you went off and explored the world like you were always talking about and found some other guy along the way.

"You're so pretty. I see the way other fellas look at you and it makes my blood boil. You don't ever seem to notice them, but I do. I've always been so proud to have the prettiest girl in town on my arm."

Her nostrils flared. "I'm not some object to be possessed and paraded around."

"I know that," he snapped. "I know," he said more quietly. This time he did take her hands. "Mary Elizabeth Trask, you are always going to be the girl I'm in love with. I'm still asking you to marry me. I still have that ring in my pocket. But I want you to know, if you need more time, take it. I'm not going anywhere. If you say yes right now, we can stay engaged for two years, if you want, before we walk down that aisle. I just want to know that you're going to be my wife and…anyway… That's what I wanted to share."

If Mary felt badly before, now she felt like a complete heel for what she'd come here to say. Still, this didn't change anything. She cleared her throat, withdrew her hands, and folded them in her lap.

"Thank you for all of that, Sam. I know it was sincere and from your heart. You're a good man, and any girl would be lucky to wear your ring. The thing is, I'm not ready to marry you." *Or maybe any boy.*

"Remember, I said—"

"Now who's interrupting," she chided. "I know you said you'd be patient. But you deserve better than waiting around for me to decide it's time. I have a picture in my head of what my life could be like. That image involves travel, and new places, and expanding my horizons." *And true love.*

"What happens when you've done all that? Then what? Sooner or later, you're going to be ready to settle down, get married, and have a family. You don't want to be an old spinster, do you?"

"Of course not. But it's a big leap from turning down marriage at eighteen to being an old-lady spinster. There's a lot of life in between. I aim to experience it."

"By working at Meyer's Drugstore for the rest of your life? Be realistic. How are you going to support yourself?"

"I don't want to fight anymore. I care for you, Sam. Truly, I do. I'm not in love with you the way I think I should be with the man I'm going to marry. I meant to spare your feelings, but you don't want to take no for an answer."

"Trust me, you'll grow to love me more over time."

"No. It doesn't always work that way." She recalled what her father said in his letter. "The fact is, you don't know what's best for me. Only I know that. And right now, I know what's best for me isn't marrying you. I'm sorry, but there it is, as plain as I can say it." She jumped up and grabbed the blanket.

"Mare—"

"My decision is final. I'm sorry, really, I am. I hope you find the right girl for you, but it isn't going to be me. Goodbye, Sam." She tucked the blanket under her arm and ran. Even when the house was in sight, she kept running. She didn't want to go home yet.

She ended up at the library. It was closed at this hour, but she sat on a stone bench. Again her hands shook, but this time she didn't feel the least bit nauseated. Instead, she felt unaccountably lighter, as if she'd been freed from a great burden. She laughed giddily.

Something Sam said bubbled to the surface. He'd assumed she would have to work at Meyer's for the rest of her life. Well, she wasn't going to settle for that. No sir. She was going to kick the dust off and forge a new path.

As she sat there, an idea began to take shape. Maybe she had a way out of this town, after all. She only wished she'd thought of cousin Louise sooner. When she'd overheard her mother yesterday gossiping on the phone with her sister, Louise's mother, in East Tennessee about Louise's new job, she should have known that this could be her big chance to get out.

She checked her watch. First, she had to get home before curfew. Next, she had to tell her mother in the morning that she wasn't marrying Sam, and if she didn't like it… Well, that was too bad. After that, she'd put her plan into action.

She fairly skipped all the way home. By gosh, Mary Elizabeth Trask was going to make her own way. *Look out, world!*

CHAPTER EIGHT

Nora picked her way carefully across the muddy street. So far, Dr. Ludlow—Del he had told her to call him—had shown her fully a half-dozen buildings under construction. He called the buildings by odd names: Alpha this and Beta that. Sometimes, he referred to the same buildings by numbers: 9201-something, and 9204-something. Now, they were on their way to Building 9731, apparently also known as the Pilot Facility. Her head spun with myriad details she was sure she'd never remember.

"I hear you're fresh out of Columbia."

"Correct." Nora sidestepped another puddle.

"You studied under Fermi?"

"Yes." Nora hoped her monosyllabic answers would discourage Del from questioning her further. That morning's lectures about secrecy were fresh in her mind.

"Dr. Lawrence sent me here specifically to train you, you know."

"I didn't know."

"He doesn't really believe a bunch of teenage girls can successfully operate the calutron machines. Heck, we've barely mastered them in the lab at Berkeley, and we've got all guys with graduate degrees working on them."

They arrived at Building 9731, a drab, unremarkable structure that sat perpendicular to several other large, partially built facilities.

"Make sure your badge is visible, and unless you want to get stuck on a massive magnet, you'll want to take off any jewelry," he warned.

Nora's first glimpse of the massive XAX prototype model calutron machine nearly took her breath away. The scale dwarfed the cyclotron she'd experimented with at Columbia.

Del laughed. "You should see the expression on your face. It's priceless."

"The alpha calutron units are substantially larger than this?"

"Massive."

Nora studied the prototype in front of her. It was a modified mass spectrometer designed to separate uranium isotopes, different in size and scope, but not in theory, to what she'd been working on in the lab at Columbia. She thought about the work Lawrence was doing, what he'd said to her in his letter, and the meeting with him, Oppenheimer, and Groves. She added into the mix the partially completed construction she'd witnessed here and the talk of Alpha and Beta machines. Could it be that the intent was to create enough highly enriched uranium—to separate enough fissionable U-235 from the more common, harmless U-238—to fuel a giant chain reaction in the form of a bomb?

She swallowed hard and her hands shook. If her supposition was correct, her work here really could help win the war. But the human cost for the other side... *Oh, my God. What have I signed on for?* She struggled to take in a deep breath. *Don't panic. Focus on the job.*

She gazed again at the calutron, then followed Del to the center of the building, where the control panel was located. She examined its many meters, knobs, and gauges. She reminded herself that the principles for operating this machine and others like it were exactly the same as the unit she knew, and she was fully qualified not only to operate the machine, but to teach her girls to operate it successfully too.

Her girls. She already thought of them as that and she hadn't even met them yet. In fact, she wasn't even sure how many of them had been hired to date. Was she allowed to ask that? Did the question violate secrecy codes? If she was going to supervise them, didn't she need to know how many of *them* there were?

She made a note to ask about the parameters of her job. But who should she ask? She realized she didn't even know for whom she worked. Who was her boss? What were her hours? Where was her office? Did she have one?

Del introduced her to several of his colleagues from the Berkeley Lab, all of whom apparently were on loan to the Tennessee Eastman

Corporation, which seemed to be in charge of what everyone called, The Plant, or Y-12.

The names, like the building numbering system, made no sense to Nora, and maybe that was the point. If they didn't make any sense to her, they certainly wouldn't make any sense to the enemy.

She blinked and tuned back into the conversation a few of the fellows were having while tweaking the knobs and levers on the machine.

"What's Tubealloy?"

Suddenly, all conversation ceased. Del took her aside and whispered, "Tubealloy is code for uranium. We're never to use the real name. Never. Do you understand?"

Nora nodded. The intensity of his expression frightened her a little bit. "Understood."

"Good."

"What else do I need to know?"

"You'll know what you need to know when you need to know it."

Nora wanted to scream. How was she supposed to work under these circumstances?

Her irritation must've shown, because Del added, "Hey. I know that a lot of this seems cryptic and vague. We all feel the same way. Focus on what you're told to do and whatever goals they ask you to meet. Don't worry about the endgame. That's not ours."

"Okay."

"Sit down and take a crack at it." He indicated the stool in front of the control panel prototype. "Make room for Dr. Lindstrom, boys. She's a Columbia girl."

The young man seated on the stool vacated it and beckoned her with a flourish.

"The object is to get maximum output of material without—"

"Degradation," she finished the sentence for the young man.

"Oh. She's a smart one."

Nora, well used to the insecure, immature, sarcasm of her male classmates at Columbia, studiously ignored the jab. She made herself comfortable in front of the board and went to work.

In short order, she had the needles consistently fine-tuned to the maximum output range.

"Bet she can't keep it there without popping the machine off," one of the Berkeley boys said.

She refused to rise to the bait. Half an hour later, having produced consistent, and consistently high-performance values, she stepped away from the machine.

"How did she do that?" one of the boys asked.

"Shut up, Harold."

"What? Our results are never consistently that good. I just want to know how she did that on the first try."

"Beginner's luck," another one said.

"Is there anything else you want me to see?" she asked Del.

"No. That's it for today."

"So, what's next?"

"I'll show you where to catch a bus. It's about a ten-minute ride to get back to the bus depot. From there you can take the fifteen-minute walk home. You're staying in the women's dorm, right?"

"Yes." She wasn't sure how he knew that, but she didn't feel like examining it too closely. Her feet were tired and she wanted to go home.

"That's right near Townsite."

"Where?"

"Townsite. Where Jackson Square is? The shopping area? Right in front of The Castle on the Hill?"

"Oh. Yes. It's near that."

"I'm bunking not far from there. I could escort you back."

"I don't want you to have to go out of your way."

"It's no trouble at all, especially since you're new around here. I'd be happy to show you the ropes a little bit."

Was he flirting with her? Nora knew she'd never been particularly good at recognizing that behavior. Perhaps he simply wanted to be helpful. "Sure."

They caught the bus, got searched as they exited through the Elza Gate, and rode in companionable silence to the bus depot.

"Watch your step. I wouldn't want you to ruin your shoes."

"Thank you, I'm fine." Nora navigated one of the many wooden walkways that zigzagged throughout the complex.

"This," Del gestured with a sweep of his arms, "is Jackson Square. You can go to the theater, go grocery shopping, the beauty parlor... Not that you need that."

She groaned inwardly. *That's definitely flirtatious behavior.*
"Pretty much most of what you need, you can find right here. Otherwise, you can take the bus to Knoxville. They've got some nifty restaurants over there, and the lines aren't nearly as long as they are here. Here, you queue up for everything, and I mean everything. If you see a line, get in it. Chances are, it's something you want."

Rosalie had told her as much last night.

"There's a rec hall for dancing. You do like to dance, right?"

"I don't know," she answered honestly. "I haven't had much practice."

"I could teach you."

You walked right into that. "Thank you. Right now, I'd like to focus on doing my job."

"Aw. C'mon. You can't work all the time."

"Perhaps after I feel more settled." There, that was neutral, wasn't it?

"Okay. Well, here you are." He stopped outside her dormitory.

"Thank you."

"I could meet you here in the morning and we could go to the plant together?"

"Thank you. I'm not sure exactly what I'm scheduled to do tomorrow. But I appreciate the offer."

"Okay. I'll see you around."

She waved and let herself into the dorm, grateful to make it to her room without further human interaction. A shower and a date with a good book sounded wonderful.

Today was going to be a big day. Mary could feel it in her bones. Initially, she had planned to go shopping on her day off and buy herself a new dress, but she didn't want to miss the mail delivery. Today would be the day she'd hear back from her cousin Louise about job prospects in East Tennessee. It *had* to be.

She gazed out the window. Could the mailman have come when she went to the bathroom?

"You've been staring out that window for hours now." Mrs. Trask rearranged the ball of yarn and resumed knitting. "Is Samuel coming over? Is that who you're waiting for?"

Guilt tore at Mary's conscience. She still hadn't told her mother that she'd rejected Sam's proposal. She'd been busy with work, and crafting the letter to Louise, and... *Those are feeble excuses and you know it. Get it over with. Don't be a coward.*

"No, Mother. It isn't Sam. You likely won't be seeing him anymore."

"That's ridiculous. Why not? Are things that busy down at the repair shop? Surely he can make time for you."

"I..." Mary took a deep breath and plunged ahead. "I told him I didn't want to marry him."

Mrs. Trask's hands stilled. "I'm sure I heard you wrong. I could've sworn you said you turned down Samuel's marriage proposal."

"No. You heard me right."

Now she stopped knitting altogether. "When was this?"

"I don't remember, Mother."

"You don't remember? I should think something as important as that would stick in your mind. You're a terrible liar, Mary Elizabeth. It doesn't suit you. You're not too old for me to wash your mouth out with soap, you know."

Mary counted to five in her head. An angry exchange with her mother served no purpose. She strived for a reasonable tone. "I'm not a child. I'm a grown woman and I make my own decisions. I told Sam no because, while I love him, I'm not *in* love with him. I refuse to marry for the sake of convenience or because you think I should say yes. I'm not going to throw my life away."

"If you turned Samuel down, you already did throw your life away. I swear, what is wrong with you? At the rate you're going, you'll die a spinster—old and alone in your misery."

"Now you sound like him." Mary rose.

"So, that's it?"

"That's it. I don't know what else you want me to say."

"Say you'll go back to Samuel right this second and tell him you plead temporary insanity. Say you'll beg him to forgive your stupidity."

Mary heard the fear in her mother's voice, and for a moment, she felt sorry for her. "I will do no such thing. I'm not you. I don't feel like I'll wither and die if I don't have a man to take care of me. I'm stronger than that."

Her mother recoiled as if she'd been slapped. "Are you saying you think I'm weak because I married your father? I'll have you know he's the one who leans on me. Not the other way around."

"I'm saying that I'm my own person. I don't need Sam or a marriage to define me. I can get along in the world fine without a man."

"The world is not kind to women like that," her mother said, derisively.

"Women like what, exactly? What are you talking about?"

"You know. Women who…prefer the company of other women."

"I have no idea what you're getting at; that isn't what this is about. Sam is not the boy for me. That's all there is to it." Mary's heart pounded. Did her mother know she'd been wondering about what it would be like to kiss Phyllis? How could she? She spied the mailman coming toward their house and ran out the front door to meet him.

"Hi, Miss Mary. You're looking pretty as a picture today."

"Thank you. Do you have anything for me?"

"I bet you're waiting for a letter from your dad. Sorry to say, nothing from the Front today. But you did get this." He held out a letter. "It's addressed especially to you. All the way from Clinton, Tennessee."

Mary's heart rate accelerated. "Thank you."

"You're welcome. Say hello to your mom for me."

"I will." Mary went back inside and made a beeline for her bedroom.

"Anything for me?"

"No, Mother."

"Where are you going?"

Mary ignored the question. She locked herself in her bedroom, slit the envelope open, and sat on the bed to read. She regretted, not for the first time, that she had decided to correspond via letter with Louise. It had taken her forever to craft her letter, and now it would take her twice that long to read and comprehend Louise's return reply.

My dearest cousin,

It was so wonderful to hear from you. You're right, writing letters back and forth is a poor substitute for spending time together as we used to do when we were children and lived next door to each other. It has been ages since we've seen each other.

I knew you weren't wild about working at Meyer's after graduation, but I had no idea you were miserable enough that you'd consider moving so far away from home. I have to say, it gave me quite a thrill to think about you being so close again.

In answer to your specific question regarding work in these parts, have I got news for you! I recently got a job not far from here doing secretarial work. I'm told that what we're doing will help us win the war, although everything else about what we're doing is very hush-hush. The pay is better than I could've imagined, and the place is like nothing I could describe. The best part is they're hiring girls just like you by the dozen, and not only for secretarial work, either. How soon can you get here?

I can put you up at my rooming house for a few days while you apply, but you'd be best off telling them at the interview that you're not local. I have to take a bus to work because I live too close to get on-site housing. But if you get a job, and they know you're from out of town, they'll give you a place to live for a song. They're not the best accommodations, but they'll do. And the social life is out of this world. They have movie theaters, bowling alleys, recreation halls for dancing, and lots to do when you're not working.

Anyway, all you have to do is get here, and I'll help you with the rest. I'm sure you'll get hired and start right away. They need lots of workers, and fast.

As for how to get here, you can take a bus to Knoxville, and I'll come pick you up. I'm so excited that I'll get to see you again! Hurry!

Your favorite cousin,
Louise

P.S. My lips are sealed. I won't tell a soul, so you won't have to worry about your mother finding out.

Mary finally lowered the letter. This really was happening. She was going to get on a bus with a packed suitcase and leave Sam, and

Meyer's, and her mother behind. The last gave her a pang. It didn't feel right to leave her mother all alone. Then again, she'd be making more money in East Tennessee, and she could send most of that home. Best of all, what she'd be doing would be for the war effort. She could do something meaningful that would help bring her father home soon. Surely, that would justify her decision. And, when they succeeded, her father would come home and her parents would have each other. She was eighteen for cripe's sake. It was time for her to be out on her own.

She began to pace. There was so much to do. She needed to pack, tell Doc she was quitting, find the bus schedule, and get a ticket. Maybe she should make a list. But if she made a list, her mother might find it. No, better to keep everything in her head.

She would have to tell Doc at just the right time, or else her mother would know something was up. That would be disastrous. She'd insist that Mary stay, and they'd have a terrible row. Secrecy was paramount. She was sure of it.

She bounced on the bed and barely kept herself from squealing with joy. Mary Trask was striking out on her own. She'd show the world what she could do, oh yes, she would.

It's the last day you'll have to be subjected to this. It's the last day you'll have to be subjected to this. It's the last day you'll have to be subjected to this. Nora kept repeating the mantra in the hope that it would prevent her from an ugly verbal confrontation with these over-confident, bilious, buffoonish boys. Every day since she'd arrived, it had been the same scenario. After today, she would graduate from training on the XAX to working with her cubicle operators. She couldn't wait to get started.

"The output would be vastly improved if the ratio…"

Nora tuned out Berkeley Boy C. She'd taken to using letters to delineate between the Berkeley Lab scientists, all of whom were convinced that they alone could improve production outputs and the efficiency and efficacy of the calutrons. Except for Del. Del had been universally respectful and kind.

"We can't even get these to behave properly. There's not the slightest chance that some barely educated teenage girl is going to be able to operate this machine."

"It's a fool's errand."

Finally, Nora had had enough. "It may well be a fool's errand, but it's my responsibility, and you can be sure that not only do I take it seriously, but I will make it work."

"It's nothing personal, Nora," Del said. "You've experienced firsthand the difficulties we've encountered. These girls aren't being trained to problem solve. They're being given a rudimentary explanation and told to keep the needle between two points. They don't understand why; they don't know the science. How can they possibly succeed, when those of us who have a full understanding of the complex scientific process are failing on a daily basis?"

Initially, Nora had wondered the same thing. Then it had come to her. Her girls didn't need to understand the science; they simply needed to get results. *Sometimes, too much knowledge can be a hindrance.*

"The Alpha-1 calutrons will be online soon, and we're not convinced we have a workable design. They're still tinkering in Berkeley," Berkeley Boy B complained.

Nora prayed for patience. "Tomorrow I'm going to get a good look at the girls and the training your colleagues have been doing with them. Once I see that, I'll know how to help them do what we need them to do. I recognize that neither you, nor your colleagues, have faith in this arrangement, but I do. When all is said and done and these girls produce the necessary results, you'll be singing a different tune."

Her words held more bravado than she felt, but Nora had never failed at anything. She wasn't about to fail now.

CHAPTER NINE

Mary glanced over her shoulder one more time to make sure no one was watching her. So far, she'd been lucky. She was able to sneak her suitcase out of the house when her mother was hanging the wash in the backyard.

You're nervous as a cat. Stop skulking around; it makes you look suspicious. She stored her suitcase in the locker at the bus station as she'd planned and managed to get out of there without seeing anyone she knew. Next, she approached the ticket counter.

The man behind the glass partition looked bored. "How can I help you?"

"I want to purchase a one-way ticket to Knoxville, Tennessee, please." Saying it out loud made her stomach flip.

"When do you want to leave?"

"Tonight, please."

The clerk consulted his map of routes and scheduled departure times. "The bus leaves at 7:05 p.m. and arrives in Knoxville at 1:30 p.m. tomorrow. How many tickets do you want?"

"One, please."

She fished the money out of her purse and handed it to the clerk. He handed her the ticket. Just like that, with a simple transaction, Mary changed the course of her life.

After her shift at Meyer's, she'd have an hour to get to the station and board the bus to Knoxville. For now, she'd have to hurry to be to work on time.

Throughout the day, she went over the plan in her head. She wished she could've given Doc more notice, but the more she'd thought about it in recent weeks, the more she came to realize that the moment she quit, someone would tell her mother. In the end, she decided the only way was to tell Doc at the end of her last shift.

She regretted lying to her mother that morning when she hinted that she might meet up with Sam for dinner. Naturally, her mother had been overjoyed. Perhaps she should've been honest and told her mother she was leaving for good. She imagined the argument that would have ensued and her mother's histrionics and threats. No, it was best to leave without fanfare and ask forgiveness later—and from a great distance away. *I'm sorry I lied, Mother. I hope it doesn't take you long to find the note I left in my room letting you know I'm safe.*

"Mary? Did you hear me? Could you please get the quinine for Mrs. Robles?"

"Sure, Doc."

"You can leave after that if you want. I'll close up tonight."

Mary swallowed the lump in her throat. She would miss Doc. She retrieved the quinine and waited on the customer. When she was done, she asked, "Doc? Can I talk to you for a second?"

"Sure, what is it?"

Mary checked to make sure there was no one nearby. "I really hate to do this to you, Doc, but this has to be my last shift."

Doc nearly stumbled backward. "Your last shift? What are you talking about?"

"I've been asked to go do something top-secret for the war effort."

"You? Mary Trask?"

"Yes, sir."

"What could you do for the war effort that you're not already doing? You're not going into battle, are you?"

"No, sir. I've been forbidden to give any details, but it's really important." She was telling the truth…sort of.

His shoulders slumped. "Are you sure about this?"

"I am."

"Well, who am I to stand in the way of you helping to win the war? I'll miss you, Mary."

"I'll miss you too, Doc." She kissed him on the cheek and handed him her lab coat. Then she retrieved her purse and headed for the bus station. Phase One of *Operation Free Mary* was underway. By tomorrow she'd be hundreds of miles away in a world no doubt very different from anything she'd ever known. She couldn't wait. *Knoxville, here I come.*

◈◈

Nora exited the dorm and headed for the bus depot.

"Haven't seen you in a while, stranger." Rosalie came up alongside her. "You must be working hard."

"I have been."

"Don't forget to have fun. We've started a bowling league. Why don't you come play with us?"

"I don't know how to bowl."

"Neither do we." Rosalie laughed easily. "But we throw the ball at the pins anyway. It's fun."

"Thanks, but I don't think that sport is for me."

"They have tennis courts. Do you play?"

"I haven't played in years. I was always too busy studying."

"Ah, a bookworm. Now I've got your number. There's a library."

"I know. I've been there."

"How about roller skating? Everyone loves to roller skate."

"I don't have skates."

"You can rent them." They'd reached the bus depot. Rosalie put a hand on Nora's arm. "Come on, live a little. I'll get a bunch of the girls together after dinner tonight and we can all go over to the roller rink together. Please, say yes."

Nora sighed. *It wouldn't kill you to get out for a bit.* The bus to Y-12 pulled in. "That's my lift."

"Come skating tonight. You won't regret it."

She was quite certain she would regret it, but it was hard to say no to Rosalie. "Okay."

"Yeah? Okay. I'll pick you up at your room for dinner. Seven o'clock?"

"Sure."

Nora boarded the bus. Her first stop this morning was Building 9201-1. Alpha-1, as everyone referred to it, was almost complete. The ninety-six "race tracks," so named for their oval design shape, ran one hundred twenty-two feet long, seventy-seven feet wide, and rose fifteen feet up in the air. She'd been warned that the electromagnets between the collection tanks were so strong that they could ruin the mechanism in a person's watch simply by standing on the catwalk above the assembly.

She walked the length of the cubicle control room. She would have to get used to the new terminology. Around here, everyone called the calutrons D units, and the girls—her girls—were being told that their job title was cubicle operator.

Her girls... Soon, they would be sitting on these wooden stools, in front of the complicated-looking knobs, dials, gauges, and meters simultaneously controlling voltage, ionization, and source heating. They'd be producing uranium-235, which Nora now believed could be the fuel for an atomic bomb, all the while not knowing or understanding a whit of what they were doing. Her job was to make sure they did that job well.

Nora put her hand to her solar plexus. The burning sensation was back. It was the same feeling she used to get right before an important exam. *Don't panic. You'll succeed. They'll succeed. It's not like the fate of the world rests on the outcome here or anything.* Except that she suspected it might.

Don't stand here paralyzed. Do something practical.

Nora exited the building and made her way to the classroom where the Berkeley Boys were training her girls. One look at the girls' faces told her their explanations and instructions were far too complicated. After standing in the back of the room for an hour, she knew she had to intervene. On a break, she pulled the trainers aside.

"This will never work if you keep prattling on over their heads."

"What are you talking about?" Berkeley Boy A asked.

"Watch." Nora walked to the front of the class. She told herself this would be a lot like tutoring the young boy down the street who'd needed help with his science lessons. *Break it down into its simplest form. Tell them only what they need to know to do the job well and get the desired results.* "Hi. I'm Nora. You gals will be seeing a lot of me. How many of you came to CEW because you wanted to make a difference and help us win the war?"

Every girl's hand shot up, and Nora smiled.

"I thought so. Me too. It's my job to help you succeed. I know you're itching to get at the real thing, but while construction is underway, we need you to master these dummy models. She indicated the mock cubicles in front of which each of them sat.

"When you get it right in here, you'll get it right out there. The most important thing you need to focus on is keeping the needles on the meters on that panel on the left, between this point, and this point." Nora drew a quick sketch of the meters on the blackboard and used vertical lines to indicate the desired position of the needles.

"If a needle goes too far to the right or too far to the left, use the knobs on the panels to make a correction until the needle is back in the 'good' zone. Don't worry. After a while, you'll know which knob to turn, how much, and in which direction without even thinking about it. Heck, you'll be doing this in your sleep."

"I hope not," one of the girls in the front row mumbled, and several others who heard the remark, including Nora, laughed.

"There are lots of folks who don't think you gals can handle this job." Nora made eye contact with every girl in the room. "I know you can. I also know that you understand that what we're doing here—what you're doing here—is about winning this war and bringing our boys home. Nothing could be more serious, or more important, than that. In your off time, have fun, enjoy yourselves, and get some rest. When you're on the job, when it's your shift, know that your country is depending on you. The work is long, and it can be tedious. Be patient, and always remember what's at stake. You're going to do a great job. Class dismissed."

"That was too simplistic," Berkeley Boy A said. "They'll never understand what they're doing and how to make course corrections with an explanation like that."

"The difference between them and us is that we see something go awry, and we understand the import; we want to know why. We endeavor to improve the process using scientific principles. These girls can't think that way. They don't have the education for it. So they use what's right in front of them. Improving the machine and the process isn't their job. Working with what's in front of them is all they have. And it's all they need. The rest is up to us scientists." Nora walked away.

"That was brilliant."

"Hi, Delbert." Nora hadn't seen Del in the classroom, but obviously he was there.

"Oh, now that hurts."

They left the room together. "What?"

"Ugh. How many times do I have to tell you, I hate that name."

"Your mother didn't, or she wouldn't have thus named you."

"True. But she's the only one who calls me that. Everyone else calls me Del. Why must we repeat this conversation every time I see you?"

"Because it's fun to see your reaction."

"You've got a sadistic streak, Nora. I like that in a woman. What are you doing tonight?"

"I've got plans with the girls."

"Nora Lindstrom is leaving her room to do something fun? I don't believe it."

She didn't mind his gentle teasing. Since that first day when he'd escorted her back to the dorm, they'd developed an easy friendship. He seemed to understand that she wasn't looking for more, and beyond an occasional compliment, he never pushed the issue. "I didn't say it would be fun. I only said that I was going out with the girls."

"Fun was implied. Where are you going?"

"I let Rosalie talk me into going roller skating."

"Oh, that does sound like fun."

"Do you know how to skate?"

"I do...not. If my mother could've wrapped me in a blanket to protect me from anything that might cause physical injury, she would've."

"No football for you, then?"

He laughed. "Are you kidding me? She thought baseball was a contact sport."

"Poor Delbert."

"Del."

"Uh-huh."

"You did a great job in there, Nora. You were right—we were losing them by giving them too many things to focus on. You cut right to the heart of it and they heard you."

"Thanks, Del. I really appreciate the compliment."

"Listen. I know some of the guys have been giving you a hard time. Frankly, I find their lack of respect appalling. Don't pay them any mind. They're threatened by the idea that you and the girls might show them up."

"What about you? Aren't you feeling threatened?"

"Heck, no! If these girls succeed, we all win. This isn't a competition. It could be life or death." They reached the bus stop. "I'm in your corner, Nora. All the way. I believe in you, and that means I believe in them."

She hugged him briefly. "I can't tell you what that means to me, Del. These five months have been hard for me. Your friendship has been a blessing."

"I feel the same way, my friend."

For the first time since she'd arrived, Nora's heart felt lighter. She understood that Del would be spending most of his time now at Berkeley, with only an occasional trip back to the Reservation. But she would enjoy his company for those times when he was here.

Mary yawned and stretched. The early afternoon sun streamed in through the bus window, and she squinted. They were pulling into a bus station.

"Knoxville," intoned the driver. "Knoxville Depot."

Knoxville? Holy cow! This was her stop. Mary gathered her sweater and purse, stepped into the shoes she'd kicked off hours earlier, and picked her way past the other passengers to the front of the bus. The driver helped her down the steps and retrieved her suitcase from the storage area.

"Mary! Yoo-hoo, Mary! Over here."

She shielded her eyes and spotted her cousin jumping up and down and waving at her. She hoisted the suitcase and ran in that direction. "Oh, Louise. It's so good to see you." Mary had forgotten how pretty she was. Louise favored her father. She was several inches taller than her, with dark, wavy hair and soulful brown eyes.

"Give me that." Louise relieved her of the suitcase, which she set down on the sidewalk. Then she hugged Mary tightly. "I missed you."

"I missed you too."

"Let me get a look at you." Louise released her and held her at arm's length. "You've lost weight, and you didn't have any to lose. You're practically melting away."

"Oh, posh. I am not doing any such thing."

"I'm glad you're here." Louise picked up the suitcase. "My God. What do you have in this thing, rocks?"

"I wasn't sure what to pack, so I brought as much as I could fit."

Louise guided them to where the local bus to Clinton idled in its assigned slot.

Mary groaned. "Not another bus."

"What with the gas rationing and all, this is the best way to get anywhere. Don't worry. We're only about thirty miles away from the boarding house."

They got settled on the bus and Louise said, "Tell me everything, don't leave anything out, and start from the beginning."

Mary laughed. "The beginning of what? In the beginning, God created Heaven and Earth."

"Not *that* beginning, smarty pants. Why are you running away? Did you tell your mother you were going? What was her reaction? Do you still have that fella? What was his name…Stanley?"

"Sam. Which question would you like me to answer first?" Mary spent the remainder of the trip filling in Louise on the details of her life for the past two years since her father had gone to war.

"Wow. That's some story." They entered the boarding house and mounted several flights of stairs.

"Do you think I did the right thing?" she breathed heavily.

Louise led Mary into her room on the third floor and set the suitcase near the closet. "Well? What do you think?"

Mary took in her surroundings. "It's nice. Cozy."

"I know it's not much, but I don't need much."

"No, I meant it. It's quaint. I like it." She sat in the rocking chair and kicked off her shoes. "My feet are killing me."

"I bet." Louise sat on the side of the bed.

"You didn't answer my question."

"Which question was that?"

"Do you think I did the right thing, turning down Sam's proposal, quitting Meyer's, and leaving town?"

"That's hard for me to say. I wasn't there, and I'm not you."

"Oh."

"From where I sit, I think you were right not to settle for a guy you're not madly in love with. You've got plenty of living to do without rushing into anything. As for quitting a steady job… Normally, I'd have said you'd lost your mind. But because I know what's available here, I'd say you made a smart choice. We know the job will have a limited life—"

"What do you mean by that?"

"I mean, when the war ends and we win—"

"I like your confidence."

"When we win, I imagine whatever work we're doing for the war effort will end too."

"That makes sense."

"Even so, we'll have gained valuable work experience and new skills. New skills and a proven work record make it more likely that we'll be employable even after our boys come home."

"When did you get to be so smart?"

"When I had to be in order to survive on my own."

"That's only until Emmett comes back from the war, right?"

"I promised I'd wait for him."

Something about the way Louise said it gave Mary pause. "You haven't changed your mind, have you?"

Louise shrugged and glanced away.

"Cousin? Have you changed your mind?"

"There are a lot of single men on the Reservation."

"What's the Reservation?"

"It's one of the things we call the place I'm taking you. It's also known as Clinton Engineer Works, or CEW, and recently they've started calling the town Oak Ridge."

Mary thought she was speaking a foreign language. What was this place?

"Anyway, there are lots of nice-looking, single men, and they're all on the hunt for us girls, because we outnumber them by so much."

"And?"

Louise's face lit up. "And there's this one particular fella. Oh, you'd love him, Mare. He's kind and considerate. He's a Yankee— you can tell that as soon as he opens his mouth. He's seen so much of the world already, and he wants to show it all to me when the war's over."

"Sounds like you're really sweet on him."

Louise nodded and tears formed on her lashes. "But, I made a promise to Emmett. His letters are all full of longing and dreams about buying a farm out here in the rolling hills and living off the land. I don't have the heart to send him a 'Dear John' letter. He's fighting for our country. I have no right..."

"You have a right to love, Louise, same as I do."

"What am I going to do?" She buried her head in her hands.

Mary crossed the room, sat next to her, and rocked her in her arms. "Shh. Shh. We'll figure something out. We'll figure out something for both of us. We're going to get our happily ever after. You'll see. Everything's going to work out just fine."

CHAPTER TEN

"Are you ready?" Rosalie asked.

"I guess," Nora replied. "It's bad enough you got me to go skating. But going to Knoxville in a cattle car disguised as a bus? I can't believe I let you talk me into this." She wasn't really miffed. It was her day off, she was much in need of some supplies, and everyone touted Knoxville as the place to go. Also, she was happy she'd be accompanied by friends for her first trip to Knoxville. Rosalie and Betty, another girl from the dorm, both had been to Knoxville several times before and knew the ropes.

They hit Miller's Department Store first. Miller's had a store on the Reservation, but the one in Knoxville dwarfed the local store in size and was better stocked.

"What do you think about this hat?" Rosalie asked. It was a sweet little pale pink number, adorned with flowers and a turned-up brim.

"I think you look swell," Betty said.

"It offsets your black hair perfectly. But it's not practical," Nora added.

"Why, oh why must you be such a killjoy? Who cares about practical?"

"I guess I do. Then again, I wouldn't have any occasion to wear something like that."

Rosalie nudged her playfully. "That's because you're a shut-in."

"I am no such thing."

"In the past month, how many times have you left your room, other than to eat or go to work?"

Nora frowned, knowing she was beat. "Several."

"Only because we made you," Betty said.

"And when are you going to let Del take you on a proper date? The guy's crazy about you."

"H-he is not," Nora spluttered. "He's a good friend."

"A good friend who'd like to be a lot more," Rosalie muttered.

"You're reading too much into it." Nora blushed to the roots of her blond hair.

Betty and Rosalie closed ranks, standing side-by-side with their arms crossed.

She needed to redirect this conversation. "You two are boy-crazy. That's all there is to it. It's all you think about."

"You have to be one of the densest women I've ever met. That boy drops hints everywhere and follows you around like a puppy dog. The only reason he doesn't make a move is because he knows he'll send you running for the hills."

"So, instead he bides his time," Betty finished for Rosalie. "Haven't you ever had a boyfriend before?"

"She probably hasn't, if she can't even figure out when a boy is sweet on her."

Nora felt like she'd been ambushed. "Whenever you two are through, let me know."

"Aw. Don't be sore." Rosalie looked contrite. "We only want you to be happy."

"I don't need your help, thank you very much."

"Are you…ladies…" The saleswoman gave them a disgusted once-over. "…planning to buy something?"

Nora, already feeling off-balance, snapped, "We might have, if you—"

Rosalie stepped in front of her. "How much is this hat?"

"Can't you read the label?"

Nora couldn't believe her ears. Never had a salesperson treated her so rudely. Again, Rosalie intervened. "I must've left my glasses in my other purse."

The salesperson told her the price.

"I'll take it."

"Don't—"

This time Betty took Nora by the hand and pulled her away. "Come look at the stockings with me."

"What are you doing?" Nora whispered harshly. "That woman was insufferable."

"You're right. Folks here in Knoxville take one look at our muddy shoes and know where we've come from. They think we're all Yankees and they despise us."

"That's absurd."

"That's a fact."

"But Rosalie's from right here in Tennessee."

"What's your point? She's not from *East* Tennessee, and that makes all the difference." Betty selected a pair of Rayon stockings. "Have I mentioned how much I hate Rayon? Nylons have spoiled me for life. Rayon sags at the knees."

"Our boys need all the nylon for parachutes. I'd rather they be safe than my hose not sag."

"Ever-practical Nora," Betty said as Rosalie rejoined them.

"In this case, you're right. It's why I plan to buy some slacks."

"Oh, that'll certainly make you a rebel."

Nora scoffed. "Me? A rebel? Hardly. I'm living up to my reputation for practicality. I'm going to buy a pair of saddle shoes too. I'm tired of losing heels in the mud."

"Me too," Betty said.

They finished shopping and stopped at a restaurant near the bus depot for dinner. "Tell us about you, Nora. I feel like I don't know anything about you. You're so shy. It's hard to figure you out." Betty twirled a helping of spaghetti with her fork.

"I'm not shy." She blushed again.

"See? You're blushing. You are shy."

"I think it's more that she's introverted."

"If I could crawl under this table right now, I would."

"Case closed. You've proven our point."

Nora squirmed. "What do you want to know?"

"Everything," both women said at once.

Nora set down her fork. "My parents emigrated to the United States from Sweden before I was born. My father is a shop owner in Greenwich, Connecticut. I have a brother six years younger than I am. He's…" Nora considered what to say about Bill that wouldn't sound terrible. "We're polar opposites."

Rosalie shook her head. "That's all interesting, sugar, but I want to know about you—Nora Lindstrom—not your family. Tell us something that would surprise us about you."

Nora's eyebrows rose into her hairline. "I don't have any surprises. I guess I'm a boring person."

"Nonsense," Betty said. "Didn't I hear someone say you were a doctor?"

"I'm not a medical doctor. I've got a Ph.D. in physics."

"See?" Rosalie talked around a mouthful of mashed potatoes. "That right there is fascinating. What made you want to be a scientist?"

Nora smiled. "I was always captivated by how things worked—the mechanics of time and space, atoms—all of it, really. The first time I swam in the ocean and my body floated without effort, I needed to understand why. I craved the knowledge." She shrugged. "I guess you could say it was curiosity that made me pursue science."

"I was curious about the world too," Rosalie said. "Usually, that curiosity landed me in hot water with either my parents or the principal."

"I can see that," Nora said. She liked Rosalie. She was different from all the other girls Nora knew. She didn't care about status, level of education, or money. She only wanted to know if you were a good person.

"We'd better get going or we're going to miss the bus," Betty said.

When she was safely back in her room, Nora pulled out her journal.

Dear Diary,

Today, I took the bus to Knoxville, the largest city around these parts (now I'm starting to talk like a local). My friends Rosalie and Betty came along, which made the outing more fun. Friends...such a foreign concept for me. Except for Anna, I've never really had any good friends. It seems odd at this point in my life that I should find some, and so far from home and my experiences.

Speaking of Anna, I had cause to think of her today. Rosalie and Betty were razzing me about a boy. He's another scientist I've told you about before, my friend, Del. The girls insist he likes me, and not as a friend, but as a potential girlfriend. I tried to pooh-pooh the idea, but if I'm going to be honest about it, I suspect they're probably right. He's a nice guy and a gentleman, unlike so many of

*the boys I've met here and elsewhere. But I'm just not interested in
him, or in any other boys for that matter.*

*Dear diary, is there something wrong with me that it's Anna that
makes my heart race and not Del? I fear that there might be.*

*Well, enough of all that. Things are ramping up here. I can't say
much about it except to say that the real work is commencing and
I'm praying we're up to the task.*

More soon, dear diary.

Faithfully yours,

Nora

≪⑥↷≫

Mary folded her hands in her lap to keep them from shaking.
She'd never seen anything like this place. She made note of the
barbed wire fencing, the guard tower, the gates, and the very
obvious military presence. Then there were the signs warning of the
need for absolutely secrecy. Even if she had trouble making out the
words, the message in the pictures was crystal clear. When the
soldiers searched the bus and scrutinized her visitor's pass, she
wanted to run, even though she knew she'd done nothing wrong.

At the bus depot, men and women of every size and shape
disembarked from a sea of buses advertising odd destinations like
Y-12, K-25, and X-10.

She leaned over and whispered to Louise, "What are those
places?"

"Don't ask questions."

Mary checked to see if Louise was kidding, but her expression
was dead serious. They disembarked. "Where are we going?"

"The Castle on the Hill."

"There's a castle? In the middle of nowhere?"

"It's the administration building. That's where you'll have your
interview." Louise picked up the pace. "Like I said, don't ask
questions. Answer whatever they ask you directly. Make sure you
emphasize that you can keep a secret. There are spies everywhere
in here, so don't let your guard down, ever. If you get hired, people
will try to get you to slip up. They'll ask what you do here. Tell
them this and that."

"But I thought you said I was supposed to answer directly?"

111

"That's just during the interview. Tell them where you went to school, what your skills are, that kind of thing."

Mary's stomach flipped. This was going to be a lot harder than she thought.

They arrived at the building and Louise led Mary to the reception desk and checked her in for her interview. "I've got to go to work. Wait here and they'll call you when they're ready." She kissed her on the cheek. "Good luck. You'll be fine."

Mary sat in one of the nearby chairs. She didn't feel at all as though she'd be fine. When Louise had said they were hiring for the war effort, she should've asked more questions. *You should've thought this through. What if you're not qualified? What if you don't want to do whatever the job is? Are you going to run back home with your tail between your legs? This is crazy.*

By the time a girl not much older than her called her name, her mood had plummeted. She had fairly convinced herself that a full-time job at Meyer's wasn't so bad after all.

"You'll be interviewing with Mr. Knutsen in personnel. He's right around the corner." They took a left. "Here we are. Have a seat. He'll be right with you."

"Thank you." The office was drab and unremarkable. There were no personal items, such as family photos.

"Hello."

Mary's hand flew to her heart. She jumped to her feet and turned to see a balding, middle-aged man in a crumpled business suit standing in the doorway. "I'm sorry. You startled me."

"I apologize. Please, sit down. I'm Mr. Knutsen, I'll be conducting your preliminary interview."

"I'm Mary Trask."

"Nice to meet you, Mary."

He pulled a pen and a folder from his desk drawer. "Let's start with your personal history. Where is home for you?"

"I hope here, sir." She thought perhaps he would smile, but he remained stoic.

"And before that?"

"Philadelphia, Pennsylvania, sir."

"How old are you?"

"Eighteen, sir."

"Do you have a high school diploma?"

"I do."

"Any prior work experience?"

She told him about her employment at Meyer's and her responsibilities.

"Very well. Do you know shorthand and do you take dictation?"

"No, sir." Mary bit her lip. Would that count against her?

He made a notation in the folder. "How is your eyesight? I see that you don't wear glasses."

"Oh, I see perfectly, sir. Nothing wrong with my eyes. I'm observant too." Mary wasn't sure why she added the last, and she wished she could take it back. *Answer the questions directly, Mary Elizabeth. Don't offer things that aren't asked.*

"That's good. Do you have any disabilities?"

"I'm not sure what you mean, sir." Mary squirmed. She had trouble reading and writing and needed to be extra careful and take lots of time with those skills, but those weren't disabilities.

"Do you have any trouble with your back, your hands, or your neck? Is there any reason you can't sit for long periods of time, or turn dials, pull levers, or twist knobs?"

"No, sir. I'm the picture of health."

"Good." He reached into his drawer and pulled out another folder. "I've got a short, written test here for you to take."

Panic welled up, choking off Mary's airway. "I-I'm not very good at written tests, sir."

He raised an eyebrow. "You said you graduated high school, correct?"

"Yes, sir."

"You can read and write?"

Mary heard buzzing in her ears. "Y-yes sir, but I'm much, much better at verbal and visual tests."

"I see." He tapped his pen thoughtfully on the desk. "Stay here, please. I'll be back in a minute."

When he'd gone, Mary's shoulders slumped. *You're doomed. Doomed.* If only she had an easier time reading. It wasn't that she didn't try, or even that she didn't enjoy reading. She loved stories.

Several minutes passed, and then Mr. Knutsen returned with another man in tow. This gentleman was nattily dressed, fit, and much younger.

"Hello, Mary. I'm Mr. Edwards. Mr. Knutsen and I have talked it over and think we have a better way to test your aptitude. If you'll come with me, I'm going to show you a machine and tell you how to work it. That will help us determine if you're suited for the job we have in mind for you. Does that sound okay?"

"Yes, sir."

They passed a classroom humming with activity. Girls sat on stools in front of massive panels. On the panels were meters, gauges, knobs, and dials. Mary knew her mouth was hanging open. What were these things?

Mr. Edwards led her into another room and sat her in front of a single similar machine. "Okay, Mary. I'm going to give you some instructions. Let's see how well you can retain the information and apply it."

Mary sat on the stool and did her best to get comfortable. Although she could hear the din from the classroom next door, she shut out everything except for the sound of Mr. Edwards's voice. When he was done explaining the task to her, she repeated the instructions back to him.

"Now, apply that to the panels in front of you."

Mary did as she was told.

Roughly twenty minutes later, Mr. Edwards said, "That's enough."

"I can do this longer, and I know in time I'll get better at it."

"Actually, you did quite well. I'm impressed, and I'm not easily impressed."

Mary smiled from ear to ear. "Does that mean you want to hire me?"

"One more thing. I know you told Mr. Knutsen that you had trouble with reading and writing. How are you with recording numbers on a log sheet?"

"Oh, I can do that, sir. It's just words that are tough."

"Show me." He produced a clipboard with a sheet of paper on it. "Write down the readings on those dials." He pointed to the left-side panel on the machine in front of her.

Carefully, she wrote down the figures. "Is this what you wanted?"

"Yes, it is. Very good, Mary."

"Now does this mean you want to hire me?"

"I do believe it does."

"When can I start? Do I have a job title? Where will I live?"

Mr. Edwards held up a hand. "Hold your horses. First, we'll get you to a clerk so that you can get an ID badge and a Townsite Resident Pass. Then you'll go to housing and they'll try to find you an open dorm room. A single room rents for fifteen dollars per month. A shared double room rents for ten dollars per occupant. The job is called a cubicle operator, and you'll have to spend some time in the bullpen and at orientation before you can get cleared to work in the plant."

"Bullpen?"

"Think of it as a holding area where you get trained while you wait for clearance to start your regular assignment."

Clearance? Suddenly, dread filled her. "They're not going to call my mother to check up on me, are they?"

The question surprised a laugh out of Mr. Edwards. "You're eighteen, right?"

"Yes, sir."

"Then no, they're not going to call your mother."

"Good." She breathed a sigh of relief. Maybe coming here was the right decision after all.

CHAPTER ELEVEN

Nora pinched the bridge of her nose, where yet another tension headache was taking up residence. She held the phone to her ear with the other hand. "We cannot continue on this way. Every day at Alpha-1, on multiple shifts, we've got equipment failures. The machines are shorting out and shutting down; the needles are going haywire... Respectfully, sir, it's not my girls that are the weak link. I've sat down at the cubicle and gotten the same results. There's something wrong in the design. It's not my job to figure out what that is, but if someone doesn't figure it out soon, we'll all be wasting our time here."

"I understand your frustration. Do the best you can. Try to keep morale up. We're working on solutions over here. I'm sending a couple of my assistants back to help you. General Groves and I are in close contact about the situation."

"Thank you, Dr. Lawrence. I appreciate your assistance with this."

"And I appreciate your honesty and your discretion. It's the reason I made sure your clearance was at the highest level. I'll be in touch."

Nora hung up the phone. Dr. Lawrence had thanked her for her discretion. Presumably, even though she hadn't said as much, he surmised that she'd examined the entire process. He would have been right.

After Nora determined that the malfunctions weren't due to operator error, she met with the supervisors who were in charge of each of the other aspects of the process. Whatever the flaw was, neither Nora nor the other supervisors had been able to identify or correct it.

She buried her head in her hands. Failure was not an option, and with the Alpha-2 and 3 and Beta-2 plants about to come on line, whatever the problem with the calutrons was, it needed to be rectified quickly.

In the meantime, she would keep her girls working, oversee the training of new hires, and try to keep up morale. It was all she could do.

❧❧

Mary hung up the last dress and arranged her shoes in the bottom of the closet. A knock on the door startled her. "Who is it?"

"It's Peggy from next door."

She opened the door. "I'm Mary. Nice to meet you."

"Nice to meet you too. Like I said, I'm Peggy. I thought I'd stop by and welcome you. The girl who had this room before you didn't last very long and I was sorry I never got the chance to meet her."

"Really? What happened to her?" Mary knew she shouldn't ask, but her curiosity was piqued. The clerk that assigned her to the dorm had said she wasn't sure she could find Mary a room since space was at a premium. Then she checked her list and remarked at how lucky Mary was that a vacancy had suddenly cropped up on the first floor in W-1. In fact, she was so surprised by the room availability, that she double-checked it with a supervisor.

Peggy sat on the bed without invitation. "Rumor has it a background check turned up money troubles and ties to the Communist Party. Nobody saw her leave, but she was living here one day and the next she was gone."

"How did they know all that about her?"

"They assigned you to the bullpen, right?"

"Yes."

"That's because they need the time to check into your history and make sure you're not a security risk."

"But they already hired me."

"Provisionally. Trust me, they're not going to put you in a job until they're sure you're clean."

"I already have an ID badge and a resident's pass."

"Which mean exactly nothing if they decide you're a security risk."

"Well, I can tell you there's nothing bad for anyone to find."

"Good. Keep it that way." Peggy got up to leave but turned back at the door. "By the way, it isn't only your background they're looking at. Here's a tip from someone who's been here a few weeks. Don't blab. Don't run off your mouth. They'll try to trip you up by asking you stuff to get you to talk. Secrecy is the name of the game here."

"Right."

"Did you get the resident's handbook yet? Read the first page. 'What you see here, what you do here, what you hear here, let it stay here,' or something like that. Anyway, I'll see you around. We all eat at the cafeteria. If you want, I'll stop by and get you for breakfast in the morning."

"That would be great. Thanks, Peggy, for everything."

"You're welcome. Don't worry, you'll be fine." She let herself out.

Mary closed her eyes. If they were going to be that thorough, chances are they would find out about Sam, and of course they'd contact her mother, even though Mr. Knutsen said they wouldn't. In fact, they'd probably contact her just because Mary seemed worried about it. *Stupid mistake, Mary Elizabeth. Louise told you not to ask questions. That was a question.* She determined that from now on, she would observe everything and say nothing.

She snapped up her toiletries, walked down the hall, and was relieved not to have to wait in line for the communal bathroom. Back in her room, she turned the lights out, laid down on the bed, and stared at the ceiling. By now, her mother would've found the note in her room, telling her that she was all right, that she had gone away for work, and would be in touch when she could arrange it. She'd noticed a telephone in the lobby. Maybe she should call her.

The more Mary thought about it, the more she liked the idea. That way, if someone from this place did call her mother, she could coach her ahead of time. *And tell her what, exactly? You can't share anything with her—not where you are, what you're doing, or where you're living...* Still, a phone call might help. It wasn't yet ten o'clock, so she could make the call before curfew.

She threw on her bathrobe, walked to the lobby, and made a collect call home.

"Hello?"

"Mother?"

"Mary? Is that you? I've been worried sick about you. What were you thinking? You quit your job? You broke it off with Samuel? You didn't tell me where you were going, or, never mind that, that you were going at all? Have you lost your mind? You come home right this minute."

She waited for her mother to take a breath so she could get a word in edgewise. "I'm fine, Mother. Truly. I haven't lost my mind. I didn't want what you wanted for me. I'm safe. I got hired to help us win the war. And the job pays seventy-five cents per hour. I can send most of that home to you. You're going to be so much better off."

"Who in their right mind would hire a girl directly out of high school to help us win the war? If that's the kind of people the government is relying on, we're in more trouble than I thought and we should surrender to Hitler right now."

"Mother! It's not like that." She knew she needed to get off the phone before her mother pressed her for more details. "Listen, I've got to go."

"Go? Go where? Where are you?"

"Someone's waiting for the phone, Mother. I'll be in touch as soon as I can. I love you. Tell Daddy I love him in your next letter to him. 'Bye."

"Mary Elizabeth—"

She hung up the phone.

"Those are always the hardest."

Mary wheeled around to see a girl about her age sitting nearby smoking a cigarette.

"I'm Doris. I haven't seen you around here before."

"It's my first night."

"Ah. Welcome to the nuthouse."

"Thanks."

"Was that your mother?"

Mary figured it was safe to say it was, since she imagined Doris must've heard some of the conversation. "It's hard since my dad's been away at war. I'm an only child."

"I've got seven brothers and sisters, and I couldn't wait to get away. My mother barely has time to miss me."

"Did you tell her you were leaving?"

"Heck, yes. She was happy. One less mouth to feed."

Mary couldn't fathom her mother feeling that way.

"Anyway, it gets easier. Your mother will come around. You'll see."

"Thanks. Goodnight." Mary escaped to her room. This time when she laid down, sleep claimed her easily.

Nora leaned against the wall at the back of the room as the latest group of new hires filed in and took their seats. They appeared so young, eager, and excited. *They look exactly the way you felt when you first arrived here.* That was before the stops and starts, the machine breakdowns and failures, and before the pervasive mud had ruined every pair of shoes she owned.

Don't be cynical. It doesn't suit you. Stay focused on the task at hand, help these girls be the best cubicle operators they can be, and get the job done.

"Grab a seat, please, so that we can get started." Richard Honeycutt finished the diagram on the blackboard and dusted the chalk from his hands.

Nora liked him. He had proven to be cool under fire as a shift supervisor in Alpha-1. Unlike some of the other male supervisors, he refrained from chatting up the girls or distracting them from their jobs. Beyond that, he hadn't balked at having to answer to a female boss. He respected her, and she respected him and gave him additional responsibilities like this one—initiating and training the girls for their assignments.

"Before we dive into specifics such as shift assignments, protocols, procedures, and the like, I'm going to introduce you to the big boss. Every cubicle operator in every building in this plant falls under her supervision. She knows more than anyone I've ever met about the D units you're going to be operating, so make sure if she says something to you, you're paying attention. Dr. Lindstrom? Would you come up here, please?"

Nora pushed off from the wall and threaded her way through the rows of seats to the front of the room. She studiously ignored the buzz of girls unaccustomed to seeing women in positions of power. Over time, she'd learned not to be embarrassed by the open scrutiny.

"Good morning."

A chorus of "good mornings" greeted her in return.

"You've all been through the general orientation, so there's no reason to waste time with that here." The sighs of relief were audible enough for her to hear. She schooled her expression to suppress a smile. Heaven knows, she'd felt the same way when she'd been in their shoes.

"One thing I will reiterate, however, is the importance of the work we're doing here. It is not an overstatement to say that, if we succeed in our assignment, we could save the lives of many of our troops, including, I'm certain, people near and dear to your hearts." As she said it, she made eye contact with every person in the room. From the looks on their faces, it was easy to tell which of the girls had loved ones in the fight.

Her eyes alit on an ethereally pretty girl in the third row. She was a petite brunette with light gold-brown eyes and an aquiline nose. Who was on her heart? Was it her father? A brother? A husband or fiancé? The girl smiled up at her and Nora's heart stuttered. Something about her reminded her of Anna. Quickly, she turned her attention elsewhere.

"As I was saying…" What had she been saying? *Focus on the job.* But all she could see was the girl in the third row. Her appearance was so different from Anna. Maybe it was the curiosity in her eyes… "You are here because you care about your country. You're here because your country needs you." *You're repeating yourself. Get on with it.* "While you're sitting in front of that cubicle, nothing else matters beyond manipulating the knobs and levers so that the needles on the dials in front of you remain in the maximum production zone you've learned about in the training process. I know the hours are long and staring at the machines can be hypnotic and tedious. Keep your minds sharp and your full attention on the task at hand. Nothing you do during this war could be more important than that."

Her gaze strayed again to the girl in the third row. She was staring up at her, full lips slightly parted, hands folded on the desk. Nora blinked. "Let me… Let me also remind you that what we do here, stays here. Do not speak of it with your friends or loved ones, or even each other. Do not write home about it, do not offer information, or participate in idle gossip or speculation. Trust your floor supervisors to help you if you run into trouble during your shift. They are your first line of inquiry to solve problems with the machines." She nodded to Richard. "I'm going to leave you in Mr. Honeycutt's very capable hands. But before I do, does anyone have any questions for me?"

The girl in the third row raised her hand. "Yes? What's your name?" Nora hadn't meant to ask that.

"Mary Trask, ma'am."

"Yes, Mary?" *Mary Trask. It suits you.*

"Will you be checking our work?"

Nora's pulse quickened. "Your floor supervisor is the person in charge on your shift. I will be visible throughout the course of your time here, and yes, I will periodically stop and visit with each of you." The room closed in on her. Air. She needed air. "Mr. Honeycutt? They're all yours." Nora strode quickly from the room.

She exited the building and gulped in the fresh East Tennessee fall air. Her heart continued to race. What was it about that girl? *It doesn't matter. Ignore it.*

"Hey, Dr. Lindstrom. Fancy meeting you here."

She turned at the sound of Del's friendly voice. The irony of the timing was not lost on her. "Hello, Dr. Ludlow. You're back, are you?"

"Couldn't stay away from you." Del wrapped Nora in a bear hug. "How've you been, Nora?"

She welcomed the chance to focus on work. "Baffled and frustrated. How about you?"

"About the same. We've tried all kinds of tweaks and permutations at Berkeley. Until we get a look at the actual configuration up close and personal, we're not going to figure out what's wrong."

"I could've told you that."

"Indeed. So maybe it was an evil plot on my part to get back here to visit with my good friend."

"You're neither that Machiavellian, nor that clever."

"Right on both counts, I'm afraid."

"You're headed over to Alpha-1?"

"I am, and by the way, later tonight there will be some other, much higher-ranking visitors stopping by. They'd like you to be available. Do you think you could do that?" He winked.

"Do I think I could be available for..." She let the sentence hang there, trying to ascertain, without asking directly, whether they were talking about the same visitors.

"Yes. It's kind of a command performance."

"I understand."

Dr. Lawrence and General Groves were on their way. *Good. Now maybe we'll get to the bottom of this.*

∽᳑᷾᠍᠍᠍᠍᠍᠍᠍᠍᠍᠍᠍᠍᠍᠍᠍᠍᠍᠍᠍᠍᠍᠍᠍᠍᠍᠍᠍᠍

Mary stared after her retreating figure. Dr. Nora Lindstrom. She was larger than life, her blond hair flowing and blue eyes brimming with intensity. *What is it about you?* She knew she shouldn't have asked that question, but for reasons she couldn't understand, the idea that she might never see Dr. Lindstrom again bothered her.

It was worth the risk. Now you know that you'll cross paths with her again. But how could she learn more about her in the meantime? It wasn't as though there was an employee yearbook with pictures and biographies.

"Mary Trask? Are you here? Last call."

Mary tuned back in. What had she missed?

"That's you, isn't it?" The girl next to her nudged her with an elbow. "You'd better go up there and get your assignment."

Mary stood up so quickly she banged her hip into the desk. "I'm Mary Trask." She hustled to where Mr. Honeycutt was waiting, clipboard in hand.

"There you are. You're going to Beta-2. Your floor supervisor will assign you to your specific cubicle when you get there."

"Will I always be at the same cubicle?"

"Yes. For the next six days, you'll be on nights—the 11 p.m. to 7 a.m. shift."

"And after that?" She didn't imagine she'd ever see Dr. Lindstrom on the graveyard shift.

"You'll work a six-day week, then you'll get one day off. When you come back, you'll be on the 7 a.m. to 3 p.m. shift, then one day off, then the 3 p.m. to 11 p.m. shift."

"Okay. Do I start that shift tonight?" After weeks in the bullpen, she was itching to get to work.

"Yes. I suggest you go home and get some sleep. It's going to be a long night."

Finally. "Thank you, sir."

Once outside, Mary turned in a circle, trying to get her bearings. For a second, she could've sworn she saw Dr. Lindstrom in the distance, walking along with a man. She took several steps in that direction before stopping herself. What was she going to do if she caught up to her?

Forget about her, Mary Elizabeth. If you want to survive your first shift, you'd better go get some shuteye. She changed direction and headed instead toward the bus stop. Somehow, she thought it would be a while before she could sleep.

NOVEMBER – DECEMBER, 1943

CHAPTER TWELVE

Nora, Dr. Lawrence, and General Groves stood behind Ruth Wixton, one of her best Alpha-1 cubicle operators, as she wrestled with the machine. No sooner had she gotten the needles in the optimal position, when the machine let out a loud "pop."

Ruth addressed Nora. "It's been doing this at least once or twice per shift."

"May I?" Dr. Lawrence took Ruth's place.

Nora wondered who Ruth thought these two men were. Per protocol, she'd never introduced them to her. She was grateful that Ruth was one of the most discreet of her girls. Not only would Ruth not ask anything inappropriate, but she also wouldn't engage in speculation with her co-workers afterward about who the men were or what they might be doing there.

Dr. Lawrence muttered under his breath. Several minutes later, he relinquished the stool to Ruth. He motioned for General Groves and Nora to follow him. When they were out of earshot he said, "As much as I don't want to suggest this, we are going to have to pull one of these apart and get a look inside. There must be some kind of contamination or some foreign matter that's causing the results we're seeing."

General Groves's jaw was set and his lips formed a straight line. "The timing couldn't be worse."

"I know, but what choice do we have? We must get to the bottom of this and improve the output, and soon."

Nora contented herself to stay in the background. Neither Groves nor Lawrence had asked her opinion, nor was she anxious to share her thoughts. The general remained silent so long, Nora wondered if he would answer at all.

"Do it," was all he said, and he marched off the floor and out of the building without another word.

Dr. Lawrence watched after him. "Don't worry. We're all under a great deal of strain. Keep doing what you're doing. We made some design changes in the Beta calutrons that should result in a more highly enriched product. We're on the right track."

"My girls are working their hardest. We won't let you down."

"I know. After all, they did best my boys by outpacing their production output." He winked at her.

"Thank you for your letter, by the way. I told you my girls could operate the machines and achieve results as good as, or better than, your Ph.D.'s. I have to say, it gave me great pleasure to show up your protégés."

"And it gave me none to admit that you were right."

"Fair enough." They exited Alpha-1. "Do you want to take a peek at Beta-2?" It was the most recently completed of the calutron plants.

"Why not?"

The interior of Beta-2 was painted the same drab light green as the rest of the buildings that comprised Y-12. It had become a running joke around the plant that when people from the outside asked what they manufactured at that big compound twenty minutes outside of Knoxville, the answer most often given was "green paint."

Beta-2, like the other Beta buildings, housed thirty-six calutrons in a rectangular configuration. The scale of everything was smaller than the Alpha calutrons. But for the cubicle operators, there might as well have been no difference at all.

Nora recognized several of the girls as she and Dr. Lawrence walked the control room floor. They were approximately halfway down the row when Nora spotted her—the fresh-faced girl from today's orientation. The bright blue uniform accented her tiny waistline.

Heat suffused Nora's body. Was it hot in here?

Perhaps the girl felt the weight of her stare, or maybe it was happenstance, but she turned as Nora and Dr. Lawrence passed and their eyes met for a brief instant.

"...fully functional..."

Nora blinked. She'd completely missed what he'd said. Should she ask him to repeat himself? That didn't seem wise. *Get a hold of yourself.*

"I think I've seen enough," he said. They exited the building and crossed the street. "Don't worry about the general. He'll do the right thing. Stick with what you're doing. Maximize the production as best you can, and trust that we'll get to the bottom of the malfunctions soon. We have to."

"Thank you, Dr. Lawrence."

"For what?"

"For entrusting me with such a vital assignment. I won't let you down."

"You haven't yet." He shook her hand and took his leave.

Nora resisted the urge to return to Beta-2 and check on her girls—especially one girl in particular.

The cacophony of opening and closing lockers, the incessant chattering of girls coming and going, dressing and undressing from their various shifts, and the military searches entering and exiting the change house, jangled Mary's nerves.

You'll get used to it. Give it time. She threw her uniform top and pants in the bin, uncomfortable knowing that someone else would be tasked with doing her laundry. She reminded herself that it wasn't only her laundry—it was all of the uniforms. They were never to leave the premises.

Wearily, she shrugged back into her dress and dragged herself to the bus stop. Could it really have been only eight hours since she'd reversed this process on her way to work? She rolled her shoulders to ease the tension that had taken up residence there. She'd known the job would involve repetition and tedium from the training. But she hadn't counted on it being so stressful.

Between trying to keep the needles in the appropriate range, making certain she recorded the readings properly, and keeping herself awake through the middle of the night, her last nerve was frazzled to a crisp.

"Mary. Hey, Mary."

She groaned and shifted to get more comfortable.

"Mary. This is our stop."

"Huh? What?" Mary pried open her eyes to see Delores, the girl who sat at the cubicle next to her. How had they reached the bus depot so quickly?

"C'mon, sleepyhead. Take yourself home and get into a proper bed. You look like heck."

Mary trudged up the aisle and exited the bus. She reached the bottom step and stumbled. Strong hands stopped her from falling forward. "I'm sor…" She blinked. *You're hallucinating.*

"Are you all right?"

Concerned, compassionate blue-green eyes regarded her from less than a foot away. "I-I'm fine. Just exhausted."

"If you're sure you're okay."

"I am. Thank you." Dr. Lindstrom—Nora—released her and stepped aside so that she could pass.

"Get some sleep. We need you to be sharp."

"I will. Thanks for keeping me from landing on my face."

"We can't have that, now can we?" Nora waved and boarded the bus.

She must be starting her day. Mary practically floated back to the dorm. Within seconds of laying her head on the pillow, she drifted off. As she did, she had a vision of arrestingly beautiful blue-green eyes staring directly into her soul.

Nora was bone tired. The reports from the floor supervisors weren't encouraging and Dr. Lawrence didn't seem to be any closer to figuring out the cause of the calutron breakdowns than he had been the last time they'd met.

"If you don't mind me saying so, you look like heck." Del fell into step alongside her on the way to the bus stop.

"If you don't mind me saying so, you need to work on tact."

"Since when did speaking the truth equate to tactlessness?"

"Since you told me I look like something the cat dragged in."

"That wasn't what I said."

"It's what you implied."

"Oh. Someone's a little touchy today."

"I'm sorry. I'm exhausted. I apologize if I sounded cranky."

"Apology accepted." He gave her a one-armed hug. "Anything I can do to make your day better?"

You can solve the glitches and get us on track. Although she couldn't say that out loud, she knew he would understand what she'd left unspoken. The continued downtime of the Alpha-1 D units was why he and several of the other Berkeley Boys were back in Oak Ridge. "A good night's sleep would do me a world of good."

They arrived at the bus depot. "Walk you home?"

"Sure." Whenever he was on site, this was their routine. She saw no harm in it. They'd fallen into a comfortable rhythm, and beyond an occasional hopeful comment, he never pushed her for anything more than friendship.

"Any chance I can coerce you into going dancing at the rec center tomorrow night?"

"You know I have two left feet."

"I do. But I'm well-used to you stepping on my toes, so that's nothing new." Quietly he added, "You're running out of excuses, you know."

Fortuitously, they reached Nora's dorm. "You're a nice guy, Del." She kissed him on the cheek. "You should find yourself a girlfriend and stop wasting your time on me." She studiously avoided making eye contact, not wanting to see the hurt and confusion she knew she'd see in his eyes. Her focus needed to be on getting the job done, and for that, she needed a clear head. At least that's what she told herself. She waved on her way into the dorm.

"Nora?"

She paused mid-step at the sound of the housemother's voice. "Yes?"

"I've got a message for you."

"For me?" When Dr. Lawrence wanted her, he contacted her at Y-12, and she'd spoken briefly to her mother just the other day.

"It came in via messenger a little while ago."

Nora took the envelope from her and read the address on the front. Dr. Nora Lindstrom, W-1. In the upper left-hand corner was the return address of The Castle on the Hill. She tore the envelope open.

Dr. Lindstrom, please see the housing clerk at your earliest convenience. You are being reassigned to a Flat Top as of today.

"Thank God!"

"Nora! Such language!" The housemother glared at her disapprovingly.

"I'm sorry." But she wasn't, really. No longer would she be subjected to the housemother's dour expression or the need to share a bathroom with the other girls.

She redirected her steps back out the door and fairly ran to the administration building, where she presented herself to the housing clerk on duty. "I'm Nora Lindstrom. I got word that my housing upgrade has gone through."

For the most fleeting of moments, as the clerk sorted through mountains of paperwork, Nora feared that her spot already had been filled.

"Lindstrom... Here you are." The clerk pulled a manila folder from the stack and removed a sheet of paper. She read it and reread it. "Huh. That's odd. You're single, right?"

"Yes."

"Wait here. I'll be right back."

Nora tried not to let her nerves get the best of her. Housing was at such a premium that her dorm room likely already had been reassigned. If this upgrade didn't come through, she could be forced to double up with another girl in a dorm room. The thought nauseated her.

"Okay. Sorry about that." The clerk sat down behind her desk.

"What's wrong?"

"Nothing. But you've been assigned a brand-new two-bedroom Flat Top. That's normally reserved for married couples with families. I thought maybe somebody made a clerical error."

Nora swallowed hard. "Did they?"

"My supervisor says this is what they've got for you. But at some point, you may have to take in a roommate."

"Okay." Someday was not today; she'd deal with that when the time came. For now, Nora was going to get her house, and all to herself too. She breathed a sigh of relief. "Where is it?"

"105 Georgia Avenue. Lucky you. That's barely a hop, skip, and a jump from here."

The clerk's accent was so thick, it took a moment for Nora to process what she said. "What?"

"105 Georgia is a straight shot up the hill over there." The clerk pointed, even though they were in the interior of the building. "About a six-minute walk, or two flaps of a wing as the crow flies."

"When can I get in?"

"It's all yours. I reckon you can get in any time you want. It's fully furnished and it's got an icebox and a stove. Anything gets broke over there, you call on over to the contractor, Roane-Anderson, and they'll get someone over there to fix it in a jiff."

Broken, not broke. Out loud, she replied, "Okay. Thank you."

"You're welcome."

Back in her room, Rosalie and Betty sat on the bed as Nora packed up her things.

"I can't believe you're leaving us," Betty said.

"At the very least, you could take us with you," Rosalie teased. "What are you going to do with all that space to yourself?"

"Enjoy taking a shower for more than two minutes."

"Jealous."

"Yeah. Me too."

"I'm going to miss you girls."

"We're going to miss you," Betty said.

"Knowing you, you'll never come out of that place except to go to work and back," Rosalie added.

"Hyperbole doesn't suit you."

"High, what?"

Nora laughed. "Don't exaggerate."

"Oh, why didn't you say it in plain English?"

"Because she's a Yankee, that's why."

It was an ongoing joke between the three of them. "I really will miss you two hooligans." And she meant it. "How about if I cook dinner one night next week?"

"Yeah." Rosalie brightened. "We could have a housewarming celebration."

"That's a great idea," Betty agreed.

Nora took one last look around the place. "I think that's everything." It felt odd to be walking out of this place with the same amount of stuff she'd come with, but there it was.

"Are you sure we can't help you move in?"

"There's really nothing to help with. I can carry my own suitcase. Apparently, everything else I need is already there."

Rosalie stood up and smoothed her skirt. "Then I guess this is it."

"I guess it is."

"You be sure not to hide yourself away too much." Betty hugged her.

"And remember to eat properly. You've lost too much weight," Rosalie said.

"Yes, Mother-May-I." She hugged Rosalie. "I love you girls."

"We love you too. We'll see you around. Don't be a stranger."

Nora hefted the suitcase and followed her friends into the hallway. She glanced over her shoulder one last time and then quietly closed the door. She wouldn't be sorry to leave this room behind, but she would miss her friends. *Imagine that. You've got real friends.*

She breathed in the chilly evening air. The weight of the suitcase made her short uphill journey that much harder. The night sky was inky black now, and she struggled to read the house numbers. *101. 103. 105.* There it was. She paused outside, taking in the old-growth trees that still dotted the land around the box-like structure. *Home.* This was her new home.

The door opened easily. She stepped inside, set down her suitcase, and fumbled for a light switch. She could see now that the windows facing the street belonged to the living room. A small table and two chairs sat under those three windows. A full-size couch sat underneath the second bank of windows. An end table with a small lamp filled the space between the couch and the wall separating the living room from the master bedroom, and a radio cabinet sat flush against the wall opposite the street. The entire room measured, perhaps, fourteen by thirteen.

Adjacent to the living room was the tiny kitchen, featuring an electric stove and oven, an icebox against the wall next to the door to a small pantry, and a double sink with cabinets above it. *Now I can cook for myself.* She didn't mind the cafeteria food, but cooking for herself meant she didn't have to mingle and socialize if she didn't feel like it.

The bed in the master bedroom was full-size and already made for her. Her clothes would fit easily in the closet, and the nightstand on the far side of the bed featured three small bookshelves for her books. *So far, so good.*

She left her bedroom and wandered into the smaller, second bedroom. As in her room, the twin bed in here also was made up with fresh sheets, a blanket, and a bedspread. The bathroom, located just off the bedrooms, was tiny, but at least she wouldn't have to share it. The idea of a hot, private shower almost made her moan with pleasure.

When she'd been through the entire place, she returned to the living room and twirled in a circle. *Welcome home, Nora Lindstrom. I think you're going to like it here.*

CHAPTER THIRTEEN

M ary whistled tunelessly to herself as she changed out of her uniform and back into her dress. There were so many things to love about the day shift. First, she didn't have to struggle to stay awake. Then there was the added bonus that, every now and again, she could catch a glimpse of the elusive Dr. Nora Lindstrom.

As she boarded the bus, she easily conjured an image of Nora, her long, purposeful strides carrying her regally across the cubicle room floor. She unconsciously tucked an errant strand of hair behind her ear as she walked.

What is it about that woman? It was far from the first time Mary had wondered this. No matter how many times she tried to put Nora out of her mind, her thoughts kept circling back in that direction. What kind of doctor was she? Where was she from? Did she have a husband? A boyfriend? Where was she living? And how could she get close enough to ask Nora all these questions?

Mary Elizabeth, this is getting you nowhere. She stepped off the bus. As she did so, she remembered Nora catching her as she stumbled getting off the bus from the night shift. Her stomach did a somersault. *Let it go. What you need is to go to a dance tonight. That'll take your mind off things.*

Of course, she didn't really know how to dance. Sam's disability made him too self-conscious to dance, so that was something they hadn't done as a couple. Still, she'd gone to a couple of dances with her girlfriends where she'd enjoyed watching the other kids dance the Jitterbug, the Lindy Hop, and the East Coast Swing. Maybe she could fake it.

Sam… Her mother's most recent letter said he still visited her regularly and they talked of this "foolish willfulness" of Mary's ending, her coming to her senses, and returning home to marry him. *In a pig's eye.* In truth, the only time Mary ever thought of Sam was when her mother mentioned him in a letter. She certainly wasn't pining for him. In fact, she didn't miss him in the least.

Again, her thoughts turned to Nora. On those days when she didn't see her, she missed her and wondered where she was and what she was doing. She'd never wondered those things about Sam. *Why are you comparing Nora to Sam?* It isn't like she was a love interest. Maybe this was akin to a crush on a favorite teacher. That must be it—a simple case of hero worship. *You know that's not true.*

As she approached the dorm, she stopped short. There was Nora, standing in the street. Only her profile was visible. She was chatting with two of the girls Mary recognized as living on the second floor. What were their names again?

Nora threw her head back and laughed unselfconsciously and Mary's mouth went dry. *You're beautiful when you laugh.* She shook her head. *Where are you going with this?*

Should she proceed into the dorm? If so, Nora and those other girls were directly in her path. She would have to say something. *You can't stand here paralyzed. You look stupid.*

Before she could figure out what to do, Nora turned in her direction. Their eyes met and Nora ducked her head.

Mary propelled herself forward, but Nora turned away, said something to her friends, and continued up the hill alone.

"Hi, I'm Mary," she said, when she reached the two girls to whom Nora had been speaking. "I live on the first floor."

"I thought I'd seen you around. I'm Rosalie, and this," she said, pointing to her friend, "is Betty. We live upstairs from you."

"It's nice to meet you." Mary bit her lip. Should she say something about Nora? These girls obviously knew her well, or at least better than she did. "That was Dr. Lind… Nora, wasn't it?" Her heart hammered in her chest and she tried to act casual.

"Yep. That's our Nora."

Our Nora?

"We asked her to come out dancing with us tonight," Betty said. "In typical Nora fashion, she turned us down cold."

"That girl needs to get her head out of a book and live a little," Rosalie said.

Mary seized on the opportunity to learn more about Nora. "Doesn't she like to dance?"

"Hard to say," Betty offered. "We've never gotten her to say yes."

"She's so darned shy. If we could just get her out of her shell." Rosalie stared up the hill after Nora's retreating form.

"If Del couldn't do it, what makes you think we can?" Betty asked.

Mary's head snapped around. "Who's Del?"

"Oh, he's a guy who's sweet on her."

"She has a boyfriend?" Mary worked to keep the disappointment out of her voice.

Both girls laughed simultaneously. "Heavens, no. She says she doesn't have time for… What did she call them?" Betty asked.

"Entanglements," Rosalie said.

"That's it. Entanglements. Honestly, that girl is more interested in the fictional worlds she reads about than she is in real life."

Mary let out a breath she didn't realize she'd been holding. Nora was single. "Where is she going?"

"Home. Lucky stiff got sprung from the dorm and got a brand-new Flat Top all to herself."

"It's a sweet place too."

"I bet," Mary said. Nora had lived in the same dorm as her and she hadn't even known it.

"Say, why don't you come dancing with us tonight?" Rosalie asked.

"Me? Sure."

"Okay. We'll meet out here at eight o'clock."

"Great, and thanks for including me." Deep in thought, Mary barely remembered to wave goodbye.

Nora had no boyfriend or husband. She lived alone in a Flat Top up the hill somewhere, loved to read, and was painfully shy. She also was beautiful and had a lovely laugh. *Nice to know something about you, Dr. Nora Lindstrom.* The problem was, those bits of information only made Mary hungry for more.

❧❧

I will not look back. I will not look back. I will not look back.
Nora lengthened her strides. Her breath appeared as puffs of condensation in the cold afternoon air. Behind her, down the hill, she imagined Mary's eyes following her movements. Even at this distance and without being able to see her, she blushed crimson. What was it about that girl that made Nora feel like an awkward teenager?

Pull yourself together. She's no different than the thousands of other girls here. But Mary *was* different. It wasn't that she physically reminded her of Anna—she didn't. But she had the same kind of confidence, carefree air, and self-possession. Nora often found herself detouring to walk through Beta-2 even when she didn't have to, just to catch a glimpse of her. She'd memorized Mary's mannerisms, including the way she unconsciously played with one of the curls at the nape of her neck as she focused on the dials and knobs in front of her.

Nora threw open the front door with more force than she'd intended. What she needed was to sit with her journal, listen to the news on the radio, and read the new novel she'd picked up at the library, *A Tree Grows in Brooklyn*. She closed the curtains, retrieved the journal from its hiding place in her suitcase underneath the bed, and settled down on the couch.

On the radio, Edward R. Murrow delivered a report from Berlin. Nora turned up the volume as he described a British Royal Air Force nighttime bombing raid. He'd been allowed to ride along with the bombers. Nora wondered whether he was brave, or a fool. Either way, she was grateful for a firsthand account. "Men die in the sky while others are roasted alive in their cellars. Berlin last night wasn't a pretty sight."

Nora sighed heavily. She imagined war was never a pretty sight. She snapped off the radio and picked up a pen.

Dearest Diary,
What a day! The difficulties at work persist with faulty equipment to blame, I fear. I do hope we get to the bottom of this, and soon. That's all I feel comfortable saying about that.
As for life here on the Reservation, I ran into Rosalie and Betty today on my way home. It was wonderful to see them. It's been far

too long, and they gave me an earful about that! They want me to come dancing with them later. Can you imagine? I have two left feet and no social skills, and they want me to come dancing. What could they be thinking? At any rate, it's ridiculous, of course. But perhaps I could go and watch them cut a rug for a minute or five. It would be something to break up the monotony. Besides, they won't let me hear the end of it until I agree to do something other than spend my time keeping my own company.

All right, dear diary. If I'm going to accommodate my friends, I'd better fix myself some supper, indulge in a chapter of this engrossing book I started reading last night, and find something to wear.

Ever faithfully yours, dearest diary,

Nora

The dance floor teemed with sweaty bodies—men in uniform, men in civilian clothes, and women of every shape and size. Some of the women, who far outnumbered the men, danced with each other.

Mary shouted to be heard over the music blaring from the jukebox. "Are these dances always this crowded?"

"No," Rosalie answered. "They're usually far more crowded than this."

Mary's mouth formed an "O."

"C'mon. I love this song. Dance with me!" Betty grabbed Rosalie's hand and the two of them disappeared in the crowd.

A handsome MP materialized out of the throng. "Wanna dance?"

Before Mary knew it, they were swallowed up and surrounded by gyrating hips and swinging elbows.

"What's your name?"

"Mary. What's yours?"

"Bill."

"Nice to meet you, Bill."

He took her hand and swung her around. The room spun. "I don't have much experience at dancing," she shouted.

"That's okay. Just relax and go with the momentum."

Mary tried to do as he said, but she was having trouble keeping up. He turned her in one direction, then looped her around the other way. By the time the song ended, she wondered if her shoulder was still in its socket.

"Thanks," she said.

"Wait. We're not done yet," he answered, as another song played.

"Oh, I think I am." She withdrew her hand and retreated to the sidelines.

"He's a good-looking guy," Betty said. She and Rosalie joined Mary in line for a Coca-Cola.

"I guess."

"Hey." Rosalie jabbed Betty in the arm. "I can't believe it. Look what the cat dragged in." She pointed toward the door.

"You're kidding me. I never thought she'd show."

Mary followed their sightline. She stood on her tiptoes to see over the crowd. Her breath caught as she glimpsed Nora standing just inside the entrance to the hall. It never occurred to her that Nora might be here; the girls said she'd turned them down.

Rosalie waved wildly.

Nora nodded in recognition and arrived a few moments later.

"Hi," she said.

Betty pinched her on the arm.

"Ow. What was that for?"

"I needed to be sure it wasn't a mirage. You're actually here."

"Very funny." Nora glanced around nervously, and Mary thought she might bolt.

"Hello," she said, and Nora turned in her direction. She smiled, revealing straight, white teeth, and Mary blinked. *Stunning.* She wore her hair swept up off her face, accentuating her high cheekbones. The blue of her dress matched the exact shade of her eyes.

"Hi. I see you're awake this time."

"Day shift this week."

"Since you're here, you must dance." Rosalie nudged Nora toward the dance floor.

"But, I have no idea how to dance."

"I'll teach you."

Whatever Nora answered, it was lost in the beat of the music.

"Let's go," Betty said, pulling Mary along with her.

They danced three or four songs; Mary lost count. For the first time in a long time, she was having fun. Every now and again, she caught a glimpse of Nora, her expression a mix of embarrassment and concentration as Rosalie taught her the steps.

"This is the East Coast Swing," Betty screamed in Mary's ear. "Triple step, triple step, rock step, rock step."

Mary twice turned in the wrong direction before she finally caught on. Once she did, they fell into an easy rhythm.

"Hey, you're a quick study. I like that."

The song ended, and Rosalie tapped them both on the arm. She mouthed, "Let's get some air. It's so stuffy in here."

The four of them spilled out into the night, and, as if by silent agreement, turned toward home.

"That was a blast!" Betty mopped her brow.

"It sure was," Rosalie agreed. "How about you, tall, fair, and shy?" She bumped hips with Nora. "Admit it, you had a good time."

Nora's cheeks stained red.

"Well? You did, didn't you? You are honor-bound to tell the truth."

Reluctantly, Nora nodded. "I confess, I had more fun than I thought I would."

"Ha! I told you so."

"That doesn't mean I'm going to let you drag me to these things on a regular basis."

"No, of course not," Betty teased. "You'd rather have your head stuck in a book."

"There's nothing wrong with loving to read."

"I know. But a good book won't keep you warm at night, if you know what I mean." Rosalie winked.

If possible, Nora's face turned a darker shade of red, visible under the streetlight. "Some of us aren't as boy-crazy as you are. Speaking of which, what happened to what's-his-name?"

Rosalie sighed. "What's-his-name turned out to have a girlfriend back home he conveniently neglected to tell me about."

"Ouch," Betty said.

"That's awful," Mary said.

"What about you, Mary? Do you have a fella?"

Mary's pulse accelerated as all eyes turned to her. Nora's gaze nearly burned a hole through her. "I... I had a boyfriend back home. His name was Sam and he worked as an apprentice to a watchmaker."

"Had? As in, past tense?" Betty asked.

"Yes." Mary fidgeted under the intensity of Nora's scrutiny.

"Well, details, girl." Rosalie pushed.

Mary wished they would drop it.

"Don't leave us hanging. He made a good, steady living, right?"

"Yes."

"He was good looking?"

"Very."

"What happened?" Rosalie prompted impatiently. "Getting information out of you is harder than figuring out what the heck it is we're all really doing here."

"He wanted to get married." Nora's expression held surprise and disappointment. Or maybe Mary was reading something into it that wasn't there at all; she couldn't be sure.

"And?" Nora asked it so quietly, Mary wasn't sure she'd heard her correctly.

"I-I didn't want what he wanted."

"What did you want?"

Mary searched Nora's face. *Why is it so important to me that you believe I don't miss or need Sam?* She furrowed her brow. *Choose your words carefully, Mary Elizabeth.* "I wanted to be in love—to really be in love. I never felt about Sam the way I thought being head-over-heels should feel." *I expected to get lost in his eyes the way I get lost in yours.* Mary swallowed a gasp.

"Here, I've been trying to find a fella to spoil me and provide for our family. I figure if he does that, I'll learn to love him," Betty said.

"And it wouldn't hurt if he was Clark Gable-handsome, either," Rosalie added.

Nora remained stoic, her expression unreadable. They arrived in front of the dorm.

"You want us to walk you home, Nora?"

"No, thanks. I can make it fine on my own."

"That's the refrain of your life, Yankee." Rosalie kissed her on the cheek. "I'm proud of you for coming tonight. I know that wasn't easy for you, and I want you to know we appreciate it. Don't we, girls?"

"We do," Betty and Mary said in unison.

Nora waved and strode up the hill as the three girls watched after her.

"I can't believe she really came."

"You owe me a buck." Rosalie held out her hand to Betty.

"C'mon, that was a friendly wager."

"A bet's a bet."

"You two bet on whether or not Nora would come to the dance tonight?" Mary asked.

"We did. This is probably the hundredth time we've asked her to join us," Betty said.

"But the first time she's ever taken us up on it. Pay up."

Betty dug in her purse and pulled out a dollar bill.

"Thank you very much." Rosalie snatched it from her.

"I can't believe you two." Mary led the way into the building. "I've got to get some shuteye. I'm exhausted."

"We're glad you came with us," Betty said. "You're fun."

"Thanks. You two sure know how to show a girl a good time." Mary bit her lip. These were Nora's good friends. Where they went, maybe Nora would go too. "Maybe we could do it again sometime?"

"You bet."

"Okay, then. Great." Mary pointed down the hall. "That's me, second door down on the left." She started toward her room, and then turned around. "Thanks again for inviting me."

"You're welcome," Rosalie said. "It isn't everyone who passes the Nora test."

"The Nora test?"

"She means that with most strangers, Nora gets so uncomfortable that she heads for the hills at the first opportunity. She must've really liked you. She stuck around."

"Huh." Mary smiled. "Goodnight."

"Goodnight."

Once she was inside her room with the door closed, she twirled around and flopped onto the bed. *I passed the Nora test.* The thought made her unaccountably happy. *Maybe I'll see her on the floor tomorrow and I can thank her for coming out tonight.* She frowned.

Don't be silly, Mary Elizabeth. She never even acknowledges that you exist at Beta-2 beyond checking your work.

Still, the notion that she might be in proximity to Nora again so soon made her heart flutter happily. *See you tomorrow—maybe—Nora Lindstrom.*

CHAPTER FOURTEEN

Nora, Del, and Chauncey Starr, Y-12 operations manager and Dr. Lawrence's liaison, sat around a conference table in the administration building on the campus. They'd gone around and around on the issue of whether or not they could afford the time necessary to send the coils from the giant magnets back to the manufacturer, Allis-Chalmers, for cleaning and repairs.

"I'm telling you, if we shut Alpha-1 down now, we'll be so far behind the eight ball we might as well hand a win to Hitler, because the Germans surely will beat us to the finish line." Chauncey's face was nearly purple with anger.

Nora gripped the edge of the table to keep her hands from shaking and gritted her teeth. *I am not going to give in. I'm right. I know I am.* Still, she was treading a fine line. Technically, she had no say here, since the issue only tangentially involved her cubicle operators. Del shot her a warning glance that she studiously ignored.

"And I'm telling you, my girls can only do so much. If we don't take this step now and shut that operation down so that the coils can be properly cleaned, we'll never get the level of production we need out of that plant."

"Stand down, both of you." General Groves swept into the room, followed closely by Dr. Lawrence.

"Sir." Nora, Del, and Chauncey stood simultaneously.

"Sit, sit." Groves threw down a thick manila folder, and the papers within cascaded out onto the scarred wood. He took a seat at the end of the table. Dr. Lawrence pulled up the chair to his right.

"Dr. Lawrence and I have gone over all of these incident reports you've compiled." He indicated the now-messy pile of documents.

Dr. Lawrence picked up the conversation thread. "We've looked at this every which way. We've tried the minimally invasive approach, but the truth is, we believe the coils are shorting out because of rust and sediment in the cooling oil."

General Groves leaned forward and planted his elbows on the table. "The only cure for that is to remove the coils and send them back to Allis-Chalmers."

Chauncey's lips formed a thin line. Nora was tempted to say she told him so, but there was too much at stake to gloat over a situation that could be catastrophic to the war effort.

"I'm hereby shutting down Alpha-1 until Allis-Chalmers gets this resolved and sends the coils back, fully cleaned and contamination-free," Groves announced.

Starr opened his mouth to say something, but Dr. Lawrence put a hand on his arm to restrain him.

"I understand what a hardship this is," General Groves continued. "It will be more important than ever to ensure that we account for the factors that are bedeviling Alpha-1 and make damn sure they aren't repeated in the racetracks coming on line now. I don't have to tell you, today is December 15, 1943. The Germans are hard at work trying to do the same thing we're doing. For all we know, they're ahead of us. Bringing those other buildings up to speed and operating smoothly is our top priority."

He turned his piercing gaze on Nora and she struggled to maintain eye contact. *This is no time to be a shrinking violet. You represent all those hard-working girls who're being maligned on a daily basis by others who try to shift blame.*

"You're confident these young girls can handle what's ahead? We don't have time for histrionics; we need results."

"Yes, sir. These girls are dedicated and determined. They're learning to problem-solve as they go. We're up to the task."

"Good." He turned to Chauncey. "The chemists, the engineers, and the rest of your boys, they're capable?"

"Yes, sir."

"All right, then. You've got your marching orders. Squeeze as much production as you can out of those racetracks that are on line or coming on line, keep downtime to a minimum whenever possible, and remember that we're all on the same team. If one of us fails, we all fail. Am I understood?"

"Yes, sir," Nora, Chauncey, and Del said in unison.

The general gathered his papers and he and Lawrence departed without saying another word. Nora slumped back in her chair as the tension of the moment dissipated.

"Listen," Del said, "Groves is right. We have to find a way to optimize Alphas 2 and 3 and Beta-2. Nora, I know your girls are working around the clock, and you're doing a great job with them." He smiled kindly at her. "Chauncey, I know you've got your boys working overtime trying to adapt the equipment and implement the new designs to compensate for the failures. We've all got to keep communicating and problem-solving as a team. Dr. Lawrence and the general are counting on us. They've put a lot of faith in us and we need to prove we've earned that faith."

Chauncey rose. "I'll do my part, and so will my boys—that means raising and maximizing production levels. You do your part." He pointed his finger at Nora. "Keep those girls from making mistakes, and everything will be as good as it can be."

Nora went through the motions of putting food on her tray. She selected an apple, a banana, and a cup of whatever the mystery soup of the day was. In truth, she had no appetite. This whole mess with the Alpha-1 work stoppage and the lack of productivity turned her stomach.

What if Chauncey was right? What if the Germans *had* gotten the jump on them? What if, right now, they were creating enough U-235…Tubealloy… She admonished herself and shook her head to clear it. Even in her thoughts, she should avoid using forbidden terminology. *Forget about what the Germans are doing. You can't control that. Focus on what's in front of you.*

It wasn't peak lunch hour, so she was able to procure a table to herself over in the corner. When she was settled, she set down the attaché case she carried over her shoulder, withdrew a folder and opened it. She reviewed the roster of cubicle operators. She would have to shift the operators from Alpha-1 over to Alpha-3 as soon as it was up and running. If the modifications to the magnets in the newer racetracks worked, things should start to go much more smoothly, with fewer glitches and greater production. Whenever Alpha-1 came back on line...

Nora paused to take stock of the room. It felt as though someone was watching at her. *You're losing your mind.* She refocused on the paperwork in front of her. Several moments later, when the feeling hadn't dissipated, she scanned the room again. This time, her eyes settled on Mary. Although she averted her gaze, Nora could've sworn that she'd been staring a second ago. *Reading people isn't your strong suit. Stick to what you know.*

She focused once again on her work and made a notation in the margin to talk to Jane Greer about the output calculations. She'd met Jane for the first time the other day and they'd clicked immediately. Jane had wanted to be an engineer, but she'd been told that wasn't an appropriate career for a woman. Instead she turned to statistics and became the first woman to graduate with a degree in statistics from the University of Tennessee. In terms of their experiences as women in male-dominated fields, they had a lot in common. Now, Jane was in charge of all statistical analysis and documentation for the project. She had the same clearance as Nora—the only other woman ranked so highly—and thus they were able to converse in ways Nora couldn't with any other females on the Reservation.

It wasn't Nora's purview to keep up with the data on the amount of Tubealloy produced—not directly, anyway. Still, how was Nora supposed to measure whether her girls' efforts were succeeding if she couldn't know whether the amount of material collected matched expectations? *That's foolish. You know full well that you haven't come close to hitting the necessary quantities.* But how much was needed? And what if she was wrong altogether in her assumptions about what they were doing here and why? *You're not wrong. You're a physicist. We're enriching uran...Tubealloy. How else are you to interpret the end goal? With a sufficiently large quantity of enriched material, presumably the chain reaction would be powerful enough to...* Nora's eyes popped open wide. To do what? Annihilate an entire people?

"Excuse me. Hi."

Nora's head shot up. Mary stood directly in front of her, looking pretty as a peach. Quickly, she shoved the papers back in the folder and tucked them in the attaché case.

"I hate to interrupt what I expect is a fascinating conversation for one." She smiled tentatively. "But you look positively awful. You're terribly thin, and that furrow in your brow doesn't suit you at all, and..."

Nora blinked. "Did you come over here to insult me?"

"What?" Mary took a step back. "No, not at all." She pulled out a chair and sat down, uninvited. "You haven't touched your lunch, and you're clearly distracted. I simply wanted to help. Sometimes a friendly face can make all the difference in the world."

"I'm sure you mean well, but I'm perfectly fine."

"No, you're not. That much is clear."

Nora frowned. The impudence! Who did this girl think she was?

"Come to another dance with me. It'll do you good to cut loose a little."

Nora's pulse quickened at the idea of spending time with Mary. She'd watched her surreptitiously the other night, dancing with Betty. She'd been jealous that Mary'd been smiling and laughing and having a good time with her friend. Jealous! What did she have to be jealous about? They were all friends out having a good time. "I-I can't. I've got too much to do, and besides, I'm not a very social person."

Mary leaned in closer, and Nora sat back as far as she could in her chair. "Well, you should be. You can't work all the time. I'm really worried about you. Please? Come dancing with me tonight. It's my last day on first shift until Christmas, so it's my only free night."

She looked so hopeful. "I'm sorry. I'm sure you can find someone else to keep you company." Even as she said it, the idea of Mary out on the town with someone else nauseated her. She closed her eyes.

"I apologize for bothering you." Mary's face was crestfallen and her voice quavered. She pushed her chair back deliberately and took her leave.

Nora stared after her. Mary was unlike anyone she'd ever met—vibrant, confident bordering on brash, and alluring. *Alluring?* Where had that come from? *Maybe you really are working too hard.*

She cleared her place. She would run over to the Pilot Facility and find Jane. Jane certainly didn't make her feel the way Mary did. She would find safe, nice, reliable Jane and talk numbers. Yes, that's exactly what she would do.

⋞⋟

Nora propped her pillow against the wall and sat up in bed. She opened the journal to a fresh page and sat with her pen poised for a long time before she began her entry.

Dearest Diary,

I'm not really sure where to start. My feelings are a jumbled mess. Perhaps it's the stress from work, which is enormous, but somehow, I don't think that's it. As much as I'm loathe to admit this, even in the privacy of these pages, it's about a girl, and it's not Anna. Her name is Mary.

What can I say about her? She's petite and pretty as can be, self-possessed (especially for one so young), outgoing, and effervescent. In other words, she's my opposite in nearly every way. Still, there's something magnetic about our connection, and I sense that's true not only for me, but for her too. When I'm near her, I experience this queer feeling in my body, unlike anything I've known before.

With a word or a glance, she flusters me, leaving me floundering and tongue-tied. I've had crushes before, dearest diary (at least that's how I would categorize them), but nothing compares to what I feel when her eye catches mine. It's as though I'm rooted to the spot, without the slightest desire to move. I find myself lost in the depths of her gaze.

I know I'm prattling on, dear diary. I wish I felt an eighth for Del, who makes his interest plain even in his restraint, what I feel for Mary. Why must I feel this way about a girl? And what I am supposed to do about it? Nothing, that's what.

Now, I'm answering my own questions. Truly, I've gone stark-raving mad. Time to lose myself in a good book, dear diary. More soon.

Ever faithfully yours,
Nora

CHAPTER FIFTEEN

Christmas Day dawned sunny and crisp, which should have made Mary happy. Instead, she moped through the morning, bemoaned the fact that she had no presents to open, and ignored the carolers crooning, "Hark, the Herald Angels Sing" outside her dorm room window. In the distance, she heard the bells of the brand-new, non-denominational, Chapel-on-the-Hill. Church never had held much appeal for her, but perhaps she should consider attending the noon service, if only to pray for her father's safe return.

She hadn't gotten a letter from him in weeks, and the memory of Phyllis and her mom crying inconsolably on the sidewalk played like a bad movie in her mind's eye. *You have to be okay, Daddy. You just have to be.* She should call her mother and wish her a Merry Christmas, she knew. But every call ended in an argument and her mother insisting that she'd gone daft for "running away," as she termed Mary's departure. Maybe she had run away, but surely her mother could show more gratitude for the money Mary sent home on a regular basis. It was far more than she ever could've earned at Meyer's—enough to ensure her mother's comfort until her father returned home.

She dragged herself to the phone in the lobby and made a collect call home.

"Hello?"

"Hello, Mother. It's Mary. I-I just wanted to say Merry Christmas." She closed her eyes and gripped the receiver tightly. She hadn't expected to get emotional. "Mother? I miss you."

"Merry Christmas, Mary Elizabeth."

"Is everything okay?" *You sound so frail.*

"I'm lonely, I guess. My husband is away at war, and my only daughter has run off God-only-knows where, to do God-only-knows-what..."

"I've told you before. I'm in Tennessee, working for the war effort." *You had to ruin the moment, didn't you? I will not feel guilty, I will not feel guilty...*

"So you've said. Frankly, I find your evasiveness highly suspicious, young lady. You're not pregnant, are you?"

"W-what?" Mary fumbled the receiver. She put it back to her ear. "What in the world would make you ask such a thing? And what kind of girl do you think I am?"

"I don't know. You disappear suddenly; you won't say exactly where you are or what you're doing; you won't say when, if ever, you're coming home; you abandon your mother at a time when she needs you... It's as if you're covering something up. What else am I supposed to think?"

"You're supposed to think I'm a morally upstanding, independent, capable young woman who takes time to call her mother, sends home a regular paycheck, and is doing her country proud. That's what you're supposed to think. Merry Christmas, Mother." Mary hung up the phone without waiting for her mother's reply. A sob escaped from her lips. How could she think and say such awful things?

"Is everything all right?" Betty stood several feet away.

Mary sniffed. "Y-yes."

"Homesick?"

"I was... Until I talked to my mother."

"I understand how that goes," Betty sympathized. "Why don't you come to services with us? Rosalie will be down in a minute."

"I don't know. I'm not much in the mood."

"Well, suit yourself. Merry Christmas."

"Merry Christmas." Mary returned to her room, flopped onto the bed, and stared at the ceiling. Why did everything with her mother have to be so darned contentious? And why did her mother always think the worst of her? She'd never done anything wild or crazy. Perhaps refusing to marry Sam made her seem a bit willful, but she had legitimate reasons for her decision.

Shake it off, Mary Elizabeth. Stop singing the blues and make the most of the day. Idly, she wondered what Nora was doing today.

Was she working, even on the holiday? Had she gone home to be with family, as some of the other girls had? Betty and Rosalie had gone to services. Did Nora go with them? Was she home reading a book? *That's a depressing thought.*

She sat up and gazed out the window. It's a beautiful, sunny day. *Stop being a gloomy Gus and take yourself for a walk.* She changed into a pretty dress to make herself feel better, donned a comfortable pair of saddle shoes, threw on her winter coat, and grabbed her picnic basket. Maybe she could collect some pine cones and make something from them. If she happened to contrive a means to run into Nora along the way, that would be fine too.

Nora never paid much attention to religion growing up. Then, as a college and graduate student, she hadn't had the time to spend several hours in church on a Sunday. Her energy was devoted to her studies, her experiments, and the occasional visit home to see her parents.

But it was Christmas Day, she had nowhere else to be, nothing else to do, and the Alpha-1 situation had her feeling just desperate enough that even she was willing to pray for a Christmas miracle. The Chapel-on-the-Hill was brimming with folks as interested in the fellowship as in the hymns. A kinship born of the circumstances that brought them all to this anonymous town, invisible to the outside world, drew them together like a family of misfits and orphans.

Nora glanced around her at the faces of the worshipers. Some of these men and women she recognized from the bus. She knew dozens of the girls because they were under her supervision. Still others were familiar because she'd seen them around town. Some, however, she'd never seen before. She found herself looking for one face in particular and was disappointed to realize that Mary wasn't there. Either that, or she was hidden from view. *Who are you kidding? She's probably off with someone who didn't stupidly refuse her invitation to go dancing.*

The idea of Mary spending time with someone else depressed her to no end. By the time church let out, Nora felt good and sorry for herself. She started down the hill toward Townsite, with no particular destination in mind. Families filed out and children, no doubt still flush with the memories of presents opened that morning, expelled excess energy by playing tag with one another. Several times, Nora had to sidestep a young one rolling like a log down the hillside.

She hopped to the side to avoid a five-year-old boy as he dove out of reach of the older boy who chased him. As she did so, she bumped into another body. "Oh, my goodness. I'm so sor..." The rest of the phrase died on her lips as she looked down to see Mary, half-sprawled on the ground at her feet, a basket of pine cones spilled beside her. Immediately, she bent to help her up. "I'm so sorry. Are you okay? Did I hurt you?" Gently, Nora lifted her to her feet and brushed her off.

Mary laughed. "Don't look so concerned. I may be small, but I'm not that fragile."

"Good thing." Nora reached down at the same time as Mary to gather the pine cones, and their hands brushed. She withdrew her hand as if it were on fire.

"Better let me get those," Mary said. She winked. "Were you on your way somewhere special?"

"Who, me?"

Mary corralled the last pine cone and returned it to the basket. "There. No harm done." She situated the basket handle back on her arm. "You're the only person I'm talking to, so yes, you."

"I was leaving church."

"So I gathered." Mary glanced in the direction of the building and Nora blushed.

"I guess that was obvious."

Mary laid a hand on her arm, and the touch seared Nora's flesh. "Don't be embarrassed. I asked the question."

"You asked where I was going, not where I'd been."

"Close enough." Mary released her hold. "You look very pretty, by the way. I love your dress."

Nora's blush deepened. "Thank you. You look quite fetching yourself. That coat is pretty."

"Thank you." Mary twirled around. "It's a little something I picked up in Knoxville on my last day off."

"It suits you." Nora bit her lip. "Do you have any special plans later?" Her heart hammered in her chest. *What could she be thinking?*

"As a matter of fact, I don't."

"I'd like to make up for running you over. There's a brand-new movie opening at the theater tonight. It's *Mrs. Miniver* with Greer Garson and Walter Pidgeon. Would you like to go with me?"

"You like the movies?"

Nora laughed. "Don't look so surprised. I adore the movies. I especially can't resist a good war movie. How about you?"

"Are you kidding me? I love the movies! Yes, I'd love to accompany you. What time and where shall we meet?"

"You live in W-1, right?"

Mary's eyes grew large. "You know where I live?"

"Let's see... You were out in front of the dorm talking with Rosalie and Betty. They live in W-1. Then you came to the dance with them. Ergo, I deduce that you must live in W-1."

Mary clapped her hands delightedly. "Very observant. I shall have to be careful not to give away any state secrets with you around."

"So, as I was saying, you live in W-1, which is closer to the theater than my place, so why don't I swing around and get you at, say, six o'clock and we'll walk to the theater together. That way we'll have time to pick up refreshments before the movie starts."

"That sounds perfect. It's a date." Mary winked, waved, and once again was on her way.

Nora stared after her. *It's not a date, it's a movie, isn't it?*

Mary stifled a scream when the Nazi soldier brandished a gun at Mrs. Miniver. Reflexively, she grabbed hold of Nora's hand and squeezed. Nora returned the squeeze. Her hand was soft and warm, her skin smooth and supple. For a moment, Mary forgot all about Mrs. Miniver's dire predicament. She snuck a peek at Nora's profile. Every feature of her face from her intelligent blue-green eyes to her aquiline nose, to her perfectly formed lips, worked together to create a vision of beauty unlike any Mary had ever seen before. *I could look at you like this forever and never get tired of the view.*

Mary swallowed hard. This. *This* was how she expected to feel when she fell in love with someone. This was what she'd never felt for Sam. Mary's breath quickened. *You hardly know this person. Besides, she's a woman. Women don't fall in love with other women.* Maybe she was mistaken. Maybe she was caught up in the heady moment of helping to win the war together. Maybe it was a passing crush.

Belatedly, she realized she hadn't relinquished Nora's hand. Then again, Nora hadn't let go of her hand, either. What did that mean? Was Nora feeling what she was feeling? Was she wondering too?

On screen, the end credits began to roll. Quickly, Mary withdrew her hand. The lights would be coming up any second now. What would happen if someone had seen them holding hands? Then, another thought, equally terrifying, crossed her mind. *What are you going to do if Nora wants to discuss the movie?* Panic welled within her. She hadn't seen or heard a thing after the Nazi in the garden. *You'll look like an idiot. A woman like Nora wouldn't be the least bit interested in someone who can't hold a conversation or talk intelligently about a movie.* Well, it was too late now. It wasn't like she could rewind the last two hours and watch it again. She would have to fudge, that's all there was to it.

"Did you like the movie?" They spilled out of the theater with the rest of the crowd and out into Jackson Square.

There it was. The very question she'd been dreading. "I really did." *Think quickly or you're going to get caught out for not paying attention. Turn the tables on her.* "What was your favorite part?" Mary quickened her pace to keep up with Nora's longer strides.

"I particularly enjoyed the vicar's speech at Carol's funeral."

"Yes, that was really moving." *There, that was no doubt true.* Still, she knew she couldn't keep up the charade for long. Perhaps if she changed the topic... "It's a beautiful night, and it's early yet. Would you like to take a stroll? We could look at the Christmas displays in the store windows."

"Sure. Will you be warm enough?"

"I think so. How about you?"

"I'll be fine." Nora wrapped her coat more tightly around her as they slowed to a more leisurely pace. "Afterward, if you'd like, we could go back to my place and I'll make a pot of coffee. That is, if it's not too late for you."

Mary's pulse quickened. "I'd love that. I told the housemother I'd be out past curfew because of the movie."

"I bet that went over well." Nora rolled her eyes. "I lived in W-1 when I first moved here. That woman has all the personality of a corpse."

She laughed. "Do you know many corpses?"

"No, but I'd bet they don't smile much."

To Mary's delight, Nora imitated the housemother's expression. "Wow. That's spot-on. I'm impressed. Do you make it a habit to study people so closely?"

Nora shrugged. "When you're as introverted as I am, you tend to watch rather than interact. I've been paying attention from the sidelines all my life."

"Really? I think you always should be front and center."

Nora stopped walking and faced her. "Why is that?"

"B-because..." *I can't think straight when you look at me like that.* "Because you're a remarkable woman. What's that old expression? Don't hide your light under a bushel."

"First, I'm too tall for a bushel to hide me, and secondly, I can't imagine what it is you think you see in me. I'm just...me."

"You're a bona fide doctor. There aren't many women doctors that I know of, nor I would guess, many women scientists. That's what you are, isn't it? A scientist?"

"Yes. I have a doctoral degree in Physics from Columbia University."

"See? That, right there, is mighty special. Heck, I don't know that I can even spell the word physics, never mind be an expert in it."

"I'm sure you don't give yourself enough credit. I've seen the way you pick up the nuances of the fluctuations in the unit and how you make adjustments to compensate. You've really got a knack for it."

Mary's head swelled with pride. "You think so? Heck, that's nothing more than dumb luck."

"Nobody's that lucky all the time. You should learn to take a compliment."

"Pot, kettle, Dr. Lindstrom."

"Fair enough." They reached the windows of the A & P store. "Are you ready to head up the hill? My place isn't more than a ten-minute walk from here."

Butterflies took up residence in Mary's stomach. "Sure. Lead the way." For the first time, she was going to be all alone with Nora—no other movie-goers, no fellow diners in the cafeteria, no other cubicle operators—just the two of them. With Sam, Mary tired of having to fend him off, so she mostly avoided being alone with him. At least in public, he had to behave himself. But the idea of being alone with Nora thrilled her. This was all so confusing. Why did she feel the way she did...about a woman? *Because she's the female version of what you've been longing for.* Warmth suffused her body, displacing the cold of the late-December night air.

"...made you want to come to Oak Ridge?"

She frowned. *If you don't quit daydreaming, she's going to think you're a complete snowflake.* "I'm sorry. What did you ask?"

"Never mind. I'm sure I'm boring you."

"What? No! Never! Please, tell me what you asked."

"I asked what brought you to this place? Where are you from?"

"Oh. I'm from Philadelphia, which sounds far more exotic and interesting than it was, believe me."

"That's a good-size city."

"Well, my neighborhood felt more like a small town." Mary proceeded to explain about her job at Meyer's, her father's enlistment, her mother's incessant badgering, and her desperate letter to Louise looking to get away from all of that.

"I see."

Mary hung her head. "I'm sorry. I'm sure that was way more information than you were looking for."

Nora squeezed her hand and released it. "On the contrary, that was the perfect amount of information." She stopped in front of a small Flat Top on Georgia Avenue. "We're here." She opened the door and motioned for Mary to precede her inside.

Her eyes flitted over the space. It wasn't big, but compared to her dorm room, it was a palace.

"I'm sorry. I know it's not much."

162

"Are you kidding?" Mary spun around. "It's perfect, and it's so quiet up here."

"Want a tour?"

"Yes, please."

Nora showed her around the place.

"Your own shower. Oh, my God, that must be heavenly."

"You can't even imagine."

"You're right, I can't." They arrived back in the living room.

"Make yourself comfortable. I'll put the coffee on."

Mary hung her coat on the coatrack inside the front door and walked over to the radio. "Can I put on some music?"

"Sure."

She switched on the radio and found a station playing Glenn Miller's "Moonlight Serenade." She began to sway to the music with her eyes closed. When the song ended, she opened her eyes to find Nora staring at her from a vantage point with her back against the kitchen sink. Mary wasn't sure anyone had ever looked at her the way Nora looked at her right now. The intensity of it made her mouth go dry. *I want to kiss you, but I know I shouldn't. I mean, it's wrong, right?*

The music transitioned to a Frank Sinatra ballad, and Mary beckoned Nora to join her.

"I-I don't know how to dance."

"That's okay. It's just the two of us, and you only have to know how to sway."

Tentatively, slowly, Nora bridged the distance between them. She placed her hand in Mary's and allowed Mary to take her other hand and place it around her waist.

Mary breathed in the scent of her shampoo, and a light floral scent she couldn't quite identify. She rested her cheek on Nora's collarbone and moved in closer. The moment their bodies touched, she felt an explosion inside—a quivering in her lower abdomen that was completely new to her—and a tingling sensation throughout her lower limbs and chest.

Nora's heart galloped next to her ear, and puffs of air caressed the top of her head.

"You're doing great," she murmured into the cotton of Nora's dress. She got no reply, but she didn't need one; she knew everything she needed to know by the beating of Nora's heart. She wasn't the only one feeling things she shouldn't.

The last notes of the song faded away, and their bodies stilled. Finally, Mary said, "I think I'll take that coffee now."

"Right." Nora backed away and tucked a strand of loose hair behind her left ear.

Mary noted that her hands were shaking. She memorized the way Nora moved as she walked into the kitchen; her eyes trailed down Nora's back to her buttocks as she reached for two cups from the cupboard and poured the coffee. Unable to stop herself, she came up behind her and ran her hands along Nora's sides. When Nora turned, her face was flushed, and her lips were parted.

Mary traced Nora's lips with her fingers. Her eyes opened wider, but she made no move to stop her. That was all the invitation required. *If this is wrong, I don't want to be right.* Mary pushed up on tiptoes, wrapped her fingers in luxurious blond locks, and pulled Nora's mouth down to meet hers.

"Wait. I'm not sure…"

Mary persisted, and any resistance fell away.

Nora's lips were soft and tasted sweet, like strawberry pie. She pushed further, wanting more, and Nora responded in kind. When their tongues collided, it was like fireworks on the Fourth of July. They melted together, their mouths moving in perfect, breathless synchrony. *How can something so wrong feel this good?*

She lost all track of time, for in this moment, in this place, time ceased to exist. Vaguely, she was aware of the two of them gliding across the floor and into the bedroom, their hands and bodies moving of their own volition. "Wait!"

Nora blinked and stepped back. "You're right. This is… I'm not sure what this is, honestly."

Mary bit her lip. In the past, when she'd envisioned losing her virginity, it scared her. Now… "I'm not sure what it is, either. I only know that I want this, whatever this is. I really, really want this." She moved back into Nora's embrace, and with a shaky hand, ran her fingers over sensitive skin.

Nora gasped and closed her eyes. "God help me, I want this too."

"I don't know what to do; I've never done this before."

"I don't either. Are you certain this is what you want?" Nora's eyes searched hers.

"I'm more certain of this than my own name."

"Okay, then. We'll learn together." Nora's fingers trembled as she unzipped Mary's dress and slid it off her shoulders.

Mary held Nora's gaze as she stepped out of her shoes, slip, and hose. Then she undressed Nora and the two of them tumbled onto the bed.

The cold sheets felt wonderful on her overheated skin. Then other things felt wonderful—otherworldly—and so very, very right.

"Mary?"

"Hmm?"

"Mary?" Long fingers traveled the length of her naked body as she rose back to the surface. Her eyes popped open to be greeted by a marvelously disheveled and equally unclothed Nora. "It's getting late. We've got to get you home before the housemother screams bloody murder."

"Mmm." She stretched languorously. "What time is it?"

"Eleven o'clock."

She sat bolt upright. "Eleven?"

"Yes."

"Oh, my God." Hurriedly, and with Nora's help in finding all her various layers, she dressed and applied new lipstick. "Do I look any different?"

"Any different than what?" Nora, now also fully clothed, leaned against the door frame.

"You know what I mean. I do look like we…" Mary bit her lip and then blurted out, "Do I look like I just lost my virginity?"

"I don't know how that's supposed to make someone look, but I can tell you that you look beautiful."

"Sweet talker." She shrugged into her coat, snatched up her purse, and ran for the door. Nora hadn't moved, so she backtracked to her. "I…" She searched Nora's face. Her eyes still smoldered, and her lips were bruised from their kisses. All she wanted was to take her back to bed. "Thank you for the most amazing Christmas ever."

"I could say the same."

Mary took two steps away and came back again. This time she kissed her thoroughly. "That was a first I'll never, ever forget."

"Me too." This time, Nora followed her to the door. "Should I come with you? Make sure you get home all right?"

"Yes. No. If you do, I'll do something I shouldn't in public and we'll both be in the soup. I'll be fine."

Nora opened the door for her.

"Will I see you tomorrow?"

"Probably. I'll be doing my normal walk-throughs."

"I didn't mean on the job."

"I know. You'd better get going."

"Nora?" Panic made her heart race. "I will see you again like this, won't I?"

In response, Nora leaned down and kissed her tenderly.

"I wish I didn't have to go."

"Me too. But the reality is that you do. Be safe."

"Dream of me."

"Of that, I have no doubt."

CHAPTER SIXTEEN

S ix strides from the living room windows to the wall with the radio, six strides back. Nora knew this because she'd been wearing out the floor from one direction to the other for the better part of an hour. Finally, she sat on the couch. Less than a minute later, she jumped up again to pace to-and-fro. "What could you possibly have been thinking?" She gesticulated wildly while berating herself. "What possessed you? She works for you—under your supervision. Do you have any idea how bad that looks? Did you think about the impropriety? No? Let's not even talk about the perception. And what if someone catches you looking at her like she's your next meal? What then?"

She plopped down on the couch again and lowered her head into her hands. She was certain it had to be the lack of sleep talking. After Mary left, she'd poured out the burnt coffee and cleaned the percolator. She'd lain down and prayed for sleep, but it would not take her. Instead, she tossed and turned for hours, reliving their time together, remembering the way Mary's back arched as she...

Nora popped up yet again. This time, she flipped on the radio to distract herself with the news. That proved to be another bad decision, since the first sounds she heard were the strains of Glenn Miller and his Orchestra. There was Mary, standing in the very spot Nora now occupied, swaying to the music and looking more sensuous than any pin-up model.

She turned the dial and tuned in the CBS Network. Perhaps she wasn't too late to hear Edward R. Murrow reporting from Berlin, or Eric Sevareid reporting from London or Washington.

Her mind strayed to Mary, sitting at her cubicle, her face a mask of concentration, assuming anyone could concentrate the night after Christmas. She checked her watch. It was almost eleven o'clock. Mary would be getting off work right about now. *Did you get any sleep when you went back to your room? Or did you lie awake wondering what just happened, as I did? Are you as confused as I am?*

In truth, she hadn't gotten a wink of sleep last night. Mary's scent lingered on the sheets and pillowcases, permeated her nostrils, and bedeviled her no matter which way she turned. Images of their evening together played like a movie every time she closed her eyes. Mary, her eyes open wide in fear when the Nazi took Mrs. Miniver hostage. Mary's hand gripping hers in the theater. Mary, her head thrown back in passion. Mary, so uncertain where she stood when they parted.

Nora knew she'd been less than fully encouraging as she ushered her out the door. But what else could she do or say? This was uncharted territory. She needed time to process her emotions—time to understand what all this meant and what to do about it. It wouldn't be fair to make promises she wasn't certain she could keep, would it?

You're making excuses for behaving badly because you're scared. That girl gave herself to you last night. Yes, it was your first time, but it was hers too, and she's a lot younger than you. She's frightened and questioning, just like you. How would you feel in her place?

She frowned. Had she been too dispassionate today on the control room floor when she'd passed Mary's cubicle without so much as a glance in her direction? No. Work was work. If they had any chance to have a relationship, they would have to compartmentalize. Nora absolutely could not play favorites on the job, nor acknowledge anything beyond a supervisor-subordinate role. Mary simply would have to accept that.

She nodded, satisfied that the parameters and boundaries were firmly set in her mind. She switched off the radio and turned off the lights. Tonight, she would get some much-needed sleep.

❦

Mary checked the area around the grove of large trees to the left of the entrance to The-Chapel-on-the-Hill for the fourth time.

"What are you doing?"

She yelped and put her hand to her heart. "Oh, my goodness. You scared me to death."

"You asked to meet here, so I assumed you were expecting me," Nora said practically.

"I was. But you can't sneak up on a girl like that."

"I wasn't sneaking. I walked right up. If you hadn't been so busy checking for spies, or whatever it is you're up to, you'd have seen me coming."

"I wanted to be sure we were alone."

Nora gave an exaggerated glance over each shoulder and stage-whispered, "I think we're alone."

"That's not funny, Nora Lindstrom. I'm being serious here."

"I'm sorry. If I had been suspicious, the way you were skulking around would've made me more so than I already was."

She folded her arms across her chest. "You're the one who's been ignoring me because you're afraid people will think something."

"I haven't been ignoring you."

"What do you call what you've been doing? It's been three days, and you haven't so much as glanced my way as you walk past."

"That's because we're working. You're supposed to be monitoring the D unit, and I'm supposed to be supervising. That's why we're here."

"You don't need to lecture me about my role and yours. I know you're smarter than me and higher ranking."

"What? That's not what I'm saying. I'm simply stating the facts. Work is work. When we're working, you're just like anybody else I supervise. I can't give you special treatment or pay you more attention than I do any of the other girls."

"I know that," she snapped.

"Then I fail to see what it is you're mad about."

"We…" Mary checked their surroundings again and lowered her voice. "We did what we did and you haven't even acknowledged that. I don't know about you, but that was pretty important to me. In fact, it's probably the most important thing that's ever happened in my life." She choked on a sob and angrily wiped at her eyes.

"Hey," Nora said softly. "It was every bit as important to me, okay?" She raised a hand, presumably to wipe away Mary's tears, but let her hand fall away without making contact.

"Don't you love me?"

"Don't I...?"

"In all the time I was dating Sam, I never once felt about him the way I felt about you in the first five minutes we spent together. I always said that when the real thing came along, I'd know it. It's confusing and confounding. I mean, we're two women for gosh sakes. But, we're the real thing, Nora. I can feel it in my heart and in my bones, but if you don't feel the same way..."

Nora sat down under the largest tree and patted the ground next to her.

Reluctantly, Mary sat next to her. *Please, don't break my heart. I don't think I could take it.*

"What transpired between us the other night was incredibly special. I've never experienced anything like it, either, and I'm seven years older than you. I'm just trying to figure out where we go from here. It's complicated—a lot more complicated than whether or not I'm ready to say I love you. And yes, the fact that we're two women makes it even more disconcerting."

"There's nothing complicated about knowing whether you're in love or you're not. It's yes, or it's no."

Nora let out a growl of frustration. "What if I am, Mary? What then? If we ever got caught—"

"We won't get caught."

"You can't know that for sure."

"We'll make sure of it."

Nora shook her head. "Impossible."

"Then, what? We forget about what happened and just go about our lives? I can't do that. I don't want to do that."

Nora stared off into the distance, and Mary was surprised to see that she, too, had tears in her eyes.

"I don't know all the answers, sweet Mary. I've spent three days trying to figure it out, and I've gotten exactly nowhere. When I'm not with you, I'm thinking about you. Does that mean I'm in love with you? I don't have any idea. I have no frame of reference by which to judge. Seems to me it's too early for that sort of proclamation after one date, but what do I know?"

"If you need convincing, go out with me again. New Year's Eve is coming. Let's have another movie date. That should be harmless enough. Friends go to the movies together all the time. I already checked. *Destination Tokyo* opens that night. It's Cary Grant and it's a war movie. What do you say? Please? Give us a chance, Nora. Please say you'll at least give us a chance."

Nora closed her eyes and pinched the bridge of her nose. She let out a heavy sigh. "How am I supposed to say no to you?"

"That's easy. You're not. So, you'll go? It's a date?"

"Okay. We'll go to the movie and I'll make us dinner at my place afterward."

"Yay! I promise, you won't regret it."

Nora flinched as the downed Japanese pilot stabbed seaman Mike to death. She snuck a peek at Mary and easily read the horror in her eyes, as well. That reaction was magnified tenfold after the American submarine came into peril, first from the unexploded bomb attached to it, and then when the Japanese discovered the sub's presence and searched Tokyo Bay for it.

Several times, she caught Mary reaching for her hand but then she withdrew it and grabbed the seat arms with a death grip. Misery enveloped Nora. *You're an insensitive jerk.*

When Mary gasped as the sub was crippled in the attack by the Japanese aircraft carrier escort, Nora couldn't stand it anymore. She eased Mary's grip on the seat arm, slid her hand underneath, and intertwined their fingers. A frisson of excitement coursed through her, reaching directly to her core. It felt so right. How could anyone think this was wrong?

The audience stood and applauded as the USS *Copperfin* cruised safely into San Francisco Bay, and Nora and Mary cheered along with them. Even after they reached the street, people continued to buzz about the film.

Nora and Mary left the crowd behind and climbed the hill to 105 Georgia Avenue. "Did you enjoy the movie?"

Mary pulled her winter coat tighter around her narrow waist. "I'm not sure *enjoy* is a word I'd use. Do you think the Japs will reach the U.S.? The movie made it seem so real. I mean, I guess I don't want to think about the fact that it could come true. After all, they bombed Pearl Harbor, and we didn't think they could do that."

Nora expelled a breath, releasing a puff of moisture into the air. She wished she could share her own fears with Mary, along with her supposition about what exactly they were creating at Y-12.

They passed the billboard that read, "Who Me? Yes You... Keep Mum About This Job." It was a grim reminder about the absolute need for secrecy. Three times this month she'd heard about people disappearing because they blabbed or speculated about what they were really working on. Then there were the rumors of disguised counterintelligence agents living among them. No, she couldn't say a word. Even if no one overheard them, it would jeopardize Mary if she knew too much and inadvertently said the wrong thing to the wrong person.

"I suppose anything is possible, but I don't think it will come to that. I trust Roosevelt and Churchill. I believe we'll get to them before they get to us."

"I wish I had your faith."

They walked along in companionable silence for a little while. "Have you gotten word from your father? I know you said you hadn't heard from him for a while."

Mary shook her head. "No, and I'm getting really worried."

"How often do you normally hear from him?"

"At least once or twice a month."

They went inside the house and hung up their coats. "What does your mother say?"

"She hasn't heard anything either, which is even more alarming."

"I'm sorry. I'll keep praying for his safety."

"Thank you. I didn't know you were religious."

"I'm not. That doesn't mean I don't have faith. They're not the same thing."

"I guess I never thought about it that way." Mary moved closer. "You know what I have thought about?"

For a moment, Nora was so captivated by her face she forgot to answer. "What?"

"This." Mary ran her hands underneath Nora's sweater and claimed her mouth.

Every cell in Nora's body responded at once. Several times, her brain reminded her that she needed to turn on the stove or they'd never get to the dinner part of the date. Finally, she pulled away long enough to say, "If we don't stop now, dinner will be ruined."

"I don't care."

Mary took a step forward, and Nora took another step back.

"I waited in line for hours to get pork chops. I wanted this meal to be special."

"Okay." Once more, she closed the space between them. "If food is more important to you than…"

Nora stilled her wandering hands. "How about if we compromise and have dinner first, and then dessert later?" She waggled her eyebrows.

"I suppose." Mary sighed and sashayed over to the couch. "I'll just have to enjoy the view, I guess."

Nora tried to act less flustered than she felt as she prepared the pork chops, the fingerling potatoes, and the green beans. She set the table and lit the candle she'd purchased as a centerpiece.

Mary didn't say a word the entire time it took her to prep the dinner and cook it, and that unnerved Nora even more. "Do you have any idea how uncomfortable it makes me feel that you're watching me?"

"Do you have any idea how much I'd rather be doing something *other* than watching you?" Mary asked.

The sultriness in her tone made Nora go weak in the knees. She plated their dinners and put them on the table.

"That looks delicious."

The words were a vibration against her back, and she shivered.

"So do you." Mary put her hands on her waist and slowly turned her around so that they were face to face.

"D-dinner's ready."

"I can see that."

If you don't stop looking at me that way, I swear I'll combust. "Sit down before it gets cold."

She did as she was told and placed the gingham napkin in her lap.

"I hope it's all right. I'm not the best cook."

Mary placed the first bite of pork chop and potatoes in her mouth and moaned. "This is heavenly."

Yes, it is. Nora swallowed hard. Was it hot in here? "I'm glad you like it."

"Mm-hmm." She devoured everything on the plate, and a big slice of apple pie for dessert that Nora had made earlier in the day.

"Where are you putting all that?"

"What? It's not every day I get such a gourmet meal."

"Did you really like it?"

"I really, really did." Mary rose and blew out the candle. "Now what I'd really like is to do the dishes and have the other part of the dessert that you promised me."

As if I could deny you anything when you look at me like that.

Sometime later, Nora forced open her eyelids and stretched. Mary was sprawled across her torso, a smile plastered on her face even in sleep. Nora ran her fingers through her dark curls and kissed the top of her head.

She started to doze again and jerked awake. What time was it? Had they missed midnight? *Midnight?* Nora threw off the sheet and blanket that partially covered them. Mary's curfew!

"Wake up!" She shook her. "You have to wake up!"

"What is it?"

"You're going to miss curfew."

"Curfew?" Mary rubbed the sleep from her eyes. "What time is it?"

Nora fumbled for her wind-up alarm clock. "It's almost midnight."

"Good. Then we haven't missed our kiss." She drew Nora toward her.

"This is serious. You have to get cleaned up and dressed." Nora pulled away and sprang off the bed. She ran around the room and collected Mary's clothes. When she glanced back at the bed, Mary was half-reclining there, a bemused expression on her face.

"I mean it. We can't take a chance on you being late. How could we explain it? Curfew is half an hour after midnight on New Year's Eve."

"All right. I'm going. I was just enjoying the view."

Nora growled. *Why can't you recognize how dangerous this is?* She set the clothes on the bed as Mary sauntered into the bathroom and paced as she waited for her to come out.

"Is it midnight yet?" Mary called through the bathroom door.

She picked up the clock. "Two minutes 'til."

Mary flung open the bathroom door and leaned against the frame. She wore nothing more than a come-hither smirk, and in spite of the circumstances, Nora's pulse quickened.

"Is it midnight now?" She walked slowly toward her, and it was all Nora could do to find her voice.

"The second hand says thirty seconds."

"Perfect." She leaned up and wound her arms around Nora's neck. "Happy New Year. I love you."

Nora closed her eyes and gazed into her heart. "I-I love you too. Happy New Year."

They sealed it with a kiss, ringing in 1944 in a way Nora was sure neither of them had envisioned.

JANUARY – JUNE, 1944

CHAPTER SEVENTEEN

Mary hummed to herself and tweaked the knob to make a correction as the needle veered too far into the red zone. Last night, Nora had said she loved her. She'd said it—out loud—at midnight on New Year's Eve. Nothing could be more romantic than that, could it?

She hadn't seen her yet today, although she'd craned her neck around every time she heard a supervisor coming to see if she could catch a glimpse of her striding down the middle of the cubicle room floor.

An alarm went off and Mary jerked back to attention. "Oh, no." She yanked the knob to the left. The needle remained flat all the way to the right. "No. No, no, no." Even as she picked up the phone to connect to the control room, the floor supervisor came running in her direction.

"What did you do?"

"I didn't do anything."

"You must've done something, or it wouldn't have spiked like that." He moved her out of the way and went to work trying to correct her mistake. "This will cost us. We're going to have to shut it down and reboot it."

Mary's heart beat hard. What if she got fired for this? What if Nora found out she'd messed up?

"This is completely unacceptable. It's your fault. You need to pay closer attention."

"Yes, sir." She hung her head.

"Don't just stand there. Make a notation on your chart. When it reboots, get back to work. Mess up again, and you're finished."

179

"Y-yes, sir." She fought back tears. For once, she didn't want to see Nora. She could imagine what her reaction would be.

Nora did her best to keep her expression neutral, even as her pulse pounded in her ears. They were woefully behind their target production levels. Alpha-1 was nowhere near coming back on line, and now the floor supervisor for Beta-2 was reporting to her about an operator error that cost several hours of downtime on Cubicle 853.

"What caused the problem?" Cubicle 853, she well knew, was assigned to Mary Elizabeth Trask.

"I'd say it was inattention, if you ask me. I think she was daydreaming."

"What action did you take?" She kept her head down and pretended to examine the operator log in front of her.

"I let the operator know in no uncertain terms that inattention was unacceptable, that she cost us valuable operating time, and that if it happened again, there would be consequences." He nodded, as if for emphasis.

"Very well, thank you."

"Do you want me to take further action?"

He seemed only too eager to do just that. "No." Nora waved him away. "I'll take care of it myself."

"But, ma'am...er...Dr. Lindstrom—"

"I said I'd take care of it, and I will." She rose from behind the desk.

"Yes, sir. I mean, yes, ma'am. I mean, sure thing."

"Thank you for bringing the matter to my attention."

"Well, you said you wanted to know if there were any instances that delayed production, so..."

"You did the right thing. Thank you." When he left, Nora slumped back into her chair. He was a new hire, and eager to make an impression. *He's also right, and you know it.* She envisioned Mary sitting at her control board, her mind on their lovemaking last night. The tips of her ears turned red from embarrassment.

How could Mary jeopardize her job, Nora's job, and the project in this way? It was unconscionable. Hadn't she already warned her?

Work was work. Nora couldn't…no, wouldn't…treat her any differently than any of the other cubicle operators.

She drummed her fingers on the desk. *What would you do if it was anybody else?* She remembered firing one of her girls a few weeks ago for a second, similar infraction. She hadn't left it to the floor supervisor to do; she'd made an example of the girl, relieving her of her assignment in person.

Fortunately, this was the first blemish on Mary's record. Still, Nora would have to address it, and right away. She rose and rotated her neck to alleviate the tension building there. Shift change would be coming soon, and she needed to get to Mary's station before that happened.

She gathered up the floor supervisor's report and the operator log, stuffed them in a manila folder, and marched over to Beta-2. As she made her way down the line, with the floor supervisor trailing behind her, she saw Mary, eyes straight ahead, back ramrod straight, staring at the control panel as though her life depended on it. Mary was aware of her presence; she could tell by the quiver in her jaw.

When she was almost directly behind her, she also saw that her hands were trembling. The sight nearly broke her resolve. But she had to do this; she had to go through with it. If she didn't, if there was any hint of personal familiarity or favoritism, someone would surely figure out the truth and all would be lost.

"Mary Trask?" She used her most authoritative voice.

"Yes?"

"Please relinquish the controls to Mr. Beck. I require your full attention."

"Yes, ma'am." Mary stood up and stepped aside as the floor supervisor took her place in front of the panel. She looked up at Nora through long lashes, trepidation written all over her face.

"I received this report just now." Nora removed the operator log and shift supervisor report from the folder and waved it in front of Mary. "Do you know what it says?"

"No, ma'am."

"It says that we lost valuable, crucial time on your machine, during your shift today. Can you please explain to me why that was?"

"No, ma'am."

"Well, I can. Mr. Beck tells me you were daydreaming, that you failed to adequately monitor your station, and that, as a result, your unit had to be taken out of operation for a period of time."

Mary cringed as Nora spelled out her infraction loud enough for the other girls to hear. Her lower lip trembled.

"Let me be crystal clear, Miss Trask. What we are doing here is vital to the war effort. That is why you're here. If you don't feel as though you can devote your working hours one-hundred-percent to that goal, then you should leave now."

Mary gasped, but did not move. "I-I can do my j-job. I can. I just took my eye off the meter for one second."

"That was one second we couldn't afford, now wasn't it?"

"Yes, ma'am."

"Right. Please make sure that never, ever happens again. If it does, I'll be forced to relieve you of your station. Do you understand me?"

Mary could barely meet her gaze. When she did, her eyes held a million questions and a world of pain. Nora replaced the papers in the folder in order to keep her hands busy so that she didn't reach out to soothe her.

"Mr. Beck? I believe Miss Trask is ready to resume her place. Back to work, Miss Trask."

Nora turned on her heel and walked briskly away. She kept walking until she was clear of the building and out of sight of prying eyes. She leaned against the back of a partially constructed support building and rested her head against the concrete. What had she done?

You did what you had to do. You had to be harder on her than on anyone else. Otherwise, you'll be found out. Even so, she thought she might throw up. *I love you, Mary. I'm sorry. You left me no choice.*

She pushed off the building and headed back to her office, where she closed the door. She didn't want to be disturbed for the rest of the day. She was feeling disturbed enough as it was.

☙❧

Mary lay staring at the ceiling in her dorm room. She wasn't surprised that sleep eluded her, even though she was dead on her feet. Five days—that's how long it had been since she'd last seen Nora. She hadn't even caught a glimpse of her at work.

She closed her eyes tightly as an image of Nora standing in front of her cubicle, disappointment etched in her features, played in her mind. It was cruel to have that be the last memory she had of her. *All I did was have a small lapse in concentration. She was cruel, cold, and heartless.*

Mary groaned, as her body replayed a very different memory. This one featured Nora, the expression on her face otherworldly, her mouth forming an "o" as her body shuddered in pleasure. She turned over and buried her head in the pillow.

Was this how Sam had felt about her? Like he couldn't breathe without her, like nothing in the world mattered except the next time they could be together? If so, she pitied him. Had she understood better what love was, she would've been kinder to him. It wouldn't have changed the outcome—after all, she wasn't in love with him— but she would've handled the situation more compassionately had she truly understood the nature of unrequited love.

Unrequited love… That wasn't what this was. Nora had professed her love the last time they were together. She'd kissed her at midnight. That hadn't changed this quickly, it couldn't have.

She rolled onto her back again. She simply couldn't go on this way. She had to know; she simply had to see her. She found a piece of stationery and a pen and carefully, painstakingly crafted a note.

I MUST see you. Please. Meet me under the tree at the Chapel-on-the-Hill after dinner tonight.

She sat back and reviewed her handiwork. It omitted any personal identifying information. She didn't sign it, but she was confident Nora would know it was from her.

She sealed it in a blank envelope. It was 8:23 a.m. Nora would be at work by now. Before she could change her mind, she dressed and hid the envelope in her coat.

Ten minutes later, after taking a roundabout route to be sure she wasn't followed and that Nora wasn't home, she slipped the note under Nora's front door.

By the time Nora left work that night, all she wanted was to curl up in a fetal ball and make the world go away. Dr. Lawrence gave them a target of one kilogram of enriched Tubealloy per month. Without Alpha-1, and with construction still underway on several of the other racetracks, she could see no way that they could even come close to hitting that target. According to Jane, barely four percent of the product was ending up in the "enriched" collection box, and even that was enriched only to twelve percent.

On top of that pressure, she couldn't stop thinking about Mary. Her body craved her, and her heart missed her. But the incident last week drove home the very point her head had been making all along—everything about this situation screamed trouble. *She's a girl. She's young, impressionable, and you're in a position of power. Not only that, what business do you have falling in love with a girl in the first place? Maybe you should give Del a chance? Maybe you could make yourself feel the same way about him that you do about Mary?* Even as she thought it, her stomach rebelled. She couldn't even consider doing the things she'd done with Mary with Del, or any other man for that matter.

What she needed was time...time to sort out her emotions, time to focus on the job at hand, and time to wrestle her rebellious body under control. She arrived home, pushed open the front door...and slipped on something underfoot. "What the...?" She bent over and retrieved the offending object. A blank envelope? Could she have dropped a piece of mail? As she examined it more closely, a whiff of perfume floated up toward her nostrils. It smelled like Mary.

Her hands shook as she carefully slit open the envelope. Inside was a note. She read it twice, anger welling inside her, mixed with longing. What time had she left the note?

Nora set down her attaché case and liberated the weekly schedule from its folder. Her finger traced down the names and corresponding shifts in Beta-2. She stopped when she found what she was seeking. Mary had worked third shift last night. Today, she was off. She could've slid the note under her door in broad daylight. Anybody could've seen her.

She checked her watch. She'd left work later than usual, and the bus had been slow tonight. It was almost 8:30. Her heart lurched. What time would Mary have gone to the tree? Would she still be there? *She must be freezing.* She threw down the schedule, re-buttoned her coat, and ran back out the door.

The night was pitch-black, and several times she lost her balance and had to recover. The semi-frozen mud squished under her heels and the wind whistled through her ears. As she approached the chapel, she squinted. A solitary figure stood huddled against the tree. *Mary.* Her breath quickened at the sight, and it was all she could do not to run to her and scoop her up in her arms.

Then the anger returned. Anger at her foolishness for freezing to death out here. Anger for the possibility of being spotted together, alone, in an isolated spot, at this hour of the night. How would it look? Anger at the thought that someone might have seen her slip the note under her door. Anger at how her heart and body betrayed her at the mere sight of Mary. Anger at the impossibility of all of it.

"Y-you c-c-came!"

Nora's eyes adjusted to the darkness. "Have you lost your mind? It must be below freezing out here." Nora removed her gloves and handed them to Mary. "Put these on. Honestly, what's wrong with you?" She shook her head. "How long have you been standing out here?"

Mary shrugged. "I d-don't know. Since d-dinner."

"You could catch your death of cold."

"C-could you please stop y-yelling at me?" Mary glanced away. When she looked back, tears hung on her lashes.

"I'm sorry." Nora softened her tone. "It's too cold for you. You shouldn't have come."

"I d-don't know any other way to get your attention. I never s-see you anymore. It's like you're av-voiding me."

"I am avoiding you." *No sense beating around the bush.*

"Why? Why would you do that?"

"Do you not realize the import of what you did? Tell me that you weren't daydreaming about us when your unit failed."

"Of course I was daydreaming about us! I haven't been able to think of anything else. I can't eat. I can't sleep. All I can think about is you, and us, and all I see when I close my eyes is you, mercilessly berating me in front of everyone."

"You made a bad error that cost us material and valuable time. I would've done the same to any of the girls who'd made such an egregious mistake."

"Would you? I don't think so. I've seen plenty of girls mess up. It's always been the floor supervisor who pulled them aside and spoke to them quietly. I think… I think you meant to scare me. You meant to make me look bad. You meant to intimidate me."

"Not my intent." Nora crossed her arms defensively. "I meant to give you a stern warning. I hope you got the message."

Mary wiped away a tear. "The message I got was that you're cruel. Why are you being so cold? Didn't those nights we shared together mean anything to you?"

"I'm trying to help us both keep our jobs. Can't you see that? Because right now, we're standing on the edge of a cliff."

"What are you talking about?"

Nora rounded on her. "Do you remember Harold Thurber?"

"Who?"

"Harold Thurber. He was the first-shift floor supervisor in Beta-2. You were on his shift several weeks ago."

"You mean the guy who disappeared after a week on the job?"

"Yes."

"What about him?"

"Do you know why he disappeared?"

"I assume he wasn't doing a good job."

Nora shook her head. "He was doing a great job. In fact, he was shaping up to be the best floor supervisor we had."

"Then, what happened to him?"

"His boss and the District Engineer—the big boss—determined that he was a sexual deviate."

"A…?"

"Sexual deviate. He preferred other men to women."

Mary's hand flew to her mouth. "They fired him for that? That's terrible."

"That's us if we don't pull ourselves together and let go of this madness. I spent all those years in school and endured too much harassment from male classmates so that I could be taken seriously as a scientist. Here, in this place, I'm in a position of authority; I'm in a position to make a real contribution to the war effort. I cannot afford to take a chance on people thinking and talking about me as they did about poor Harold. He's a fine man, and he's finished now. I have no idea where, or how, he'll find work. I'm sure he doesn't, either. Well, that's not going to be me."

"What about me? What about how I feel and my life?" She jabbed at her chest. "You only care about yourself!"

"Hardly," Nora scoffed. "If you lose this job, you'll probably have to go right back home to your mother—right back where you started from—right back where you don't want to be. You'll either have to take a menial job to support yourself, find a way to go to college, or marry what's-his-name or someone else just like him. Is that what you want?"

Mary gasped. "Of course not. But you don't know that any of that is going to happen. You're scared!"

"You're darned right I'm scared. We have to protect ourselves." They were practically nose-to-nose, both of them breathing hard.

"What are you suggesting? That we forget about what happened? That we don't see each other anymore?"

Nora rubbed the sore spot over her heart. There it was—the only solution that made any sense—except it made no sense to her heart. She cleared her throat as emotion threatened to muffle her words. "Yes."

"What did you say?"

She straightened to her full height. "I said, yes. Yes, I think it would be best if we didn't spend any time together or see each other, even casually, at least until this business with Harold settles down."

Mary slid down the tree and sat at the base. She lowered her head to her knees and rocked herself in mute comfort. "You can't mean that. You simply can't." She raised her head and turned pleading eyes on Nora. "I love you. I refuse to believe you don't love me back. I know you do. I know you have a heart in there, Nora Lindstrom, and I know it beats for me just as sure as I know mine beats for you."

"I wish it could be different; truly, I do. But this is the way of the world. It's not our time. I wish it was, more than you'll ever know. I'm sorry." She smiled sadly down at Mary. "Take good care of yourself." She pivoted and started down the hill. Tears rolled down her cheeks.

"You forgot your gloves," Mary called after her.

"Keep them." She didn't turn around. She couldn't. "I love you," she whispered. "God help me, I love you."

187

CHAPTER EIGHTEEN

The bus ground to a halt and Mary exited. As had become her routine, she headed directly for the dorm. The shift had been uneventful, as so many had been for the past several weeks. She'd done what Nora had told her to do, focusing solely on her work and keeping her head down. She hadn't seen Nora even once, not a brief glimpse of her in the distance, nor a sighting of her in the cafeteria at lunchtime, nor walking the cubicle room floor. And it was tearing her apart inside.

Was she okay? Had she decided to date that Berkeley boy who'd been following her around? The idea of that nearly doubled Mary over. No, she couldn't...she wouldn't...would she? Mary didn't think so, but then again, she wouldn't have thought Nora would disappear completely from her life either.

"Hey. You're in your own little world." Rosalie came up alongside her as they entered the dorm.

"Sorry. Long day."

"Tell me about it. I've seen you in the distance a couple of times, but not close enough to shout. Are you okay? You've been really scarce."

"I-I'm fine, why?" Had Rosalie heard or noticed something?

"Because you're starting to remind me and Betty of our ghost-friend, Nora."

Mary's step faltered at the mention of Nora's name before she caught herself. What did she mean by that? *Is Nora all right?* She knew she couldn't ask it out loud, although she badly wanted to.

"You've both lost a lot of weight, you look like heck, and neither one of you has shown up at a dance, or the bowling alley, or even at the movies. They must be working you really hard over there."

"Yeah, they are." Mary smiled in relief. So, Nora hadn't been out running around with that boy after all. She was moping too. *Thank God.*

"Say, why don't you come dancing with us tomorrow night? Betty's got her eye on a fella and she wants back-up."

"I'd love to, but I can't. I've got to work." It was only a small white lie. She did have to work tomorrow, just not second shift.

"Oh, that's too bad. Well, I guess I'll see you around."

"You bet." Mary waved as she disappeared down her hallway. Once safely inside her room, she slid down the door to the floor and buried her head in her hands. *Oh, Nora. I miss you so much. We have to find a way to be together. We can't go on like this—at least I can't. What are we going to do?*

After several moments of feeling sorry for herself, Mary started to formulate a plan. It worked before, she posited, so why wouldn't it work again?

It was obvious that Nora was intentionally avoiding Beta-2 whenever Mary was on-shift. Most likely, she was steering clear of the cafeteria in case they should run into each other there, as well. The movie theater probably reminded her too much of their time together. Mary passed on going to the movies for the same reason. Where was the one place almost everybody went on Sunday? The-Chapel-on-the-Hill.

She nodded. It felt right that she should arrange to intentionally run into Nora just as she had on Christmas Day, although this time she would avoid a direct collision. Just two people who happened to be going and coming from church at the same time and pass each other on the lawn. Yes, that would be her best bet. Surely, Nora couldn't ignore her then.

A knock on the door startled her. "Who is it?"

"It's the housemother, dear. I know you've been waiting for word from your father. I thought you'd want to know right away that you have a letter postmarked from Italy."

"I do?" Mary jumped up and flung open the door.

"Here you are, dear. I'm happy for your sake you've heard from him. So many others haven't been as lucky, you know."

"Thank you." Mary didn't want to be rude and slam the door in her face, but she was anxious to be alone to read what her father had said. She closed the door and flopped onto the bed.

January 3, 1944
My dearest Pumpkin,
I got word that you are somewhere in Tennessee, working for the war effort. That was a surprise!

Mary sounded out the letters, taking her time with each word.

Your mother tells me that you left without saying goodbye and without so much as a word to Sam. That's my strong-willed, hard-headed girl! I'm not saying that I approve of what you did or how you did it, but I am proud that you followed your heart, that you're doing something to help us boys over here, and that you're happy. You are, aren't you?

Mary lowered the letter and blinked away a tear. "I *was* happy, Daddy—deliriously so—but that seems so long ago. What would you make of me and Nora? Would you turn your back on me? Would you cast me out? I know Mother would."

Thank you, by the way, for at least breaking down and giving your mother a telephone number and an address so that I could write you a proper letter. I know letters aren't your strong suit, but I comfort myself that at least it's a way we can keep in touch. I wish I could call you and hear your voice, but that's not possible from here.
Please know how much I love you, Pumpkin. I long for the day when I can gaze upon your pretty face again. I'm sure you're all grown up by now and I'll hardly recognize you!
Love,
Dad

P.S. I know you're like oil and vinegar, but please try to take pity on your mother. Being alone is hard on her.
P.P.S. I know the mail is much delayed, and I have no idea when this will reach you. We're in Italy at the moment. I'm sure it would be a beautiful country if we weren't in the middle of a war zone. I am praying to God to bring me home safely to your mother and to you too, even if you're in some secret location in Tennessee.

Mary read and re-read the letter to be sure she understood every word. Her father was safe. He was safe. Well, he was safe as of a month ago. She closed her eyes and said a prayer of thanks.

Now, if she could only get Nora back, she would truly believe in miracles.

෫ඁ෬

Sunday dawned cold and clear. Frost covered the lawn leading to The-Chapel-on-the-Hill. Nora wrapped the scarf tighter around her neck. If she attended the first service of the morning, the likelihood of running into Mary was slim.

Not that it was at all likely that Mary would go to church on a Sunday. She'd been collecting pine cones and surely hadn't been on her way to or from the chapel when Nora had run into her on Christmas Day. If one didn't go to church on Christmas, when would one go? Nora shook off the memory of nearly capsizing Mary's basket and their subsequent date. It seemed like a lifetime ago.

A wave of sadness threatened to swamp her, as so often happened these days. *It won't do you any good to dwell on what cannot be.*

She sat through the service in the back pew and barely listened to the sermon. She had told Mary the truth—she wasn't religious, but she did have faith. Heaven knew she could use God's help now. She closed her eyes and prayed. *God, please help me to have the strength to get through these days, help me to have the knowledge and the wherewithal to help us win the war, and help me to know your guidance so that I might follow the path you choose for me. Please help me to know what that path is.*

Church let out, and she allowed the other parishioners to precede her out the door. It was her day off, and she wasn't in a rush to be anywhere, although she was enjoying the biography she'd just checked out, *Madame Curie*. She'd wanted to re-read it in preparation for the release of the new film of the same name, starring Greer Garson and Walter Pidgeon.

The thought of going to a movie now, without Mary to hold her hand, brought on a renewed bout of self-pity. *Get over it.*

She exited out into the sunshine and stopped short. There, several feet in front of her, was Mary, looking thin and gaunt, but still breathtakingly beautiful.

"Hi."

"Hi, yourself."

"It's good to see you." Mary shifted uncomfortably from foot to foot and her gaze darted everywhere but at Nora.

"It's good to see you too."

"I... Can we go somewhere to talk? Please?"

She appeared so small and uncertain, and alarmingly pale. Although Nora's head screamed at her to run the other way, her heart could not allow it. "Let's go back to my place." It was the most private place she could think of, even as her mind reminded her that it also was the most dangerous.

Neither of them said a word on the brisk walk. When they arrived at the Flat Top, Nora checked both sides of the street, then ushered Mary inside as quickly as possible. She closed every blind and locked the front door.

When she finished double-checking her handiwork, she turned around. Mary stood in the center of the living room, tears streaming down her face.

"Oh, my God. What? What is it? Are you ill? Did somebody die?"

Mary shook her head. "I-it feels like we d-died. Like love died. I c-can't go on like this. I don't eat, I don't sleep, I worry constantly that something bad has happened to you."

Nora helped her out of her coat and led her to the couch. Then she hung up her own coat and joined her, making sure to leave space between them. Mary's head was bowed and her tears splashed onto her clenched fists.

Nora retrieved the box of tissues from the bathroom and handed them to her. "Look at me." She lifted Mary's chin with two fingers and was shocked, at this distance, to see the dark purple circles under her eyes.

You did this to her. A mournful moan caught in her throat. "I'm sorry. I'm sorrier than you'll ever know. I never should've let anything happen between us. I should've been smarter and stronger than that. All I've done is hurt you."

Mary shook her head as her lips quivered. "You showed me what love is. I never would've known if not for you."

"I caused you more pain than anyone had a right to. Mary..." She closed the distance between them. Seeing her in such agony pierced her heart and overrode her fears. "I love you. You were right. I loved you from the start. That doesn't change the fact that this is a perilous path we're on, and one misstep could mean our ruin."

"I'm willing to risk it if it means I can be with you."

"That's naïve."

Mary shrugged. "That's love."

Nora couldn't stand it any longer. She wiped away Mary's tears with the tip of her finger. Mary leaned into her touch, setting off a cascade reaction in Nora's body.

Want, need, remorse, fear, desire, all warred within her. "I—"

Mary trailed her fingertips across Nora's lips, and then replaced her fingertips with her mouth.

Nora wanted to object—she wanted to back away and tell her to stop—but her body and heart had other ideas. She rose to meet her, and her carefully cultivated façade of restraint and indifference shattered in an instant.

Afterward, as Mary dressed, Nora's sense of foreboding returned. "Promise me, you'll not take any chances with being seen with me unless it's here, under cover of darkness. At work, we will continue to have absolutely no contact or interactions. You must pay strict attention to your D unit. On the job, your concentration must be absolute."

Mary rolled her eyes. "Of course."

"This is beyond serious, Mary. The slightest hint of impropriety will be our downfall. Some of the girls already resent me for my position. They'd love an excuse to have my head on a platter."

"They can't have it; it belongs to me." Mary, now fully clothed, kissed her one last time. "I give you my word that I will do my best to divert suspicion. I'll come and go only at off times when I have the least chance of being seen." She shrugged into her coat and shoved her hands in her pockets. "Oh, I almost forgot. I heard from my father."

"You did? That's great!"

Mary held out the letter and let Nora read it.

"I bet you are much relieved."

"I am."

"I'm glad for you." She handed the letter back to Mary, who stuffed it back in her coat pocket. She paused in front of the door.

"What is it?"

"It's daylight. I have to leave now or I won't be able to get any sleep before my shift tonight, and the big boss wants me to concentrate."

Nora frowned. She searched around until she found the book she was looking for. "Take this. If anyone sees you, you can say you came to borrow this book from me."

"Okay." Mary leaned in and kissed her once more. "I love you. Thank you for giving us a chance. I don't think I could've gone much longer without seeing you."

"I missed you too."

Mary slipped out the door, and Nora fell back on the couch. *Oh, how I missed you.* She hadn't realized until she saw her standing outside the church just how true that was.

"Mary? Mary, are you in there? Come quick, there's a phone call for you. She says it's urgent."

Mary roused herself from a deep sleep. She'd been dreaming that she was still wrapped in Nora's arms.

"Mary!" The pounding on her door continued.

"Wh—" She cleared her throat. "What is it?"

"Urgent phone call for you. Hurry up, already."

"Oh, my gosh!" She jumped up, threw on her bathrobe, and flung open the door. The housemother, curlers still in her hair, had her fist raised, no doubt ready to knock again. Mary ran right past her and down the hall to the lobby, where the phone was off the hook.

"Hello?"

"Mary?"

Her mother was crying. Dread pooled in the pit of her stomach and tears sprang to her own eyes. *Not Daddy. Please, God, don't take Daddy.* "Mother? What is it?"

"It's your father…"

She gripped the phone tighter. "What about Daddy?"

"He's been wounded."

"Is he…" She couldn't bring herself to ask it.

"He's alive, but he's got multiple gunshot wounds. They're evacuating him from a hospital in Italy right now and sending him home. He'll be here tomorrow."

"He's alive, Mother! That's great news."

"He's badly hurt. I need you to come home right now. We need to be here for him."

The buzz in Mary's ears was so loud she missed the next thing her mother said. Come home? That would mean leaving Nora and the life she was building here.

"The officer who gave me the news says he's lucky he made it out alive. It was the Battle of Rapido River; we lost almost 2,000 men there."

Mary shook her head to clear it.

"When you get here, we'll have to see about you getting your job back at Meyer's. I imagine it will be a long time, if ever, before your father can go back to work. We'll need the money you can make."

Blood pounded in Mary's ears. *No, no, no. I can't go back to that life. Not now.* "But I can make more money here and keep sending it home like I have been."

"Mary Elizabeth? Did you hear me? Your father was nearly killed. We're lucky to be getting him back at all. You *will* stop this foolishness and come home right this minute. How selfish can you be? Your father needs you. This family needs you. I expect to see you in this house by tomorrow night."

This time, it was her mother who hung up without saying goodbye. Woodenly, Mary made her way back to her room. She sat on the bed, staring off into space.

Her father was coming home. Yes, he wouldn't be in one piece, but he wouldn't be in a box, either. Tears of gratitude sprang to her eyes. She inhaled deeply. Daddy was coming home for good; he wouldn't be dying in some foreign country, he would be home with Mother and everything would return to normal.

A breath caught in her throat. Normal. Everything would return to her mother's version of normal. *Nora. I can't leave Nora. I can't.*

I just can't. Her hands trembled and her teeth chattered. What was she going to do?

Nora. She had to get to her; she would fix everything. It was almost 7:00 a.m. She'd be heading to the bus depot now. She could find her before she got to work. Nora would know what to do. She threw on the dress she'd worn the night before and some shoes and ran full-tilt, heedless of the cold and the mud. When she arrived at the depot, she searched madly through the throng of people boarding buses for the early shift. Finally, she spotted her.

"Nora! Nora!" She waved and ran in her direction, threading her way through the crowd until she arrived in front of her just as she was boarding the Y-12 bus.

"Nora," she said breathlessly. "It's my father. Please. I don't know what to do. I don't—" Tears flowed freely down her face and she threw herself into Nora's arms. She barely registered her shocked expression.

"There, there." Nora patted her back awkwardly as she clung to her for dear life. "What's happened?"

"My mother called. My father was badly wounded in battle. He's in a hospital in Italy and they're flying him home. My mother insists that I come home right away. I don't know what to do. I don't—"

Nora pulled back, grabbed her by the sleeve, and steered them away from the bus and away from the depot. "Let's get you a cup of coffee, young lady, and I'll see if I can help you sort through your problem. Pull yourself together. I'm sure everything will be all right." She practically shouted the words, as if broadcasting them for all the world to hear.

Mary's brow furrowed. Why was she addressing her as though she were a near-stranger? Belatedly, she took stock of their surroundings. *Oh, my gosh.* Everyone was watching them. This would be Nora's worst nightmare come true.

Nora was walking so quickly it was hard for Mary to keep up. She pulled them behind a nearby building, out of sight of prying eyes. "What were you thinking?"

"I-I'm sorry. I'm not thinking clearly. I only knew I needed to get to you. You'd know what to do. I can't... I c-can't..."

Nora sighed. "Come on." She walked them to the Flat Top via a back route, avoiding the major streets, pedestrians on their way to the depot, and passing cars. They arrived at the Flat Top and Nora sat her down on the couch and pulled the blinds shut.

"It's the end of February and you ran out without your coat. You'll catch your death of cold."

"I don't care." Mary's teeth chattered.

Nora wrapped a blanket around her and rubbed her arms and back. "Is that better?"

"Yes. Thank you."

"Now, slow down, take a deep breath, and tell me what happened."

When Mary finished recounting the conversation with her mother, she threw herself again into the safety of Nora's arms. "I won't leave you. I won't leave this. But my father... What am I going to do?"

Nora sighed heavily. Quietly, she said, "You have to go."

Mary stiffened. "But—"

"There's no choice here, Mary. He's your father, and your parents need you. You have to go."

"No." She choked on a sob. "If I go, my mother will never let me come back. She'll insist that I marry Sam and my life will be over. Our time together will be over. I can't stand the thought of never seeing you again, of us not being together."

Nora pulled back and caressed her face. "Then you'd better make sure you come back to me."

"But, how?"

"I don't know yet. You're over eighteen and not a minor, so they can't physically keep you there."

"Nothing can keep me there. My heart is here." She placed a hand in the center of Nora's chest. "How am I going to live without you?"

"We have to get you a train today."

"Today?"

"Yes. It's the fastest way to get you there, and still, you'll just make it in time for your father's homecoming. We'll make it an open-ended round trip. That way, you can tell your mother that work requires you to return."

"I like the way you think." She rested her cheek on Nora's chest. "I'm going to miss this heartbeat." She felt her sigh.

"I'm going to miss you."

"I... I'm sorry about before. I wasn't thinking clearly. The bus depot was the absolute worst place... Do you hate me?"

"I could never hate you, Mary Elizabeth Trask."

"Still, I know how much you worry—"

"You leave the worrying to me. Now is not the time to focus on that. Can you get to the train station and get your ticket? I really have to get to work. I'm already late and I don't want to have to explain why."

"I can."

"Do you need money? I can pay for it."

"No. I've saved enough."

"Okay. Go home and pack your things first. I'd lend you my coat to get back to your place, but..."

Mary laughed for the first time in what seemed like forever. "It would be a little big."

They rose together. Nora swept an errant strand of hair off Mary's face. "I'll miss you."

"Not as much as I'll miss you."

"You call me when you can."

"I will. I wish I could spend one more night with you."

"You know that can't happen."

"A girl can hope."

"Don't worry about work. I'll take care of it for you."

"I wish you could see me off."

"I do too, but that's impossible."

"I know."

"Come back to me, Mary."

"Count on it."

They kissed deeply. "You have to go."

"Yes."

They stood there a moment longer, and Mary refused to believe it would be the last time. She would find a way to come back. She had to.

CHAPTER NINETEEN

Nora rubbed her eyes. She was exhausted from lack of sleep, too many hours spent trying to reduce the percentage of unit shutdowns due to operator error, the continuous influx of new hires, scheduling headaches, and this new wrinkle with Mary, who should be arriving home anytime now.

At the moment, all Nora wanted was to catch her breath. What she needed, she decided, was a lunchtime walk in the fresh air. She stood up and stretched. "You spend entirely too much time hunched over behind a desk," she muttered to herself. "What's going to happen when you get old? That's assuming you get old. At the rate you're going..."

"Dr. Lindstrom?"

"Yes?" She was surprised to see her boss's secretary standing at her door.

"Mr. Pierson would like to see you in his office."

"I'll be right there." Trepidation flowed through her. If Travis Pierson summoned for her, bad news was sure to follow. He was a hard man, somewhere in his forties by Nora's estimate, sent by Tennessee Eastman Corporation to keep things running smoothly, on track, and on time. He was practical, efficient, emotionless...and condescending. But he also was fair and not given to histrionics or overreaction. In other words, he was mostly well-suited to his position—except for the condescending part. He made no bones about the fact that he didn't believe a woman had any business being in a supervisory position, "even a smart city-slicker like you," he'd told her the first time she met him. She hoped that by now she'd done a good enough job to win him over.

His office was only a few doors down from hers, but as Nora took the steps, she couldn't help but wonder if this was the walk of a condemned woman. She knocked on the closed door.

"Come," he bellowed.

"You wanted to see me, Mr. Pierson?"

"Come in and shut the door behind you, sweetheart."

The term of endearment grated on her, but there wasn't a thing she could do about it. She folded herself into the chair opposite his desk and did her best to appear comfortable.

He chomped on a cigar, and idly she wondered where he'd found one of those during this time of sacrifice and rationing. She blinked as the smoke irritated her eyes and waited for him to look up from his paperwork. This tactic of making her wait, which she perceived as a form of intimidation, was another annoying habit she resented.

Finally, after several minutes, he set down his pen. He took a puff of the cigar, blew the smoke in her direction, and put the cigar in the large ashtray on the corner of his desk.

"Listen, Miss Lindstrom."

Nora's nostrils flared. *That's* Dr. *Lindstrom to you.*

"I hate to do this because I really like you. I didn't think a woman had the balls to do this job, but you've made a believer out of me."

Fear stuck in her throat and dread settled in the pit of her stomach. He was going to fire her. All of her hard work was going to be for naught.

"Now, let me start by sayin' I don't believe a word of it. Not one word."

She swallowed hard. Here it was, the one thing she'd feared above all else.

"But a complaint has been brought to my attention that you might be one of them sexual deviates."

Although she wanted to cry, she sat as tall and still as she could manage. She schooled her expression so that she appeared completely nonplussed, as though she were confident of her innocence. She also resisted the urge to issue a hot denial. Don't protest too much. Wait him out.

"So, here's the way I see it." He leaned back and steepled his fingers. "The girl who made this here complaint gets jealous because you're prettier than her—you are, by the way—and she files a complaint. She's got her eye on this fella, and he's got his eye on you. If she can get you out of the way, she's got a clear run at this ol' boy."

If he hadn't been sitting right in front of her, Nora would've rolled her eyes at the ridiculous presumptions inherent in his theory. Instead, she continued to sit ramrod straight and say nothing. Outright lying wasn't in her nature, even if keeping secrets was something to which she'd uncomfortably become accustomed.

"Best to watch your back. There are girls here that are gunning for you, and they ain't going to quit until they have your scalp." He picked up the cigar again. "The good news for you is, as long as I'm sitting in this here chair, I've got your back. But you best be careful out there, Miss Lindstrom. The world is full of snakes."

She realized she was being dismissed. "Thank you, sir. I appreciate your confidence in me. You can be sure I'll be careful. Thank you for letting me know. I'm certain no disciplinary action will be necessary against the complainant. She was just doing what she thought was right."

"That's mighty generous of you, Miss Lindstrom. I don't know that I'd be as generous in your place. She's a lucky girl."

So am I. Nora took her leave.

"Hi, Daddy." After the doctor finished his examination, Mary crept into her parents' darkened bedroom and sat on the side of the bed. "Can I get you anything?"

Henry Trask stared up at the ceiling without answering.

"How about some water? Or maybe something to eat?"

Again, he didn't answer. It had been like this for the better part of a week. Gone was the kind, gentle, easy-going father who'd kissed his wife and daughter goodbye on a mid-December day in 1941. The man before her was sullen, withdrawn, and angry.

"Mother will be in a little later to re-dress your wounds."

He grunted in reply.

"Well, I'll be right outside if you need anything."

He acknowledged her with a slight nod.

"I-I love you, Daddy. I'm so glad you're home." On an impulse, she bent over to hug him.

"Argh!" He raised his arms reflexively and shrunk away in fear.

"I'm sorry. I'm so sorry, Daddy. I just wanted to hug you. I would never hurt you."

He remained with his arms over his face and she retreated to the living room, where her mother was meeting with the doctor.

"His physical wounds will heal. Within a month or two he should be able to resume his conductor duties."

"That's great news," Mary said.

"And the rest? He's so...different."

"Mrs. Trask—Mabel—your husband has seen and done things no man should have to see or do. Those things are ingrained on his mind and in his heart. We can't erase any of that. All you can do is love him, talk to him, give him time to acclimate to being home again and to heal his body. The rest is up to God."

"Thank you, doctor."

"You're welcome. I'll be back around next week to check on those wounds. In the meantime, keep them clean and let me know if you see any redness or signs of infection."

"I'll see you out." Mary walked him to the front door. In a low tone she asked, "Do you really think he'll be able to go back to work so soon?"

"I do. Physically, he had almost a month to heal at the hospital in Italy before they shipped him home. He'll most likely always carry a limp, but he'll be able to walk just fine, and the wounds in his stomach and back are almost healed now."

"I tried to hug him a little while ago and it terrified him." Mary's eyes welled with tears. "I just want my daddy back."

"I know." He patted her on the shoulder. "Give him time. He's got a gentle disposition and that wasn't what he needed in the Army. He'll rediscover the man he was again."

"I hope you're right."

"I hope so too. Take care of your folks, Mary. They're good people."

"Yes, sir."

As Mary watched him go down the walk, a familiar figure materialized in the distance. *Sam.* Her pulse pounded in her ears. "Mother?" she hollered.

"I'm in here."

Mary followed her voice to the kitchen. "Any idea why Sam would be walking this way?"

Her mother looked up from rinsing the lettuce in the sink. "I invited him to dinner."

"You…what?"

"I invited him to dinner, of course. Mary Elizabeth, you've been home a whole week and you haven't even left this house. How was Samuel supposed to know you were back if I didn't tell him?"

Her ears turned red and she clenched her fists. "If I'd wanted to see Sam, I would've arranged it myself."

"I know, dear. You just needed a little push, that's all." Her mother resumed preparing dinner.

Mary stalked away, went to her room and fumed. In another minute, Sam would walk through their front door. It was her worst nightmare. What should she tell him? "Sam, I'm sorry, but I've met someone in Tennessee. We're deeply in love." If she told him that, he'd want to know *his* name. Then he'd tell her mother she'd said that, and she'd get the third degree. *Think, Mary Elizabeth. Think quickly.*

The doorbell rang. Her time was up.

"Hi, Samuel. It's so good to see you. Oh, what lovely flowers. I'm sure Mary will love them. Mary? Samuel is here. Come say hello!"

Mary rolled her eyes. There was nothing for it. She couldn't very well climb out the bedroom window, although she was sorely tempted to try.

She checked her face and lipstick in the mirror. "Coming!" She plastered a smile on her face as she came around the corner. "Hi, Sam."

"Hi, Mary. You look…pretty."

"Thank you."

"These are for you." He held out the flowers to her.

"Thank you. Those are very nice. I'll just put them in some water and be right back." She took them into the kitchen. "Mother," she hissed, "you don't get to run my social life anymore. Don't you ever interfere again."

Her mother rounded on her. "Don't you ever talk to me like that again, young lady. Just because you spent a few months away from home on your own doesn't make you an adult. You get out there and be charming. You're lucky that nice young man is still available."

"Samuel," she called. "Mary's forgotten her manners. Would you like something to drink?"

"No thank you, ma'am."

"Get out there. Now." She shooed Mary toward the living room. She sat in the chair opposite him. "So, how've you been? How's the watch business?"

"It's fine. Lots of new customers."

"That's good."

"We have a little time before dinner. Why don't you two go for a walk?" her mother called.

Mary gritted her teeth. "It's March, Mother. It's cold outside."

"Bundle up."

Mary prayed for patience. "Do you want to go for a walk, Sam?"

"Sure."

She grabbed her coat from the coat closet, along with her scarf. She felt in the pockets. Nora's gloves were still there. She put them on as if they were a shield.

As if by mutual agreement, they headed toward the park. "So, you like it wherever you are?" he asked.

"I do."

"What is it you do over there?"

"I'm working for the war effort." Her mother had grilled her much the same way. Mary was proud of herself for deflecting their questions and keeping the secret. She hoped Nora would be proud of her too.

Nora. She missed her so much it was a physical ache. She glanced sideways at Sam. He would never be Nora, that was for sure.

"What kind of work is it?"

"The kind I can't tell you about." The words came out harsher then she intended. It wasn't his fault he wasn't Nora. More softly she said, "I'm sworn to secrecy."

"You're sworn to secrecy for knitting sweaters or something? That's ridiculous."

Anger blossomed in her chest. How dare he assume she was doing something trivial!

They walked a little further in silence and the awkwardness between them grew.

"You're different, Mary."

"I am?" Her heart raced. He couldn't know, could he? Nora said she didn't look any different. It shouldn't be obvious that she and Nora were... Her breath came in shorter bursts.

"Yeah. I can't put my finger on it, but..."

Before he could say anything else, she blurted, "Nothing's changed, Sam. I still have no intention of marrying you. I'm going back to Tennessee. I'm going back to my life there."

His eyes opened wide in shock. "But, your mother said—"

"My mother says a lot of things. She's not in charge of my life. I am. I'm going back to Tennessee." She said it with enough force that even she believed it.

"Okay. You don't have to get nasty about it."

They turned back toward the house.

"I apologize. It's just... My father isn't doing well, and my mother is an interfering bother. I'm sorry if she gave you the wrong impression by inviting you to dinner."

"I'm sorry too. I don't think I want to stay for dinner, if that's okay with you. What's the use? Clearly, you've already made up your mind. You've got plans and I'm not part of them."

Guilt niggled at her conscience. She remembered how it felt when Nora rejected her. "I don't mean to be ungrateful, Sam. You're a wonderful guy. You deserve a girl who's madly in love with you. Someone who will make a wonderful wife and mother to your kids, someone you can build a life with. Unfortunately, that someone isn't me."

He nodded. The house came back in sight.

"Are you sure you don't want to stay for dinner? I'm sure my mother cooked one of your favorites."

"No, thank you." They stopped at the walkway. "I guess this is where I say goodbye."

"I guess so."

"Well, good luck, Mary."

"You too, Sam."

He stuffed his hands in his pockets and walked away with his head down. Mary inhaled deeply. She was one step closer to her real home.

"We did it." Jane Greer jubilantly waved a piece of paper in front of Nora's nose.

"Which *it* did we do?" Nora appreciated her friend's enthusiasm. Numbers made her simply giddy.

"We produced two hundred grams of material...finally. I thought we'd never get there. March, 1944. It took us almost a whole year to come up with two hundred grams—one fifth of the stated goal of one kilogram per month. Still, the big boss seemed pretty happy when I gave him the latest calculations."

Nora knew Jane had no idea why two hundred grams of sufficiently enriched Tubealloy was significant. She only knew that they'd achieved one of the target numbers she was told they needed.

In truth, Nora didn't know what they were going to do with two hundred grams of twelve-percent-enriched U-235, either. But she at least had the background to make an educated guess—a guess she'd shared with no one.

"We should go celebrate."

Nora shook her head. "I wish I could, but I have schedules to manage. Every time one of the girls gets married, a baby inevitably follows and poof, there goes my cubicle operator."

"Oh, stop complaining. It's nice that love is in the air. You ought to try it sometime." Jane breezed out of Nora's office with a wave and a wink.

Nora heaved a heavy sigh. "You ought to try it sometime," she muttered under her breath. It had been almost three weeks since Mary had left, and apart from one hurried phone call while her mother was out hanging the laundry, she'd heard nothing. They'd agreed not to send letters. The censor would've had a field day with those.

Tonight, she vowed. If she hadn't heard anything more by tonight, she'd make the phone call. She worked for several more hours and then finally called it quits.

By the time she dragged herself through the front door, it was almost 8:30 p.m. She made herself supper out of a can of baked beans and a ration of bacon she'd waited in line several hours to get.

She'd just finished washing her dish in the sink when the phone rang. Her heart skipped a beat. *Please be you, my love.* She picked up the receiver. "Hello?"

"Collect call from Mrs. Roosevelt," the operator intoned. It was the signal they'd agreed on.

"I'll accept the charges, operator," Nora said.

"Hi," Mary whispered breathlessly on the other end after the operator had clicked off the line. "I miss you."

Nora held the receiver closer to her ear in order to hear. "I miss you too."

"My mother finally went to bed, but I don't think I should stay on long."

"How's it going?"

"Eh. My mother is still mad at me for telling Sam to pound salt. My father is almost fully healed but still not himself, and I miss a certain someone so much I think I'm going to combust."

"That certain someone feels the same way. Come home, Mary."

"I want to, more than you can imagine. My father goes back to work next week. I think that's the perfect time to tell them I'm going back to Tennessee."

"What do you think your mother will say?"

"I think she'll pitch a fit, but in the end, she'll have to let me go."

"Do you still have the other half of your train ticket?"

"Are you kidding me? I carry it in my bra."

Nora laughed. "Excellent hiding place."

"There's a problem, though."

"What's that?"

"I heard from the housemother that they rented out my dorm room and put my stuff in storage. I don't have a place to live anymore."

Nora had been afraid of that. With hundreds of people being hired every day now, living space was even more at a premium than ever. She bit her lip. "I may have a solution for that."

"What's that?"

"You could come live with me."

"Nora Lindstrom! Not that that wouldn't make me the happiest girl in the world, but how in the world do you think you're going to pull that off?"

"You leave it to me. Just promise you'll come back to me when your father goes back to work."

"I cross my heart and swear to God."

"That's good enough for me."

"Uh-oh. I think I hear my mother. I've got to go."

"Okay. I'll take care of everything on this end. You just get here."

"I will. Soon. 'Bye."

"'Bye." Nora held onto the receiver long after the line went dead. A plan took shape in her head. With any luck, it might even work.

Nora sat across the desk from Mr. Pierson and the housing director, Mr. Truett. "I'm trying to make the most of my resources. Alpha-1 will be coming back online in the next two weeks; Beta-1 is starting up this Tuesday; construction is underway on Alpha-5... We need every experienced cubicle operator we can get. Right now, I'm looking at a well-trained, seasoned operator, already security-cleared, who went on medical leave to tend to her father, who was seriously injured in battle. She's nursed him back to health, thank goodness, and now wants to come back to work. That's a Godsend."

"I agree this girl sounds like a perfect re-hire," Mr. Pierson said.

"The problem is," Mr. Truett broke in, "we have nowhere to put her. I don't know how else to say it. We're plum out of housing options right now."

"What if..." She tapped her forefinger on the dimple in her chin and pretended to consider. "What if I were willing to rent this girl the second room in my place? I'd be willing to make the sacrifice for the good of the war effort if it meant bringing in someone I didn't have to pluck out of the bullpen to train to do a job that vitally needs doing." *Please let this work. Please let this work.*

Mr. Pierson sat back, his mouth hanging open. "Well, I'll be. Now that's one I never thought of. You'd be willing to do that? Give up part of your place so this girl could have her job back?"

Nora nodded solemnly. "It seems to me she and her family have suffered enough hardship, sir. My understanding is that she's an only child, and she sends home the money she makes to support her folks. If we're not willing to support our wounded soldiers, then..." She let that hang in the air, daring them to deny Mary her job back.

Mr. Pierson looked to Mr. Truett. "It works for me if it works for you."

Mr. Truett shrugged and addressed Nora. "It's your space, and if you're willing to take in a renter, I don't see anything wrong with it."

"Thank you, sirs. I appreciate your flexibility on this."

"Seems to me you're the one having to be inconvenienced," Mr. Pierson said. "Suit yourself. I'll get the paperwork in place and she can start back anytime you're ready."

Nora took her leave before they could change their minds. She barely managed not to skip down the hall. Not only were she and Mary going to live together, thus avoiding scrutiny, but she learned that the snitch that turned her in hadn't implicated Mary as a sexual deviate. If she had, Mr. Pierson would've flagged Mary as unemployable and prevented her from returning.

Now all she needed was for Mary to come home.

Mary hadn't expected to be so nervous. Maybe coming a day early wasn't the best idea. *What if Nora doesn't like surprises? What if she has plans tonight? What if she doesn't like my new dress or my haircut? What if you just ring the doorbell and find out, Mary Elizabeth?*

The blinds were down and the lights were on, so most likely Nora was home. Mary took a deep breath and set down her suitcase. *Here goes nothing.* She rang the doorbell. She heard movement inside.

"Just a second," Nora called out. A moment later, she opened the door.

"Hi." Mary stood rooted to the spot, her heart pounding out of her chest. *You're even more beautiful than I remembered. How is that possible?*

Nora's smile turned radiant. Without saying a word, she hefted the suitcase and pulled Mary inside.

"Wh—" Mary felt herself being lifted off the ground and spun around in the air. Then Nora set her back on her feet.

"I can't believe you're really here."

"I know I'm a day earl—"

Nora drew her in and kissed her.

The softness of her mouth, the scent of her shampoo, the solidness of her body… Mary drank it all in. This was where she belonged. This was home.

"Thank you for coming early. Did everything go all right? How was your trip? What did your mother say? How's your father doing? Were your credentials all in order?"

Mary laughed. "Slow down, for Heaven's sake. Since when did you become so talkative?"

Nora laughed too. "Since I haven't had anyone to talk to in more than a month." She took Mary's hand and led her to the couch. "Come, sit down and tell me everything. Wait. You must be worn out. Do you need to rest first?"

"I'm fine. You, on the other hand, look like you haven't slept in a month." She meant it. Nora looked even thinner than when she left, and the dark marks under her eyes belied her exhaustion. "I'm worried about you."

"Don't. I'm better for seeing you." Nora caressed her cheek. "I can't believe you're really here. I know, I said that already. I can't get over it."

"Didn't you think I'd come back for you?"

"I hoped you would. I dreamed you would. But I guess I was afraid to trust it until now."

Mary kissed Nora's eyelids, her forehead, her nose, and finally her mouth, reveling in the taste and feel of her. "I made my girl a promise. I tend to keep my promises."

"Are you hungry? Do you need something to eat?"

"The only thing I'm hungry for is you." She took Nora's hand and led her toward the bedroom. Fleetingly, it dawned on her that for the first time, she was going to be able to spend the entire night wrapped in Nora's arms. There was no curfew, no need to hurry to find her scattered clothes and get dressed for a mad dash down the hill, no need to rush their time together. The two of them had all the time in the world. They were home.

212

CHAPTER TWENTY

I'm home," Nora said. She laid her attaché case on the table. "Where are you?"

"I'm in here," Mary answered. Her voice was muffled.

Curious, Nora followed the sound. For a moment, she stood enjoying the view. "What are you doing with your head in the closet?"

"Ouch!" She backed herself out and rubbed the sore spot where she'd hit her skull. "I was rearranging my shoes."

"I'm sure that was worth the headache."

"Very funny. I wouldn't have a headache if you hadn't come up behind me."

"I wouldn't have come up behind you if you weren't so irresistible." Nora pulled Mary to her feet and into an embrace. "Where's my welcome home?"

"Right here waiting for you." Mary kissed her and the stress of Nora's day melted away. After two and a half months of co-habitation, they'd developed a comfortable routine.

The exigencies of shift work made spending time together challenging, but they'd found ways to share at least one meal a day and carve out precious moments for themselves that didn't revolve around work schedules, house cleaning, or other household chores.

They walked hand in hand into the living room, where Nora turned on the radio. Each night they were home together, they listened to the CBS Radio Network for news of the war. Lately, the reports had become more optimistic. Nora knew they could use all the good news they could get.

"Dateline France. June 6, 1944, D-Day," the reporter intoned. "This is a day to rejoice."

213

Mary squeezed Nora's hand.

"At the time of this broadcast, Allied troops have taken the beaches at Normandy."

Nora let out a cheer.

"It began with paratroopers and gliders securing bridges behind enemy lines and cutting off German exit routes, followed closely by a surprise amphibious attack at dawn this morning, and continued with wave upon wave of Allied troops safely reaching the shore and securing a toehold on French soil at beaches code-named Gold, Juno, Sword, Omaha, and Utah. Yes, there were heavy casualties. The price of war is high. The cost of freedom and victory is priceless. Tonight, we are a step closer."

Nora snapped off the radio and spun Mary around. "Finally, something to celebrate." She kicked off her shoes and patted the seat next to her. Mary joined her and they snuggled into the back of the couch.

"I checked out a book today I think you'd really like," Nora said. She kissed the top of Mary's head, surprised when Mary stiffened beside her. "I know how much you love mysteries, so I picked up the Raymond Chandler mystery, *Farewell, My Lovely*. I thought we could read it to each other at bedtime."

"I love when you read to me."

"Well, it shouldn't always be one-sided. I'd love it if you read to me too."

Now Mary sat up. "I prefer it the other way around." She didn't make eye contact.

"Sweetheart? Why is it that every time I talk about books and reading, you get uncomfortable?"

"I don't get uncomfortable. Maybe I just prefer the radio, or movies." She got up and straightened the already-straight picture on the wall.

Nora went to her. "Hey. Look at me." When Mary did, there was fear in her eyes. "What's wrong?"

"Nothing."

"That's not nothing. Talk to me."

Mary closed her eyes and leaned against her. "You promise you won't laugh or make fun of me?"

Nora pulled back so she could see her. "Never."

"There's something wrong with me."

"What do you mean?" Alarm bells rang in Nora's head. "Do you feel all right?"

"I'm fine." Her face reddened. "It's just… I can't read. Well, I mean, I can read, but I'm not any good at it. I can't make out the words. I don't know why. I guess I don't see them the way everybody else does." She finished in a rush and hung her head.

Nora hugged her close and stroked her hair. "There's no shame in that, sweetheart. Why didn't you tell me before?"

"I know how important reading is to you. I didn't want you to think I was stupid or anything."

"Mary Elizabeth Trask, I would never think you were stupid. How could I?"

"I don't know."

Nora could feel her misery. "What if I could help you?"

"You can't help me. Everything gets jumbled up."

"Has anyone ever tried to help you?"

She shrugged. "Not really. I've always managed to convince teachers to give me an oral test instead."

"Do you wish you could read well?"

"Of course. Who doesn't want to read well? I love stories."

Nora nodded. "Well, I think we ought to find a way to help you."

"What makes you think you can?"

"We won't know unless we try, now will we? How about if we set aside an hour two or three times a week to read together?"

"I don't want to waste your time."

"Why on earth would you think it would be a waste of time?"

"What if I can't learn?"

"We'll find out together. There's no reason to be embarrassed, Mary, and if anyone ever made you feel that way, shame on them."

"I love you." Mary snuggled in closer.

"I love you too. How about if we start right now?"

They sat down with the Raymond Chandler book, and Nora read the first paragraph out loud. Then she handed the book to Mary and asked her to do the same. She watched her struggle with word recognition.

"Let's break it down into the sound each letter makes and see if that helps."

It took a while and more than a few stops and starts, but they fell into a rhythm, and, after some trial and error, they discovered a system of explanation and practice that worked for them.

"You know, I might even learn to enjoy reading."

Nora loved seeing the light dawn in Mary's eyes when a concept or word clicked for her. "You know, I might even enjoy reading with you." She winked and pulled Mary to her. "I need you to know, there isn't anything you can't tell me. You never need to be embarrassed or afraid where I'm concerned. I love you, Mary. Nothing changes that."

"Can we always stay this way?"

"You mean together as a couple?"

"Yes."

"I'd like that very much."

"Me too."

"Right now, I'd like to take you to bed and get some sleep."

"Count me in."

They got ready for bed, crawled under the covers, and Nora turned out the light.

"Thank you," Mary mumbled as she began to doze.

"For what?"

"For loving me, believing in me, and putting up with my flaws."

"We all have flaws. That's what makes us human. Goodnight, sweet Mary."

"Goodnight, sweet Nora."

MARCH – APRIL, 1945

CHAPTER TWENTY-ONE

Mary pretended not to notice Nora passing by her D unit with several men she didn't recognize. She'd seemed in an unusual hurry this morning when she left for work, and more scattered than Mary ever could remember her being. *Is this why you've been so distracted, sweetheart?*

After a year of living together, she could easily read her. Something was afoot. She would never ask who these men were, nor what they were doing here. Mary long ago had learned to respect Nora's position and the need for them to keep their work and personal lives separate. They managed to work around the unusual nature of their jobs and the secrets between them this place required.

Still, Mary couldn't help but be observant. Nora was spending significantly more time at the plant, at all hours of the day and night. It was hard for her to watch, as day by day Nora became more and more focused on work and spent less and less time at home.

Some part of her understood that what Nora did, she did for the war effort. But the bigger part of her selfishly wanted to take Nora away from here—to ease her stress level—and to return to those fun-loving days when they danced carefree in the living room.

There was no sense talking to Nora about it—she'd tried. The response was always the same: this was her duty and she needed to see it through. Well, at least they both were scheduled to be home for dinner tonight. It would be the first time this week.

Her shift ended, and she slogged through the change room, the bus ride, and the walk home. She had no idea what time Nora would arrive, probably because Nora didn't know either. It had been months since their last night on the town—a screening of Judy Garland's *Meet Me in St. Louis*—and Mary missed their occasional outings. At least they still found time to read together several times a week.

By the time she walked through the door, Mary's mood was as dark as the clouds overhead. She kicked off her shoes as she headed for the second bedroom, or as she and Nora called it, the place where her clothes lived. She was halfway there, when she smelled something delicious in the air.

"Are you going to walk on by, or are you at least going to say hello first?"

Nora was seated at the table with her chair facing outward. Her eyes twinkled in the candlelight. *Candlelight?* For the first time since she walked through the door, Mary took a good look around. The table was set with fresh flowers and a lit candle for a centerpiece. Something in the oven smelled fabulous, and Nora... Well, she looked ravishing.

Mary put her things down. "Hello." She walked in between Nora's knees.

"That's better."

"What's all this?"

"Do I need a reason?"

"No, but in my experience, you always have one."

"I hate that you know me so well." Nora pulled her down for a kiss.

"Do you?"

"No, but I do hate being predictable."

Mary indicated the scene. "I sure didn't predict this."

"Go wash up. Dinner's ready."

As she washed her face and hands and changed clothes, Mary wracked her brain. What was she missing? In the living room, she heard the strains of the new song, "Sentimental Journey," by Les Brown and his Orchestra and a new vocalist named Doris Day.

She emerged to find Nora standing in the middle of the living room, her arms open in invitation. They danced cheek-to-cheek and Mary forgot her foul mood.

"Do you remember the first time we did this?" Mary asked.

"I was horrible at it."

"No. You were just inexperienced."

"Mm-hmm."

The song ended and Nora led her to the dinner table.

"Roast? Wherever did you find a roast?"

"I'm resourceful."

"With real gravy?"

Nora laughed. "With real gravy and real butter for the rolls."

"I think I've died and gone to Heaven."

"I certainly hope not."

They ate in companionable silence. Mary couldn't remember the last time she'd had a meal this good. "I'll do the dishes."

"No, I've got it. Find us some more music."

She found their favorite big band station and made herself comfortable on the couch. Nora joined her soon after.

"Do you know what today is?"

Again, Mary searched her memory banks. "I give."

"What's the date?"

"March 23, 1945."

"Exactly."

Mary shook her head. "I know I must be missing something, but for the life of me, I don't know what it is."

Nora took her hands. The intensity in her eyes gave Mary goosebumps. "Mary Elizabeth Trask, on this day, exactly one year ago, you walked into this house with your suitcase after the longest month of my life. I took one look at you, and I knew that in you, I'd found my forever home. And every day since then, I've thanked whatever God there is in Heaven for delivering you back to me."

Mary swallowed hard. This was the Nora she'd been missing. This was her Nora.

"I wanted to do something to mark this occasion, this anniversary. I got you something. I hope you like it."

Nora produced a small velvet box from her pocket and opened it for her to see. Inside was a perfect ruby solitaire. Mary gasped and put her hand to her mouth.

"That's for me?"

"That's for you. It's a symbol of my love for you. Of course, you won't be able to wear it on your left hand, but you can wear it on your right, and we'll know that it's our engagement ring."

"I-I don't know what to say. It's gorgeous. I can't believe you bought this for me."

"May I?"

"Yes!" Mary held out her right ring finger, and Nora slipped the ring on it. It fit perfectly. "How did you know what size?"

Nora chuckled. "I didn't. I just knew it had to be about two sizes smaller than my finger."

Mary turned the ring in the light and watched it sparkle. "It's amazing, sweetheart, but not as amazing as you. I love you."

"I love you. I'm sorry. I know I've been a little distant lately. You know I can't talk about work, but I need you to know and trust that I will never, ever, ever lose sight of you or of us. I swear it."

"But I don't have anything for you."

"You're my gift, sweetheart. You're all the gift I need."

This time it was Mary who took Nora by the hand. "Then you'd better unwrap it, don't you think?" She blew out the candle and led them to bed.

✑✎

At midnight, Nora felt the bed move as Mary poured herself into it after her shift. She rolled toward her and kissed her. "Welcome home."

"What are you doing up? You couldn't have gotten home much before me."

"We've had so little time together lately, I wanted to be awake for you when you got here."

"You've been burning the candle at both ends over there, sweetheart. They're working you too hard."

"It's the nature of the job. More racetracks in operation equals more cubicle operators, equals more work for Nora. It's a math problem."

"It's a sleep problem, if you ask me."

Nora turned on her back and invited Mary to snuggle against her shoulder. "Get some sleep."

"You first."

The shrill sound of the alarm clock startled them both awake. Nora grabbed it and turned it off, but the ringing continued.

"The phone. It's the phone," Mary mumbled.

Nora bolted out of bed and ran into the living room to answer it. "Hello?"

"Dr. Lindstrom? G.G. and E.L. are here. They'd like to meet with you."

Dr. Lawrence and General Groves were here? She hadn't known they were coming. She looked at her watch. It was 3:23 a.m.

"I can be there in twenty minutes."

"I'll let them know."

She stripped off her nightgown and jumped into the shower. When she got out, Mary was standing there, her arms crossed and a dour expression on her face.

"What are you doing?"

"I have to go."

"It's three thirty in the morning. You barely just got to sleep."

"I know." Nora applied her makeup and selected a dress Mary had picked out for her at a department store in Knoxville last week.

"You're getting awfully dolled up for a meeting."

"I don't have time to explain. Please, let me finish getting ready."

"Is it your family? Is something wrong?"

"No."

"Then, what? I could go with you and help you with whatever it is."

"Absolutely not. Mary, please, go back to bed. There's no need for both of us to be awake." She kissed her briefly, scooped up her attaché case, and hustled out the door.

There were several men on the bus with her. She didn't recognize any of them, but she felt a kinship to them. They all looked as sleep-deprived as she was.

When she exited the bus, she was surprised to see that they got off too. And when they headed in the direction of the administration building at Y-12 along with her, she became downright curious. What was going on? Had they all been summoned for this meeting?

She announced herself to the secretary in the reception area.

"Have a seat, Dr. Lindstrom. They'll be ready for you shortly."

As she sat, the others from the bus piled in. No one said a word to anyone else beyond a nod or a polite greeting. No one introduced themselves. She noted that all of their badges indicated high clearances, which made sense given who they were meeting with.

"If you all would come with me, please." The secretary led the way to the makeshift conference room. General Groves, Dr.

Lawrence, and the District Engineer, Colonel Kenneth Nichols, were standing over what appeared to be a map of Oak Ridge.

"Come in, come in," General Groves said. "Take a seat and we'll get started."

Nora selected a chair from which she could see the map. The size and scope of the installments surprised her. What didn't surprise her was that she was the only woman in the room.

"First, thank you all for coming in the middle of the night. We recognize how hard you are working on behalf of the war effort, and we thank you for all you are doing.

"Each of you is here for your unique skill set and your scientific knowledge. Together, we have one goal in mind—to win the war. As you've no doubt heard on the news, the tide is turning in our favor, but we are a long way from victory. Time is of the essence, which is why we've taken the extraordinary step of bringing you all together at once, rather than addressing you individually. I don't have to tell you, what we say here, what you see here, what you know here, what we do here, stays here. Now more than ever, your commitment to maintaining secrecy is vital to our success.

"In your own specific areas, you may have been frustrated that we haven't yet been able to achieve our goals. Yes, there have been setbacks and delays. Yes, our process is not perfect. Frankly, we are learning as we go along. What we thought might work in theory, may or may not prove to be true in reality. That is why we have been simultaneously working on several approaches here at Oak Ridge.

"We have the greatest minds of our time on our side. We will succeed."

General Groves continued. "I was reviewing the data with some of our best scientific minds, and it occurred to us that we had been looking at this all wrong. We were thinking that what we needed was for a single process to succeed. The truth is, each process has succeeded but not to any appreciable extent. What if we took the slightly enriched Tubealloy you each have been able to produce using different techniques, and cycled it through a second time with what has so far proven to be the most-successful technique, thus further enriching it?"

Murmurs of agreement buzzed throughout the room. *It could work.* Dr. Lawrence made direct eye contact with Nora as he took over the meeting. "We propose to take the slightly enriched Tubealloy from each of your plants and feed that into the calutrons in the Beta racetracks here at Y-12. We have modified the designs of those racetracks based on our earlier experiences with the Alpha units, and we are confident that we now have in place the design we need to achieve the desired level of enrichment."

Nora nodded at him. She understood. It would be up to her girls to finish the job everyone else started. She would need her best operators manning the D units in the Beta buildings. Already, she was calculating the adjustments she would have to make.

General Groves moved forward again. "What we need from each of you, and from your people, is everything you've got, and everything they've got. Now is the time to bear down and squeeze out every ounce of enriched product you can. We're counting on you. Your country is counting on you."

The meeting broke up, and Dr. Lawrence hailed Nora over. "The Beta units are ideal for this purpose, Nora."

General Groves joined them, along with Colonel Nichols, whose job it was to oversee all of the Reservation.

"Beta-4 is getting up to capacity," the general said. "Whatever resources you need, you tell Colonel Nichols directly. Anything, do you understand?"

Nora straightened to her full height. "Sir, I've already been going through the rosters in my head. My plan will be to move my very best, most capable and consistent operators, over to the Beta buildings. Many of them already are there. I won't have to do much shuffling."

"Excellent. We're going to need your girls to put in a lot of overtime. Do you think they can handle that?"

"Respectfully, sir, from the outset, the dedication and abilities of my girls have been called into question. They've been doubted, denigrated, and under-appreciated. And yet, they've gotten the job done without complaint. I'm here to tell you, sir, yes, indeed, I know my girls are up for the task."

She blinked. She hadn't meant to say that much, and yet, she thought she saw a ghost of a smile from Dr. Lawrence.

"Good," was all the general said.

✎✎

Nora checked her watch—6:00 p.m. In another hour, Mary should be home from her shift. If she could finish the latest operator schedule for next week, maybe they could have time to do something fun together.

Fun. Nora wondered if she remembered what that was. With the new edict, it seemed that she'd been spending all her time arranging and rearranging shifts, accommodating those girls who had families and couldn't work overtime, those who were pregnant and needed their rest, and those very few who flat-out refused to stay late. When she removed them from the mix, that meant she had to overlap shifts and juggle personnel to ensure maximum production and minimum disruption. *It's like the most challenging game of chess I've ever played.*

She closed her eyes. When was the last time she'd played a game of chess? She and her father used to love to sit down to a good game on a Sunday afternoon. Afterward, the loser would buy the winner an ice cream cone. Now on Sundays, she called home solely to share a perfunctory and politely neutral exchange with her parents, who seemed more like strangers to her every day.

"Sentimental Journey" came on the radio and Nora smiled. That song always lifted her spirits. Since the night of their anniversary, it had become *their* song. In her mind's eye, she pictured them in the middle of the living room, sharing their anniversary dance. *You're getting mushy in your old age.*

She spied Mary's ring on the window sill where she left it every time she had to go to work. The magnets made it impossible to wear jewelry of any kind on the job, unless, of course, you wanted to spend your shift pinned to a giant magnet. The ring sparkled in the early April sunshine slashing through the window curtain. She'd chosen it as an enduring token of their relationship, and because she'd chosen it with such care, she knew that the ring would always remind both of them how deeply in love with each other they were.

She owed Mary an apology. Lately, she'd been irritable and inattentive. Mary didn't deserve that. It wasn't her fault they were like ships passing in the night. *No, that's your doing.* It wasn't as though she could give Mary preferential treatment and the best shifts so that they could spend more time together. As it was, she heard the backstabbing comments of girls who believed Nora favored Mary because they were roommates.

Since when are your thoughts so manic and scattered? You really do need some sleep.

"We interrupt this broadcast with a breaking news bulletin."

Nora put down her pen and set aside the schedule.

"The White House has announced that today, April 12, 1945, at 3:35 p.m., President Franklin Delano Roosevelt, age sixty-three, passed away in Hot Springs, Georgia, where he had retreated to recover from exhaustion. The cause of death was a massive cerebral stroke."

Oh, my God. The president is dead. Nora's hands trembled. FDR was her hero.

"We are told that First Lady Eleanor Roosevelt was given the news while in the White House. She received Vice President Harry S. Truman at the Pennsylvania Avenue entrance to the White House and informed him of the president's death. Shortly thereafter, Vice President Truman was sworn in as the thirty-third president of the United States."

The president was dead. God help them all. What would happen now? Time slowed to a crawl as Nora sat glued to the radio, listening to the reactions of people just like her.

"Nora?" Mary burst through the door. "Is it true?" Her eyes were misty and glazed over in shock.

Nora nodded, stood, and opened her arms to receive her. "It's terrible."

"What are we going to do?" The reaction had been much the same from mourners everywhere.

"We have a statement from the White House, from President Truman," CBS newsman Bob Trout broke in to the coverage.

"Here is what the statement says. 'The world may be sure that we will prosecute this war on both fronts, east and west, with all the vigor we possess, to a successful conclusion.'"

Tears streamed down both of their faces. "We go on," Nora said. "We go on, and we finish what the president started."

Mary burrowed more deeply into her embrace. "We have nothing to fear but fear itself, right?"

"That's what the greatest president ever said, and they're words to live by."

Nora kissed the top of Mary's head. She wondered idly if this horrific turn of events would change their mission in any way. She supposed she would find out soon enough. But for now, all she wanted was to shut out the rest of the world and hold Mary close.

❧❧

Ever since the news of the president's death, Mary and Nora tuned in religiously to the news. The first order of business when one or the other of them arrived home was to turn on the radio. Today, Mary was listening to a description of the Battle of Berlin. According to the commentator, Soviet troops were closing in on the city from two fronts, and Berlin, the heart of Adolf Hitler's empire, was sure to fall.

Nora breezed in breathlessly and dropped her ever-present attaché case on the floor next to the coat rack. "Hi. I've only got a few minutes before I need to get back. I thought we'd grab a quick bite of dinner together." She skidded to a halt in front of Mary and kissed her.

"I figured you were going to say that, so I heated up a can of soup and some beans. They're on the stove."

"You're the best." This time Nora kissed her on the cheek. "How was your day? Anything big happen in the news?" She grabbed the dishes out of the cupboard and set the table.

"Looks like Berlin is about to fall to the Russians."

"Wouldn't that be something?" Nora finished setting the table and turned up the volume on the radio.

"But there have been so many civilian deaths. Those innocent people are just going about their day, and then *poof*, their lives are over. Why? Because they're in the wrong place at the wrong time? It seems so unfair."

"It's war. War isn't fair."

"Well, I wish it didn't have to be that way." Mary hesitated before addressing the other thing on her mind. They'd all been told that what they were doing, they were doing for the war effort. If the war ended, where would that leave them? She knew she was wading into dangerous territory, but Nora didn't have to explain anything off-limits in order to answer the question. "Does that impact what we're doing here?"

Nora paused with the serving spoon in mid-air. "Not as far as I can tell. Even if Berlin falls, that doesn't mean the war is over. If the Germans surrender, we still have to deal with the Japanese."

Mary bit her lip. Nora had been so remote of late. She hated to ask the next question, but it had been on her heart and mind for weeks, so… "Nora?"

"Mm-hmm?" Nora continued to ladle out the soup.

"The war will end, right?"

"At some point, yes."

Mary took the bowls of soup from her and placed them on the table. Then she stilled Nora's hands. "When it ends, what happens to us?"

Nora stiffened. "What do you mean?"

"Well, I assume that when the war ends, whatever it is we're building or making here won't be necessary anymore. We'll have finished what we came here to do. When that happens, what about us?"

They sat at the table and Nora blew on her soup. "Honestly, I've been so focused on the work, I hadn't really thought about what's next."

Mary struggled to ward off the impending sense of doom that had been hanging over her for weeks. "The war's almost over. We're winning. I should be rejoicing. Instead, all I've been doing is crying about us."

Nora's eyes opened wide. "Why would you be crying about us? We love each other. We'll find a way to stay together. We'll figure it out."

Mary shook her head. Those felt like empty promises. "I learned a new word today."

"Oh? That's great. You know, I love that you've been working so hard on your reading and vocabulary. I'm really proud of you." Nora shoveled in another spoonful of beans and swallowed. "What's the word?"

"Placate. It means to say something you don't necessarily mean in order to keep someone happy." She smirked.

Nora dropped the spoon into her bowl with a clang. "What are you saying, Mary? That you think I don't mean it? I do. You think I don't love you? I do. You think I don't care as much about us as you do? You're wrong. Dead wrong. I don't know what else I can say to convince you, but I do know that I don't have time right now to debate it with you. I've got to go." She shoved her chair back and rose. "You can leave the dishes. I'll do them when I get home."

When she'd gone, Mary threw herself on the bed and sobbed. What had become of them? Where was the passion? What happened to the days when they couldn't get enough of each other, when it was all they could do to get through the day until the next time they could be together?

She stared at her ring. Had that been an empty gesture? It hadn't felt like that at the time, but now... *You're being overly dramatic. She said she loved you. She said you'd stay together after the war. Why isn't that enough for you?* She blew her nose and sat up. As long as she was being miserable, maybe she should call home and see how her father was doing.

"Mother?"

"Mary, is that you?"

"Is there anyone else that calls you Mother?"

"Don't be smart."

"I'm sorry." Her mother was right—that was uncalled for. "Can I talk to Daddy?"

She could hear her mother put down the phone. "Henry? Your daughter would like to talk to you."

A minute later, he picked up the line. "Hello?"

"Hi, Daddy. I miss you."

"I miss you too, Pumpkin."

She gasped. It was the first time he'd used that term of endearment since he'd returned from the war. "Daddy? How are you feeling? How is work going?"

"I'm doing okay. Doc says I was really lucky that the bullets and the shrapnel missed everything major. Except for my leg, I'm good as new. The railroad is still treating me like I'm some kind of hero, and they even upped my pay."

"That's great. You sound good, Daddy."

"And you sound like you're down in the dumps; I know my little girl. What's wrong, Pumpkin?"

Mary closed her eyes tightly as a tear leaked out. "Nothing. I'm just tired, I guess. I'm working a lot of hours."

"My hero-daughter is winning the war for us."

"Oh, Daddy. Don't exaggerate."

"I know that what you're doing must be important, or you would've stayed here with us. I want you to know, Pumpkin, you can always come home. We love you and miss you."

Mary's smile was bittersweet. This was her father—the man she'd seen off to war. *Thank you for coming back to me, Daddy.* "I love and miss you too."

"Well, you'd better get going. This is costing you a fortune."

"I just wanted to hear your voice."

"You come home anytime. I know you and your mother don't see eye-to-eye, but deep down she loves you and misses you too."

"Okay, Daddy. I'll call again soon. 'Bye."

"'Bye, Pumpkin."

JULY – AUGUST, 1945

CHAPTER TWENTY-TWO

N ora let herself in as quietly as she could. The only light illuminating her way was a side lamp in the living room. She kicked off her shoes at the door and tiptoed to the door of the bedroom. There was her Mary, snoring lightly, her arms wrapped around a pillow that should've been her.

She slid her night table drawer open and fished below several books for her journal and pen and then returned with them to the living room.

It was so hard, not being able to talk to anyone about what was going on. Although she couldn't say much that was specific in her diary, at least she could pour out her heart.

July 22, 1945
Dearest Diary,
It's been almost three months since the Russians marched into Berlin, a firing squad exacted justice on the Fascist Mussolini, and that most awful of monsters, Hitler, killed himself. It's been almost that long since the Germans surrendered unconditionally in Reims, France.

Still, even though we Americans won the Battle of Okinawa, the war goes on in the Pacific. And so, we go on with it. G.G. held a meeting with the Select Few here and told us nothing had changed. Our objectives remained the same, and we were to double our efforts.

Honestly, dear diary, my poor girls (including my Mary!) are working themselves to the bone. I don't know how much longer we can keep this up. I feel horrible for all of them. The hardest part is not being able to share any reasonable justification or rationalization with them for the increased hours and intense pressure. I know I alone must carry this burden, but my shoulders are sagging.

Worst of all is the growing chasm I feel between me and my beloved. I have no words of wisdom to ease her anxiety about the future, for we cannot yet plan for the future without knowing the outcome of our present. I know without doubt that I love her with all my heart, and that I would walk through fire for her if that were required of me.

I cannot say where the path we're on will lead. Will my future in the scientific community be assured after this? I can neither know nor say. One thing is clear: if we are to make it in this world, I will have to make sufficient income to support us.

Where would we go? Where in the world would a love such as ours be accepted? Where would we not be ostracized or worse? Here, we are somewhat insulated by the unique circumstances. I fear the same will not be true in the world at large, and I don't know what to do to protect us—to protect her.

Mary continues to sink deeper and deeper into despair. Her insecurity about my love for her and my intentions are fueled by my inability to spend the necessary time to allay her fears.

I feel trapped between love and duty. While it may sound overly dramatic, I believe the fate of the world hangs in the balance based on the work we are doing here. I must stay focused, with a steady hand on the wheel, and pray that when all this is over, I will be able to speak freely and that Mary will understand and forgive me.

It is getting late, dear diary, in so many ways, and I must at least try to sleep, for the days and nights ahead are bound to be long.

Ever faithfully yours, dearest diary.

Nora

She closed the journal, shut off the light, and tiptoed back into the bedroom. For long moments, she stood there gazing down at Mary. In sleep, she appeared so young and innocent. Tears formed on Nora's lashes, and she brushed them away. She returned the diary to its hiding place, changed into her nightgown, and slipped under the covers.

Unconsciously, Mary reached for her and snuggled against her. Nora drank in the scent of her skin, her shampoo, and her perfume. "I love you, sweet Mary, and I always will. Sweet dreams, my love."

"I love you too," Mary murmured in return.

Nora smiled a bittersweet smile, closed her eyes, and prayed for her dreams to take her somewhere where she and Mary could live carefree and in love. Within seconds, she was asleep.

Nora hurried down the hall toward the conference room. She was in such a rush that she nearly ran over Jane, who had just emerged from a side office.

Jane squeezed her hand and winked. When Nora cocked her head in inquiry, Jane simply smiled.

Nora's stomach flipped. *Did that mean what I think it meant?* She knew Jane couldn't, and wouldn't, tell her. But the fact of her presence, the sheaf of papers she carried, and the broad grin gave Nora goosebumps.

They arrived in the conference room to find General Groves, Colonel Nichols, and the middle-of-the-night group Nora secretly had dubbed The Select Few, already there.

"Close the door, please," General Groves instructed.

Jane closed the door behind them. She walked to the front of the room and presented the general with the sheaf of papers.

He took a moment to review them and nodded. "Gentlemen, and ladies." He nodded to her and Jane. "I am happy and relieved to report that your extraordinary efforts here have reaped the desired outcome. After several years of hard work and dedication, we have reached our target goal. Congratulations."

Everyone in the room broke out in smiles. The men clapped each other on the back and shook hands. She and Jane hugged.

"Hold on a second." The general held up a hand. "I want to be clear. We must stay the course and continue our production unabated. This is not the end, but the ascertainment of an important milestone. I am counting on all of you to keep your people pressing forward. And remember…"

The group repeated, "What you see here, what you hear here, what you do here, let it stay here."

"Dismissed."

Outside the conference room, Nora breathed a sigh of relief. Whatever they had done, indications made it appear as if it would all be over soon.

⋖⋗

Mary thought she'd never been as glad to see home as she was this morning. Normally, third shift was challenging, but with the additional hours of overtime on the front end, tonight had seemed interminable.

She opened the door and slipped inside, fully expecting to hear the shower running and Nora getting ready to go to work. But the house was quiet. Maybe she'd already caught the bus. In any event, Mary was looking forward to falling into bed for a few hours before she had to go run some errands in Jackson Square.

She went first into her room, stripped, and threw her dress in the hamper. It was a humid early August morning, and she didn't feel like putting on a nightgown, so she didn't bother. She brushed her teeth and headed for bed.

"I thought you'd never get here." Nora lay in the center of the bed, her head propped up on her elbow, wearing nothing but a bemused expression.

"Argh!" Mary's hand flew to her heart. "You're still here. You nearly scared me to death." Her mouth went dry. Even after all this time, and all they'd been through, the sight of Nora like this set her on fire.

"It is my house, you know. Occasionally, one should expect to find me in it. And yes, reports of my demise have been greatly exaggerated."

"That's not what I meant. Why aren't you on your way to work?"

"Because my girl had a really long night, we haven't had nearly enough time together lately, and I wanted to surprise her. Surprise!"

Mary crawled across the covers and landed on top of her. "Really? You're not going to get up and run out on me, are you? No emergencies? No mysterious disappearances?"

"The president himself couldn't drag me from this bed." She flipped Mary over, surprising a laugh out of her. "Not until I've made love to my girl. That is, if she'll have me."

Her voice cut right through Mary, sending a bolt of lightning directly to her core. "Let me see if I have time for you in my schedule."

Nora nibbled on the sensitive area just below her ear. "Well? Do you…" She changed direction and moved further down Mary's body. "…have time for me?"

Mary moaned and arched back. "I think so. Keep going and I'll let you know."

All of the angst, all of the anger, all of the uncertainty and frustration of the past few months dissolved in an instant, leaving in its wake the only thing that mattered—their love.

"I love you, Mary Elizabeth Trask. You make my life complete in a way I never imagined possible. Please say you haven't given up on me…on us?"

"I could never give up on you, Nora. I loved you from the moment I first laid eyes on you. That will never change."

Mary closed her eyes and surrendered to the moment, to love, to Nora, and to their life together.

Afterward, she stirred as Nora disentangled herself. Mary checked the clock. It was 8:45 a.m.

"I'm sorry. It is a Monday, and I really do have to go to work."

"Spoil sport." Mary stretched languorously and Nora leaned over and kissed her tenderly.

"I love you. Thank you for the perfect morning."

"Thank *you*, Dr. Lindstrom. Now go save the world."

"What are you going to do while I'm off saving the world?"

"I have a few errands to run. I'll pick us up some groceries and stop at the bank."

"That sounds like a lot more fun than going to work. But, alas…" She rose and headed for the shower. "Will I see you before your shift?"

"I don't see why not. I'll probably leave around ten thirty. I should be back here by mid-afternoon. If you get home by six, we could have dinner together."

"You know I'll do my best."

"I always do," Mary said at the same time Nora said it.

"You know I hate that I'm so predictable."

"I consider it more like…reliable, and I find it charming."

"Thank God."

"I'm just going to catch a few winks before the errands."

"I'll be quiet as a church mouse. You won't even hear me leave." Nora came back for one more kiss. "I'll see you later. I love you. Sweet dreams, sweet Mary."

The last thing Mary saw as she drifted off to sleep was Nora's beautiful face smiling down at her.

Nora whistled all the way to Y-12, and even once she reached her office. She pulled out the scheduling manifest and went to work. If she focused, she could knock out the new schedule for next week in several hours. After that, she would walk through Beta-2 first, since Mary wouldn't be there to distract her, and then Beta-4, the newest plant.

She had no idea how much time had passed when Jane came flying into her office without knocking.

"Here's your hat, what's your hurry?" she joked.

"What are you still doing sitting there?"

"Where else would I be?"

Jane shook her head. "You're either the coolest customer ever, or you're living in a cave."

Nora knew she must look as puzzled as she felt. "What in the world are you talking about?"

"Haven't you heard?"

"Heard what?"

"Oh, my God. You *are* living in a cave. It's all over the news and all over town!"

"What is?"

"We dropped an atomic bomb on Japan, on some city named Hiroshima! And the fuel for that bomb was made right here in Oak Ridge, by us! Apparently, that's what I've been doing all this time—calculating percentages of enriched uranium. I had no idea!"

Nora sat back and tried to absorb that information. "We dropped a…"

"Uranium!" Jane shouted. "That's what the Tubealloy is! It's enriched uranium, and we made it right here. The president said so in an official statement. Put your head out the window."

Nora went to the window. A sea of jubilant people crowded the streets.

"Come on, we have to go celebrate!" Jane tried to tug her along.

"I'll be out in a minute. I've got to tie up a few things here."

"Okay. See you out there!" She practically floated out the door.

Nora slumped in her chair. They'd done it. They'd actually done it. She'd been right. Their purpose had been to convert enough harmless U-238 into reactive U-235 to create a massive chain reaction—one big enough to wipe out an entire population. They'd brought Japan to its knees. Surely, the Japanese would have to surrender now. She and Mary were going to get their happily-ever-after.

Mary. She needed to get home to Mary. Nora jumped up. She had to tell her. Now she wouldn't need to keep secrets anymore. They could talk about it openly. They could celebrate that the work they'd done likely had brought an end to the war. Now the Allied soldiers would be able to come home. She gathered her papers and stuffed them in her desk. Heck, she didn't need to hide what she was doing from prying eyes anymore. Apparently, the whole world knew.

She needed a radio. She needed to get home, see Mary, and they could listen to the radio together. She ran out and down to the bus stop, jumped on the first bus she saw and was on her way.

Out the windows, she could see workers pouring out of buildings and swarming the street. As they got closer to the bus depot, even more townsfolk lined the wooden walkways. Everyone was hugging and cheering. They pulled into the bus depot and it was pandemonium.

Nora fought her way through the crowd. All she could think about was getting home to Mary to tell her the war most likely was over, they'd won, and she'd helped make it happen—they both had.

"Excuse me, pardon me, excuse me." She pushed against the tide of humanity until she was in the clear. Then she ran all the way to 105 Georgia Avenue and flung open the door.

"Mary! Mary! Did you hear?" When she got no reply, she ran through every room. Then she remembered, Mary would've gone to Jackson Square to run errands.

She checked her watch. It was almost noon. She headed for the door, changed her mind, spun around in a circle, headed for the door again, and changed her mind one last time. She flipped on the radio and stood in front of it.

"At 11:00 a.m. Eastern War Time, President Harry Truman, in a statement delivered at sea, announced that the United States unleashed the fury of the world's first atomic bomb on the Japanese city of Hiroshima on August sixth, at 8:20 a.m. local time… That's some seventeen hours ago.

"According to the president, the bomb contained more power than twenty thousand tons of TNT."

Nora put a hand to her mouth. It had been even more powerful than anything she could've imagined. It would've decimated an entire city.

The announcer continued. "The president's statement goes on to say—paraphrasing here—that secret sites, including Oak Ridge, near Knoxville, Tennessee, Richland near Pasco, Washington, and Los Alamos, near Santa Fe, New Mexico, have been working for more than two years on the materials to produce this bomb, and that it was the facility in Oak Ridge that played the principal role in the creation of this, the most powerful weapon ever used in war."

Outside the window, Nora heard shouts of joy. Should she wait here for Mary? No. If Mary was in Jackson Square, she'd find her. Just in case they missed each other, though, she should leave her a note.

She found a notecard and a pen.

My dearest, darling Mary,

As you probably know by now, all of our hard work has come to fruition. We did it, sweetheart! We did it. And now we can share everything. No more secrets, no more clandestine, middle-of-the-night meetings. Now I can explain everything. Now I can share that what we've been doing here was creating the fuel for the bomb that brought the Japanese to their knees. Now they will have to surrender, and our troops can come home. You should be so proud of what we—what you—did, darling.

Oh, my love. There are so many places I want to show you, so many things I want us to do together. I can't wait to get started! I want to give you the world.

You must be out running errands. I know it's crazy to brave the crowds, but I have to see you. I'm going to Jackson Square to find you, even though I imagine it will be like looking for a needle in a haystack.

If I somehow miss you there and you get back here and I'm not here... WAIT here! I'll come back for you. I can't wait to hold you in my arms.

All my love always.

Nora sealed the envelope. For once, she wished she could throw caution to the wind and sign the note, but they were ever mindful of someone else finding their correspondence.

She exchanged her dress for practical slacks and a blouse, and her high heels for saddle shoes. Then she propped the note up on the table where she knew Mary would see it and headed back out the door.

The crowds were so thick she couldn't see her own feet. Still, she kept pushing forward. People she didn't know hugged her and kissed her on the cheek.

"Did you hear? We won the war!"

"And Oak Ridge is on the map!"

"Uranium! We've been making uranium!"

"We got the Japs good! We brought 'em to their knees!"

Nora let the words wash over her. She looked left and right. She squeezed through the tiniest of openings. She finally reached the bank's front door, only to find that the place was mobbed. After multiple tries, she was able to get inside. She searched every teller station and line—no Mary.

She left the bank and worked her way around the square to the grocery store. The crowd was dozens of bodies deep. She couldn't even get close.

"Nora! Hey, Nora!"

She whirled around. "Mary?"

Rosalie grabbed her by the hand. "Isn't it great?"

"It is. Have you seen Mary?"

"Who?"

"Mary. Have you seen her?"

"Oh! Sorry, I couldn't hear you with all this noise. No, I haven't seen her. If she's in this mess, good luck finding her." Rosalie got carried away by the swell of the crowd.

Nora raised up on her toes. She looked left and right, up the square and down. Finally, just as she was about to give up, she saw a figure in the distance. She wore a beautiful, bright yellow dress just like one Mary owned. Even though she could only see her from behind, Nora was certain she'd know that body anywhere.

It would take a herculean effort to get from here to there, but they had time. In fact, they had all the time in the world. Nora pushed through the crowd, never losing sight of that girl—her girl—the one she would spend the rest of her life with.

THE END

Want to find out how
Nora and Mary's story ends?

Pick up your copy of

Chain Reactions

The best-selling sequel to
Secrets Well Kept

About the Author

Lynn Ames is the best-selling author of *The Price of Fame, The Cost of Commitment, The Value of Valor, One ~ Love, Heartsong, Eyes on the Stars, Beyond Instinct, Above Reproach, All That Lies Within, Bright Lights of Summer, Final Cut, Great Bones, Chain Reactions, Secrets Well Kept,* and one of five authors of the collection *Outsiders.* She also is the writer/director/producer of the history-making documentary, "Extra Innings: The Real Story Behind the Bright Lights of Summer." This historically important documentary chronicles, for the first time ever in her own words, the real-life story of Hall-of-Famer Dot Wilkinson and the heyday of women's softball.

Lynn's fiction has garnered her a multitude of awards and honors, including five Goldie awards, the coveted Ann Bannon Popular Fiction Award (for *All That Lies Within*), and the Arizona Book Award for Best Gay/Lesbian book. Lynn is a two-time Lambda Literary Award (Lammy) Finalist, a Foreword INDIES Book of the Year Award finalist, and winner of a Rainbow Award for Lesbian Romance. *All That Lies Within* was additionally honored as one of the top ten lesbian books of 2013.

Ms. Ames is the founder of Phoenix Rising Press. She is also a former press secretary to the New York state senate minority leader and spokesperson for the nation's third-largest prison system. For more than half a decade, she was an award-winning broadcast journalist. She has been editor of a critically acclaimed national magazine and a nationally recognized speaker and public relations professional with a particular expertise in image, crisis communications planning, and crisis management.

For additional information please visit her website at www.lynnames.com, or e-mail her at lynnames@lynnames.com. You can also friend Lynn on Facebook and follow her on Twitter and Instagram.

Published by
Phoenix Rising Press
Phoenix, AZ

Lynn Ames books are available in multiple formats through
www.lynnames.com, from your favorite local bookstore, or
through other online venues.